THE WITCHES
OF ALL SAINTS

ALSO BY JILL TATTERSALL

The Wild Hunt
Midsummer Masque
Lady Ingram's Room
Lyonesse Abbey

The Witches of All Saints

JILL TATTERSALL

William Morrow & Company, Inc., New York   1975

TAT

Copyright © 1975 by Jill Tattersall

Printed in the United States of America.

1 2 3 4 5 79 78 77 76 75

Library of Congress Cataloging in Publication Data

Tattersall, Jill.
  The witches of All Saints.

  I. Title.
PZ4.T222W13   [PR6070.A68]   823'.9'14   74-22076
ISBN 0-688-02890-X

To my parents, who allowed me
to spend so much of my childhood
in the churchyard of All Saints,

and to

Virginia Morshead, Marilyn Beazer,
Viola Lloyd, Ann Hazel, Emma Barry,
without whose efforts I would never
have had time to write this book.

THE WITCHES
OF ALL SAINTS

ONE

It was cold in the chaise. Wisps of fog seeped in through the ill-fitting window and the heat had long since drained out of the hot brick on which my feet were resting. The muffled sound of the horses' hooves slowed and stopped, to proceed cautiously again. I could understand now why the postilion had gloomily insisted that four horses would take me to my destination no quicker than two, though I had thought him absurd to be speaking of fog rolling in from the sea later in the day when, as we left the last posting-house, the pale February sun had been shining out of a clear sky. Now, however, it was not only fog but twilight pressing in about the carriage and I wondered unhappily just how late I would arrive at Pheasant's Hall.

The postilion began to sing a mournful dirge, to keep his spirits up, I assumed, or to encourage his horses. I strained my ears to make out the words:

" 'O, the hangman waits for you and me,
Alas!

9

O, the hangman waits for you and me,
Alas!
He waits for us by Tyburn Tree—' "

There was a sudden scuffle and the song broke off. I caught my breath and then, curiosity gaining over apprehension, I lowered the window with some difficulty and put out my head.

"What is it, Hodgkin?"

" 'Tis only the horses shying at a signpost, miss. Come up, Lady, that 'ont hurt you, girl." He stood in his stirrups and peered at the offending board. "Darnation!" I heard him muttering. He dismounted and kicked about the grass at the base of the post. A moment later he stumped up to my window, his feet, no doubt, even colder than mine.

"Tain't no manner of use our going on, miss," he assured me with an air almost of triumph.

"Why, are we lost, Hodgkin? But what of the sign?"

"That tells us where we come from, miss, and that tells us what lies down that tiddly little track yonder, but t'other arm is broken off and gone, like." He paused as if waiting for me to congratulate him. I sighed, and my throat felt raw as I inhaled the cold fog.

"Well, what does lie down that track?"

He hesitated, as I thought; but then I saw that he was blowing his nose in a voluminous red handkerchief. "All Saints Church, miss, so it says," he eventually replied.

"What day is it? Oh, to be sure, a Saturday. How unfortunate it is not Sunday."

"You'd not be travelling on a Sunday, I should hope, miss. No, 'tis Saturday, February second, 1811—the Feast," he added oddly, "of Candlemas."

"Candlemas! Do they hold services for that? But not at

10

such an hour and in such weather, I suppose. Well, if there is no one about to direct us, we shall just have to try the anonymous road, shall we not?"

He pushed back his tall white hat and scratched his head. "I dunno, miss. That road might not be fit for horses, and that might be a long way afore you'd meet another soul, on such a night. I'd sooner walk back to where I saw that glimmer through the trees, like as it might be a house—tidy step though it is."

"No doubt you are right, but do you mean to leave me here?"

"Someone has to stay with the horses, miss, and you couldn't go off down that road alone."

"Very well, if you think it best. But I must warn you that I know very little about horses."

"They'll stand quiet enough, with you at their heads, though it would be better for them if you was to walk them, slowly like."

"But where would I walk them? I would be afraid of trying to turn the chaise. What if I got a wheel into the ditch? No, I think, if they will not catch cold, I'll hold them standing."

I saw a gleam in Hodgkin's eye as he looked past me into the murky interior of the chaise. "If so be you'd lend them your rug, miss, 'twould keep off the cold."

I looked regretfully at the comfortable travelling rug which reminded me so much of my late aunt, and told myself this was no time to become possessive. Besides, now I was rich, I could afford to buy a dozen such. "Very well, Hodgkin. But tell me just what I must do. Are you sure that the horses will stand still? They will not bite me?"

He looked pityingly at me. "Not if you hold the rein close by the bit—Lady's rein, for Prince will take his orders from

11

her, in a manner of speaking, for 'tis what he's accustomed to." Hodgkin opened the door and let down the steps. "Out with you, then, miss."

I stepped down to the rutted ground, hard frozen, and huddled my cloak about me. Hodgkin led me to the horses' heads and put the rein into my hand. "Just talk to her, like, miss," he advised me.

"But what do I say?"

"Just you tell her everything will be all right by and by, and that Hodgkin will be back soon—if the glim I saw ain't a will-o'-the-wisp, that is," he added lugubriously. I shivered and bit my lip, wishing I had taken more interest in horses during my country childhood. My father's ill health had reduced us to the kind of poverty that did not own horses, but my grandparents had kept their carriage and I might have ventured into their stables more often when I had had the chance. I tightened my grip on the rein. Lady rolled an eye at me and shook her head so the bit jingled and little beads of damp flew off her mane. Prince snorted nervously, and I trembled.

Hodgkin leaned closer. He smelt strongly of horses, leather, linseed oil, hay and manure—an amazingly comforting mixture, I decided, wishing I could keep him there.

"Here, miss," he said in a somewhat furtive tone, thrusting his hand within his waistcoat, "you'd best hold this, I reckon."

He pulled out a villainous-looking firearm and attempted to push it into my left hand.

I recoiled. My father having died young, and without providing me with brothers, I was no more accustomed to guns than I was to horses.

"Now see here, miss, you be so young and pretty-like, what will you do if some vagabond comes by? There may be footpads hereabouts after your purse, or horse thieves. I'm not

12

saying 'tis likely, mind, in this fog; but 'tis well to be prepared."

"I don't need your pistol," I told him. "I—have a dagger." I could feel the weight of it in my reticule. It was slightly curved and came from India in its fine embroidered sheath, and Aunt Layton had made me promise to keep it by me on this journey to which, on her deathbed, she had consigned me.

"A dagger?" Hodgkin exclaimed. He looked rather taken aback but soon persisted. "Now miss, a dagger may be very well for some purposes, but that can't let me know if you need help, not like a pistol can."

"You really think I might need to summon you?"

He pursed his thin lips and looked away. "I've heard some ugly tales about these parts," he owned reluctantly. "No, you just keep the barker—and mind, for 'tis loaded. Then all you have to do if aught troubles you is fire it and I'll come running back."

"But—what do I do?"

"You just curls your finger about the trigger—this here, miss, and squeeze it, gentle-like—whoa there!" he cried, skipping aside in alarm as I began to follow his instructions. "Not now, miss—and not while 'tis aimed at me, neither!"

"Oh dear, I am sorry—I forgot you said it was loaded."

"Point it down, miss," he implored me.

I obeyed. "That is easy, it is so heavy. Well, you had better go, I suppose, but please be as quick as you can."

"Just a minute, miss, while I throw the rug over them." He did not throw it, but rolled it and laid it cautiously across the horses' withers before slowly unrolling it to cover their backs. I realized that he was taking pains not to alarm them by sudden movements, and felt apprehensive at this evidence of his respect for their sensitive natures.

13

All too soon he had done and was lurching away down the road with his peculiar bowlegged gait. I tightened my grip on the rein and let the pistol hang limply from my other hand. There was utter silence apart from the muffled sound of the postilion's receding steps, and a soft dripping somewhere. It was almost dark but I could just make out the looming shape of the hedgerow, swathed in mist. Prince snorted again and I shifted my weight uneasily to the other foot, already grown numb with cold. I turned to glance at the faintly re-assuring glow of the carriage lamps, lit by Hodgkin an hour ago. What was I doing here, lost in a Sussex lane in a cut-down mourning gown with a fat purse in my reticule and a pistol in my hand? It seemed a far cry from either of my previous modes of existence, first as the protected daughter of the widow Tremayne who, though impoverished, yet had the security of living in the Essex village where her family had dwelt for generations, and next as the pampered companion of my late mother's eldest sister, the Admiral's widow, at a respectable address in Kensington. Now she too was dead, and I was on my way to my other aunt, the one whom I re-membered from years before as being happy, gay, and confi-dent in her belief that life was a fairy tale with herself as the heroine. Would her second marriage have changed her, or would I find—but here Lady sharply recalled my attention to the present moment by impatiently stamping her hoof. With a pang of guilt I remembered that I had engaged to talk to the horses. Feeling remarkably foolish, I followed Hodgkin's instructions in the matter, assuring them that all was well and that he would soon be back.

Silence fell again. After having heard the sound of my voice, it seemed worse than before. I cleared my throat to speak again, but before I could do so, disaster struck.

A large bird flew up out of the ditch with an unearthly

14

cry and went rocketing away under the horses' noses. Lady flung up her head, snatching the rein from my numb grasp and painfully jerking my wrist. As she wheeled away, taking Prince with her, the rug slipped. She plunged in terror, and it flapped. An instant later both horses were in full flight, the carriage lurching at their heels, the lamps growing dimmer as they raced into the fog.

I hurried in pursuit, stumbling over the ruts of the poor track they had taken, the way to the church. I came to a corner and, just beyond it, another division in the road. There was no sign of the chaise and the hard ground held no impression of its passing, though I thought I could still faintly hear the drumming of hooves.

I peered at the sign, barely visible in the deepening dusk. One arm pointed left to the church, the other to the Home Farm. The horses, I supposed, if they were capable of constructive thought, would be more likely to make for their own kind and I had actually taken a step towards the farm when a queer muffled sound made me start and pause as I identified it. A great bell had begun to toll slowly, distorted by the fog. It was impossible to tell from which direction it came, but common sense suggested it must be connected with the church. There was something eerie about the sound, but I could not allow that to deter me. Even if it were a passing bell tolling the dead, a live hand must be ringing it, I reflected; and I turned resolutely instead to walk down the hill towards All Saints.

It was still very cold and the pistol was heavy in my hand. I considered firing it to summon the postilion, but just as I had not done so earlier for fear of further alarming the horses, so now I did not want to frighten the bellringer and possible congregation, whom I was hoping to persuade to come to my assistance. Besides, I did not think I had the

15

courage to face Hodgkin again until I had found his horses.

I sniffed, and paused to blow my nose. It was then I made the dismaying discovery that my reticule was no longer about the wrist of my right hand. I could not believe I had been so stupid as to drop it, but it was certainly possible that the strings had caught on some part of Lady's harness as she leaped forward, in which case it might now be almost anywhere in this inhospitable strange land. It was a mishap of the first order, for all my money was in it, and the letter from Aunt Prendergast offering me a home at Pheasant's Hall, to say nothing of my comb, my best handkerchief, and my fine Indian dagger.

It did not take me many minutes of peering about the road and feeling in the ditch to persuade me that it was a hopeless task to find such an object in the dark, and soon I relinquished the attempt and began to hurry more urgently towards what I took to be the direction of the tolling bell.

Presently I came to an open gate, sagging from a mossy post. The track ran down more steeply here, across a field; and with no hedge to follow I should have to be careful not to lose it. The bell sounded erratically, now seeming to come from one side, now from the other. A bird called on a high piping note, and a horse whinnied quite near. My heart leapt in hope that it might be Lady or Prince, and I stared until my eyes watered at some vague shape that appeared to come and go through the swirling mist. A puff of cold wind momentarily cleared the fog but the glimpse I dimly caught was of a saddled horse, a long-tailed grey, which seemed to be tethered with one or two others to a fence. It certainly began to seem as if there were to be a service at the church. I hurried on, remembering to be grateful that at least the track was dry, while the bell grew louder. Suddenly I realized I had lost the path. My feet were on grass instead of

16

frozen mud. I went forward cautiously and stopped abruptly as I almost stumbled into a stone wall. I felt along it with my hands, and began to walk beside it. I came to a corner, and soon afterwards my right hand slipped downward as the wall ended in a tumble of stones. Then I discovered I was standing among reeds, stiff and tall, on the brink of thinly iced water, beneath which a wide river flowed slowly, presumably southward to the sea.

I was trembling from the narrowness of my escape, near to tears from losing not only a chaise and pair and a valuable rug but also my precious reticule. I found myself wondering what were the ugly tales men told about these parts, and even wishing for the company of my mournful postilion, rightfully furious though he would be with me. I bit my lip hard to regain control of myself and began to follow the wall back. It led me round the corner, under a shadowy yew to a lych-gate, hanging open and in sad need of repair. A path, much overgrown with rank weeds, led from here towards the dim bulk of the church. My heart bounded with relief as I saw light glowing within, a pulsing light as if that of a fire.

The bell had stopped, I realized, for I could hear voices coming indistinctly from the building, and music—music that, I became incredulously aware, was far from sacred: the thin haunting music of a flute that rose and fell, flirted and beckoned, among a medley of other sounds, a strangely pagan note, indeed.

I walked with hesitant feet towards the church. Suddenly the mist swirled away to reveal a startling glimpse of a fair-haired girl through a window, her yellow locks streaming in abandon over her white grown, illuminated by the flaring torch she held aloft. As I watched, a hand took the torch from her and she came into the arms of a dark and terrifying figure, a man dressed in a loose black robe, his head concealed

17

in a black hood with slits for eyes that seemed to stare at me as the couple began to dance, as if he were as arrested by my sudden unexpected appearance as I was by his. I was aware of the girl's face, wanton and oddly vacant as she pressed her cheek to her partner's shoulder, and of others behind them, particularly one great figure with a lolling head. An icy breath of wind dispelled the fog still further and revealed, as in a nightmare, torn walls, a tumbled tower in which, halfway up, the bell still swung, though silent now —and then a grey cloud swept about the ruined church as completely as if it had removed it, and left me horrified and alone.

With an inarticulate cry I turned and ran, heedless of direction, stumbling over fallen headstones and mounded graves, tearing my skirts on sticks and brambles, caring nothing that I might fall into the river or lose myself entirely, only so that I escape the ruined church where such people danced to pagan music and tolled a muffled bell—if indeed they were living people, and not ghosts.

Something loomed up before me. I leapt away, tripped, and fell, dropping the pistol. Snatching it up in my right hand, I staggered to my feet and turned to where I believed the gate to be.

"Stay, not so fast!" cried a man's deep voice, and a hand caught at my left arm.

My heart seemed to come into my throat. I looked round, eyes wide with terror, and nearly swooned when I saw my assailant, for he was gowned and hooded in black—no doubt the man I had seen dancing, now come to silence me.

Shakily, I raised the gun. "Stand back!" I stammered. His hand dropped and he started aside with a rough oath just as I fired. There was a stab of flame, a sound like thunder—

and I was again alone as I stumbled on with ringing ears about that frightful churchyard in search only of escape.

All at once my feet refused to move. They were slowly sinking, held by the mud of the river bank. I struggled free and stood with my hands to my mouth, crying in earnest. I must have dropped the pistol again, for my hands were empty. After a while I braced myself, knowing that at least my feet had found the firmer ground away from the bank and fearing that if I did not move I should soon be dead of cold.

I strained my ears, but all was as quiet as if I had dreamed the whole. I tried to remember what I had heard in those frenzied moments just after I had fired the gun. Voices, I thought; a cry from the man who had accosted me—I had not killed him then, I realized with relief, for though I had not aimed at him anything seemed possible on this accursed night. What else? Further cries, the sounds of running feet, a woman's wild scream, quickly muffled. I shivered and drew my cloak tightly about me. Whoever that devil's brood had been, it was certain they had gone. All was now quiet and dark. I had surely nothing further to fear from them, at least. Now I had somehow to make my way back to the road and find poor Hodgkin, who must be frantic with anxiety by now, on behalf of his horses if not for me.

I began to move away from the water's edge but my knees were shaking so much I soon sank down. This would not do. If I stayed here I would no doubt be dead of exposure by morning. I must find the pistol and fire it again to guide the postilion towards me, in case he had not heard my former shot. On my hands and knees I began to search among the frozen swathes of grass but was soon forced to acknowledge it as hopeless as my hunt for my reticule had been. I was on the verge of despair when it occurred to me that I had been led to the church by the tolling of the bell. What could be simpler than for me to do the same for Hodgkin?

I made out the jagged outline of the ruined church, even darker than the starless sky. I tottered towards it, and found the black hole of the entrance porch. The door swung ajar from rust-eaten hinges and let out a bloodcurdling screech as I pushed it wide. I waited, my heart beating uncomfortably loud, but no sound came from the dark interior of the church. I forced myself to go in. My footsteps rang echoing and hollow on the worn flagstones and when I turned to the right I blundered first into a stone font and next into a splintered pew. I persevered, and some paces farther on something furry touched my hand, and I let out a gasp of such terror that it frightened me again. Then I realized that I had found the bellrope. Thankfully, I pulled it. It came down and by the change of weight I felt the great bell move, but it made no sound. I pulled again, but still the bell was mute. I began to pray, the tears running down my cold cheeks, and a faint clangour answered my prayer. At last, at last the bell began to ring, a lone cracked note.

I could not guess for how long I tolled that bell. My arms began to ache and grew stiff, each time it rose I was almost lifted off my feet, and I was in a sorry state by the time I became conscious of a lantern glowing in what was then the full dark of the night. It swung nearer, and suddenly recognizing the bowed legs of the postilion as he approached me, I dropped the rope and sank half-fainting to the floor.

"Hodgkin," I croaked. "Oh, thank God!"

"Ay, 'tis me, miss," he said flatly. He turned and called out to someone behind him. Then he advanced towards me. "What brought you here then, miss, to this place? And where's my horses, what I left with you—and my gun, miss," he added

20

even more sharply as the lantern light fell on my empty hands, "where is my gun?"

"Please, Hodgkin," I sobbed. "I will tell you all, only give me time. You do not know what has happened since you left me—"

He gave an audible sigh. Then, looking over his shoulder, he called out again. "You there, the parish constable; give me a hand with the young lady, then. What ails you, standing there like a stock?"

There was a murmur from the porch and I realized that several persons were waiting there. A man was pushed forward by the rest and approached us reluctantly, starting at shadows and swinging his lantern this way and that.

"This is no place for honest men," he grumbled.

"Why," said Hodgkin, a new note in his voice, "is this the very church, then, what I've heard men speaking of? That did pass through my mind that might be so, but somehow—let us get Miss out of it, then, and be off—"

"Ay, let us," agreed the constable fervently. " 'Tis unhallowed ground these days, and they do say that on that very altar there—" He swung his light towards the other end of the church and I wondered why he did not finish what he was saying. Then his voice came, high and shrill.

"What is that—thing—upon the altar?"

"Oh, my God!" cried another voice from the porch, and one or two went running out into the night, and others pressed forward, crying out. I pulled myself upright and looked down the aisle in the light of the lifted lanterns.

There upon the altar something lay, bundled in white. My breath caught painfully. The lantern swung and I saw it was a woman—no, a girl, in a white gown. Her face was turned towards me, and I recognized it. If it had seemed

21

vacant when I had spied it through the window earlier, it was now doubly blank. The long yellow hair fell untidily about her, one arm hung limp, the other clutched a spray of red roses on her breast.

Roses, in February? Those red flowers were not roses, I thought slowly. They were wounds.

"Murder!" cried Hodgkin, as I fainted.

TWO

I came to my senses an instant before a hatful of dank river water was flung into my face. As I coughed and spluttered under its icy impact I was aware of Hodgkin's angry voice.

"Magistrate or no magistrate, I'm after my horses. There's no sense to be got out of Miss, but she must have let them go and I've been delayed long enough from looking for them."

"But his Honour will soon be here," objected the constable. "Jem ran to the farm to borrow a nag—it won't take long to fetch him and what will Squire say if he finds I've let you go?"

"Lord save us," said Hodgkin disgustedly, "you don't suspect me of having aught to do with this, do you? I'm not in the habit of carrying a dagger—" He broke off and turned to stare at me where I lay, damp and shivering, a wretched sight, no doubt. "I'm off," he said abruptly.

Carver put out a protesting hand. "But where shall we find you?"

The postilion shrugged. "If I don't find the horses I'll

be somewhere about, looking for them. If I get them back safe, my address is care of the King's Head, Horsefield." Shaking the constable's hand off his arm, he strode out of the church.

"Oh dear, oh dear," moaned the constable. "I've never known nothing like it, not in all my born days. I didn't ought to have let him go—"

"No, that you didn't, Sim Carver," cried a female voice harshly from the doorway. "Catch hold of that man, you fellows there! Look sharp about it! Arrest him in the King's name as a witness, for Squire will want to hear his evidence, that's certain."

The constable's face cleared. "Ay, that's right, Maggie Smith. Have they got him, then? You, Tom, Ezra—"

"They have him fast," she reported, "and small thanks to you. I'll say this to your face, Sim Carver, you're a better wheelwright nor what you're a constable."

"I wish I'd never been appointed, Maggie, and that's God's truth. And to think there's ten months more of my year to run! It would have been worth paying a proxy, that it would."

" 'Twill soon pass, I reckon, as time does at our age— and you're not likely to see anything like this again. Poor Farmer Holford," she added soberly. "I shouldn't care to be the one to tell him what has come to Polly, nor I wouldn't want to break it to Peg—nor Mother Holford neither, for all she's something simple in the head. 'Tis cruel hard to lose a child in such a way, and I wouldn't be in Jem's shoes for much, for he'll have to tell Farmer at least if he's to borrow a horse from him—"

"I've nothing to say, I tell you," protested Hodgkin as he was half-dragged back into the church. "No, I can't vouch for the lady's character—never set eyes on her before today. Seemed a nice enough young lady to me at the time—

24

came off the London to Brighton stage and asked for a chaise to take her to Pheasant's Hall—"

At this there was an outcry, for some reason, and I heard a voice shout, "A ruse! A ruse!"

"Well, it may have been, for all I know." Hodgkin shrugged. "She did seem a stranger to the county, that I can say. How was I to guess she knew her way to the church, and in a fog, too? Come to think of it, maybe she didn't—for how was she to know I would stop the chaise just there and leave her with it?" he added belligerently.

The faintness had cleared from my head by this time, and I sat up, stiff and wet and miserable. I glanced towards the altar, to see thankfully that the body had been shrouded by a coat.

"So you're awake, are you, miss?" cried Hodgkin. "Now see here, where are my horses?"

I found my voice. "I am extremely sorry . . . they took the turning for the farm, I believe. I only came this way because I heard the bell—"

But Hodgkin was not concerned with my adventures, only with his missing possessions.

"And my pistol, miss? Cost me a mint of money, that barker did, and shoots straight, what's more. I wouldn't part with that gun, I wouldn't, not for all the tea in China."

"It's—not lost, I think, but I fear I dropped it in the churchyard." I cleared my throat, for my voice was strangely weak. "You should find it outside the church, somewhere near the river."

"No examining the witnesses till Squire is present," cried the constable, suddenly officious as a bustle in the porch announced an arrival of some importance.

"Good evening, Squire," said Maggie Smith, dropping a curtsy. "You've come very quick, if I may be so bold."

25

The squire appeared in the doorway, a tall heavy man, his probably once-handsome face ruined by good living and hard weather, carelessly dressed in chalk-stained hunting pink, his stock wrenched aside and his silk hat over one ear. "You may, Maggie Simpson—Smith, that is to say. H'm, you may make so bold. Bold as you please." He swayed and I realized with a sinking heart that he was very drunk. "Ay," he went on, looking about him with a foolish smile, " 'twas a lucky thing young Jem found me when he did. Been hunting, you know—had a good scent earlier in the day, despite the sun, but our fox was chopped by a pesky waggoner. Cast about for a goodish while but had to call hounds off when the fog came down. Sent 'em home with Stevens and followed more slowly myself. Spare the horse, you know—and then I had a little business at the Green Man and one or two other ports of call —hic! Was just thinking I must try for home when Jim— Jem, whatever the fellow calls himself, I've no head for names as everybody knows—but where's the constable, eh? What's this Jim told me of a body? Dashed unlikely tale, as he told it . . ."

" 'Tis true enough, sir, I fear. Poor Polly Holford."

"Ay, so Jem said. Well, lead me to it, man."

"Here 'tis, sir, just upon the altar, as you see. Nothing has been touched, your Honour, barring covering the face of the deceased—"

"I told him to do that," put in Maggie Smith, folding her arms complacently. "For I recalled your telling poor Smith as much, when he was alive and constable in his turn, God rest him, that time old Clement died at market."

A small bespectacled man who had entered after the squire now stepped forward and took him by the arm. "This way, sir. Mind the step."

"Ay, thank you, Badcock—Baldock." The squire stopped abruptly. "God! Look at it, clerk. And on the altar, too!"

"Yes, sir. A bad business, I fear."

The squire loomed over the body, bracing himself, before drawing back the concealing coat. "H'm, 'tis Polly Holford, right enough. And not much doubt either as to the cause of death."

The clerk leaned forward. "These stab wounds here, your Honour."

"Ay, just so. Any sign of the weapon, constable? What do we look for, Baldock? Knife, or sword?"

"If you will assist me to turn the body, sir—"

They lifted her between them and after a moment lowered her again.

"A dagger, then," declared the squire.

"A dagger?" echoed Maggie Smith. "Now there's a fine thing! Why did this postilion here say *he* was not the one to be carrying a dagger—and made to run off, after? How did he know what the weapon was, if he'd only just come to the church, like he made out?"

"Any fool could see as the girl had been stabbed," Hodgkin pointed out morosely. "As for the dagger, this young lady said she had one and naturally, putting two and two together—"

"Do no such thing!" cried the clerk. "Your evidence will be heard in due course, and at the proper time."

The squire put out a hand to steady himself on the remains of a choir stall. "Quite right, Badcock—Babchick? We must do this in the proper form. Constable! Oh, you are there, man. You say it was you who discovered the body? Write this down, clerk."

"Ay, your Honour." The clerk opened his ink and began to scribble on a tablet, resting it against the lectern.

27

Carver cleared his throat and said in an unnatural tone, "I discovered the body, sir, in the presence of this man Hodgkin, and the young person over there, and all them as is in the porch—Tom Jenkins, Maggie Smith, Ezra Johnson, they all saw me swing my lantern and—discover the corpse, sir, as you might say."

"Quite so. You, then—Hodges, did he say your name was?" The squire advanced heavily and peered into the postilion's gloomy face. "I don't know you, do I? You are not from hereabouts? Who are you? A postilion, certainly, by your dress—but where's your chaise?"

"Ah, sir, I'd give a deal to know that myself. I left this young lady holding the horses while I walked back to enquire the way—"

"Yes, yes, we'll have those details from you in good time. For now, where are your stables?"

"The King's Head, Horsefield, sir. You ask anyone round there—they all knows Abel Hodgkin on account of his ill-luck. You may say I'm something of a legend, sir: this ain't the first time I've been connected with a violent death, not by no means. I was held up once by a highwayman, and two passengers shot behind me, poor souls. One time I nearly ran over a body in the road, been dead for days, he had—and that's not the end of it, sir. Why, if I was to tell you all the mishaps as have occurred to me, all in the way of my work, like, I daresay as you'd hardly believe it. 'You'll end up at Newgate,' my old mother used to say to me, 'you see if you don't,' all on account of my bad luck, sir. But I don't know nothing about this here murder, that's God's truth—and you may hang me if I lie."

"I certainly shall, Hedgehog," returned the squire pleasantly, rocking a little on his heels. "Yes, if I find you lie it shall be my pleasure to send you to the quarter sessions, and thence to the high court, and thence—h'm! But if I understand the matter aright you came down to the church in the company of Cartwright here and these others, and found this —er—" for the first time he peered drectly at me—"this young lady here alone with the body?"

"Yes sir, 'tis so, and I'm bound to say that does look bad. If you ask me—"

"But I have not done so, Hedges—Hodges?"

"Hodgkin, sir. But I was only going to say—"

"Pray don't," said the squire in a dignified manner, "for I believe I am conducting this, er, preliminary enquiry, and not you. Hic! H'm . . . where was I? Ah, yes, your name, madam? Write this down, clerk."

"Tansy Tremayne, sir," I replied, between chattering teeth.

"Train?" he queried, frowning. "Well, no matter. Be good enough to tell me how you come to be here in All Saints with Polly Holford on such a night."

I realized wearily I would be hard put to account for it, so much had happened to me this evening that would sound incredible in the telling. After a good night's sleep, perhaps . . .

"Hurry, girl," said the squire sharply. "We don't want to be here all night."

"It was the fog," I muttered, clasping my hands together in a vain attempt to keep them warm. "It was as Hodgkin told you. He got down to walk back to a house in order to enquire the way, and left me with the horses—"

"Ah, yes, the missing horses." The squire turned to Hodgkin. "Do you wish to prefer a charge?"

The postilion looked baffled and Mr. Baldock, if that was his name, nudged the squire gently in the ribs. He looked round. "What's that, clerk? Oh, the enquiry first, ay. So you were left with the horses, miss, which have since—hic—vanished. Well, go on."

"A—a pheasant flew out of the hedge and startled them, so they ran away. I followed—"

Hodgkin interrupted. "But why didn't you fire the pistol, miss, like I said to do?"

Haltingly, I made my explanation to him, while the squire regarded me very suspiciously indeed.

"And now for the dagger," he said suddenly. "For I understand that, not content with the pistol, you were also in possession of a dagger—and for reasons that are no doubt obvious to you, it is the dagger which interests us particularly. I demand to see your dagger, young lady."

Weakly, I shook my head. After a moment I found the strength to whisper that I had lost my reticule, and the dagger with it.

"You lost it, you say? Mark that, Babchick. So you have not now the dagger, nor any proof of your identity, come to that?"

"N-no. But perhaps, if word can be sent—"

But the squire was listening to Baldock, who whispered in his ear. "Ay," he murmured pensively, and then, raising his voice, called out, "Step up here a moment, Mrs.—er, Smith, if you'll be so good. I wish you to run your hands over this young lady to make sure she has not the weapon on her."

"Ay, sir, that I will," cried Mrs. Smith, coming forward with alacrity. "Stand up, miss, if you please."

I submitted to the indignity of the search; but worse was to follow. "Hold her on a charge of vagrancy, you suggest?" the magistrate was saying to his clerk. "No visible means of support? Gives us time to look about a little. Well, we'll see. Now, miss, think carefully what you say and tell us what happened when you came here to the church—and why you came, indeed."

I closed my eyes. "I came because I heard the tolling bell . . ." Hold me—on a charge of vagrancy? What did that mean? Arrest, and imprisonment? Or would they send me to Bedlam when they had heard my tale?

"Yes," said the squire impatiently, stamping his feet on the cold flags. "So you heard the bell? Odd, that. Dashed odd!"

Flatly, prepared for disbelief, I explained how I had come to the church and seen lights, heard music, and glimpsed people within—the girl who now lay dead, and a tall man, and others moving behind them; but if the squire was skeptical, the villagers were not and my tale was told to the accompaniment of gasps and squeals and furtive crossings. I told how I had fled across the graveyard, and then some belated instinct for self-preservation halted me as I came to the moment when the tall man accosted me, and I fired on him. If I confessed to that, would not the charge on which they held me be attempted murder? Praying that the man had indeed escaped unscathed and that they would not find his body lying out there among the weed-grown graves, I said only that I had fired the gun to guide the postilion to me.

"Unlawful possession of a firearm!" cried the squire enthusiastically. "Is that not so, Badcock? Quiet, you—er, Hedges. Let Miss Trayle finish."

"Tremayne, sir," I ventured to correct him, but immediately wished I had not done so.

"Trelawney, Train, what's in a name?" he muttered angrily. "Well, go on. Where is this gun? Or can you not produce that either?"

I continued with less and less certainty as I became ever more aware of the squire's impatient incredulity. There was

31

a pause when I had done. Then the constable ventured to say, in my support, "I have heard tell as powerful strange things go on here at All Saints, sir—"

"Not so strange as the tale we have just heard, I think," the squire returned implacably.

For the first time I became fully aware of the gravity of my situation. I had been found here in the church alone with no one to bear witness for me—alone save for the dead body of a girl who had been murdered by dagger wounds—and I had owned to possessing a dagger but I could not produce it to prove that it was innocent of blood. Now indeed I understood why the squire had mentioned vagrancy. It was to give himself a charge on which I could be committed to jail so I should lie safe while he prepared a case against me—and what evidence should I ever be able to find to clear me when the only witness to the truth of my story was a masked man at whom I had shot and who would hardly be eager to appear before the law on behalf of one who had, even if unwittingly, spied upon him and his companions?

To my dismay I found myself half-swooning again. I had eaten little in the course of a day spent travelling, and was further weakened by cold and fear; nevertheless I was able to struggle for consciousness and regained it in time to hear the squire conclude a sentence which appeared to be addressed to me.

"—satisfactory account of yourself?"

I gazed up at him blankly and shook my head to clear it.

"Brrh!" exclaimed the squire, striking his hands together. "Let us be done with this business, Babchick, for the moment at least. Constable! Have a waggon sent for to remove the body; and ask poor Holford for the loan of his gig on the King's business—he'll be glad enough to lend it when he understands it is to be used to convey the chief suspect to jail, I'll warrant!"

The clerk leaned towards him and murmured at some length while these orders were being carried out.

"Very well, man," the squire assented at last. To me he added brusquely, "Well, girl, do you understand me? Do you still refuse to speak?"

"Speak? Speak?" I repeated wildly. "What can I say but the truth, and that you have already heard!"

"Have you any proof of identity, or means of support?"

"I told you that I lost my reticule—"

"Then I have no choice but to sign the committal—unless your postilion here cares to stand bail for you?"

This was taken as some sort of jest by the villagers, and drew an emphatic disclaimer from Hodgkin. After a moment, however, he added grudgingly, "I can witness that Miss owned a fur rug, before she lost it with the horses—ay, and she had a fat purse, too."

"*Visible* means of support," snapped the squire. He turned to the clerk again. "Well, man, give me the form—and your pen and ink."

The paper was produced, and they bent over it together. Could it really be a warrant for my arrest, I wondered numbly. I was not left long in doubt. Mr. Baldock fixed me with a steady stare, the lamplight dancing on his spectacles so I could not see if there were pity in his eyes.

"You are to be committed, then, on the charge of vagrancy, to Hallchurch Gaol. Your full name?"

"Tansy Amanda Tremayne," I faltered. "But—but, sir— my box—it is on the chaise—"

The squire, already at the door, looked back to answer me. "Lord, girl, you won't need to make a good appearance where you're going—but we'll send your clothes after you if we find them, you may depend upon it—and your reticule, of course. Come, clerk," he added impatiently, "what do you stay for? I'm ready for my own fireside and a bowl of punch, if you are not. We've visitors expected, and my son is with us at the moment."

"Excuse me, sir," said the constable timorously. "Where am I to put the body, sir?"

"You'll put it nowhere, for you are to take the prisoner in your charge and deliver her to the jail, on the remand side, of course. Have the body sent to the church hall—and mind they guard it well. As for the rest of you, you may look to be subpoenaed later."

With that he washed his hands of us all and strode unsteadily into the night, followed by the clerk as soon as he had hastily shut up his ink and handed the form to the constable.

Hodgkin hurried after them, crying, "What about my horses?" in a plaintive voice. I sank down onto a pew and picked splinters out of the wood unthinkingly, oblivious of the stares and murmurs from the porch.

Some time later Maggie Smith called out that the gig was come. "Look sharp, Sim Carver," she cried. "The sooner that girl is set before a fire, the more like she is to survive for the trial."

I was led outside and down the path. The constable lifted his lantern and revealed a farmer's gig with a bright-eyed lad holding the reins, who looked down at me, first with interest and then with amazement.

"That's right then, Jem; hand the young lady up," said Carver, pushing me forward.

"Lord," cried Jem, "but she's the prettiest piece they'll have seen in Hallchurch Gaol this many a year!"

"Handsome is as handsome does," returned the constable sagely.

I hung back. "Where is Hodgkin? I want him to take a message for me."

The postilion loomed out of the thinning fog. "Here I am, miss, and hereabouts I'll be until I find that dratted chaise—"

"A chaise, mister?" said Jem alertly, twisting in his seat. "Be you a-looking for a chaise and pair?"

"Why, I thought as the whole county would have known that by now," said Hodgkin sourly. "Do you know aught about 'em, then?"

Jem scratched his head. "That went clean out of my mind, on account of the fuss that came after, when I gave Farmer the news about poor Polly—but when I ran in to borrow a horse for to take the message to Squire, Farmer met me and said to tell Squire as he'd found a chaise and pair and to tell him he'd stabled the cattle and would bait them if Squire would be so kind as to refund him—only afterwards, with Mother Holford crying and carrying on so, and Peg going off in a swoon and all, dang me if I didn't forget to tell Squire about it—" He broke off. "Now where's the fellow gone?" he asked indignantly. "One minute he was standing here, and next—"

"Never you mind about that postilion, Jem," said Carver. "He'll have gone after his horses, same as you would do yourself. Don't keep us standing about, lad, but make haste to drive us to the jail—and don't spare poor Holford's cob."

"Here, one minute," cried Maggie Smith, bustling forward and dragging off the black frieze coat she wore. "Put this round the child, for she's wet through—only mind you bring that back, Sim Carver, for that belonged to my late husband, as well you should know, seeing as it was your cousin Trimble made it up for him."

The warmth of the coat revived me a little and I sat shaking in it as the gig bounded through the darkness, telling myself that in the morning my reticule would surely be found

35

and then there would be no excuse to keep me imprisoned. In the morning, too, my uncle would certainly set up a hue and cry for me—my uncle! I thought with a pang of remorse. I had meant to send a message for him by Hodgkin, but the postilion had left too quickly for me. Perhaps if I begged the constable . . .

"Are you acquainted with a gentleman by the name of Sir Abraham Prendergast?" I enquired hopefully.

To my surprise the constable gave me an odd look, then nudged the driver with his elbow. "Miss is beginning to wander in her mind," he muttered. "Can't you get a better pace out of that cob?" To me he said severely, "Now never mind that, miss. There's no call for you to be talking—plenty of time for that when Squire comes to question you again, as no doubt he will on Monday, if not tomorrow. And while we're on that subject, there's one or two matters I should mention to you if so be you have not been in prison before."

"No," I said faintly, "indeed I have not." But it was with an awful feeling of despair that I realized I should never again be able to make the same assurance. Always from now on I would have a secret to hide or be known as a jailbird, and in the latter case my reputation would be utterly ruined, no hope of honourable employment possible—and it was not beyond the bounds of possibility that Aunt Prendergast might now withdraw her offer of a home for me.

"In that case, miss, I'd better warn you as you'll be given one or two little tasks to carry out, since you've no money for garnish, and it won't be very comfortable for you, no question—but you'd best make up your mind to do what they ask, for if you don't they have punishments and work the like of which you've never known, from the look of you—"

"Whoa—whoa!" cried Jem, reining in the cob. "There you

are, Mr. Carver—and the captain himself couldn't have drove you quicker, I reckon."

"So soon?" I cried.

" 'Tis just down the road from All Saints, miss, in a manner of speaking."

"I—am not ready," I protested, in a ludicrous attempt to postpone the evil moment.

"There's worse jails than Hallchurch, miss," said the constable gruffly.

I bit my lip and stared at the dark huddle of buildings, unrelieved, as far as I could see, by any window or any glimmer of light. There was a stout nailed door with a grating in it, and a great iron bell beside it, which Jem proceeded to ring. As the melancholy clang reverberated from it a horrible scream sounded from within the prison, followed by incoherent sobs and cries and moans.

Aghast, I shrank closer to the constable, who moved uneasily away from me. Then I heard the tramp of heavy footsteps and the clink of keys, followed by the sound of bolts being slowly drawn, as the jailer responded to the summons of the bell.

"Who's that?" a rough voice cried out through the grating.

" 'Tis I, the constable, Sim Carver—with a committal from the magistrate."

"Lord, at this time of night?" the jailer grumbled, but inexorably the great door swung open while behind it, the screams redoubled in volume.

THREE

"You've done it now, Sim Carver," the jailer complained, while the constable helped me to descend. "We have the pleasure of Mad Maudie's company tonight, as you can hear, and the least disturbance sets her off. I thought we had her settled for the night and now you've come along and roused her—" He broke off, lifting his lantern high. "Well, well," he added in a different voice, "and who do we have here?"

"Tansy Amanda Tremayne," announced the constable, glancing at the paper in his hand, "to be held for vagrancy—and don't be too hard on her, George, for 'tis my belief she's gently bred."

"Ha! Them is always the worst, in my experience," declared the jailer.

"Which as we know is considerable, George," said Carver placatingly. "But I don't think Miss will give you trouble."

The jailer laughed. "None that I can't deal with, I dare say. But she'll have to be broke of her fine lady airs. What brings her here, in any case? She has gloves, I see, and her handkerchief would fetch a shilling or two."

"Ah, well, I won't hide from you that there's more to this than meets the eye. You won't have heard the news yet, of course—a rare gossip we'll have by and by. But first you'd better get young Miss settled, for she's halfway to a swoon, I'm thinking."

"Well, she'll not be the first to swoon on this ground—not by a long chalk. Nor she wouldn't be the first to succumb, neither—but we'll trust it does not come to that, for it don't look well on the books to lose a prisoner, and then there's the cost of the funeral to be defrayed."

"A pauper's funeral don't cost too much—but Squire will be fair put about if you lose this one, George."

"Oh, is that so? Wants special treatment for her, does he?" The jailer leered at me horribly. "I hope as you're well-feathered, miss, for that makes a vast deal of difference to your comfort here."

"Vagrancy, George, remember."

"Oh Lord, so you said." The jailer's face fell. "Has she nothing to her name? Nothing to buy her a mattress of feathers—or even chaff? Nothing to buy a meal—for 'tis but a loaf a day as is provided here, as well you know, and the daily broth. Not so much as will secure her a room to herself?"

"Steady there, George," said the constable. "You won't frighten this one into bringing out the sovereign sewn into her hem—for wouldn't the likes of her have shown it to Squire if she did have means of support before it went so far as this? You must give her a room to herself without charge, for we both knows as the jail is half-empty just now. You'd best give her a mattress, too, and a shovel of fire for the grate—for Squire will want a reckoning if this one dies."

"What, and no garnish in it for me?"

"I daresay Squire will slip you something for your pains, when she comes safe to court."

39

"Well, I make no promises, mind; it will be straw to lie upon, and bread and water for her fare—"

"Just as you say, man, only get her to a fire."

"Mrs. George will see to it," said the jailer sulkily, and let out a bellow for his wife that set the madwoman to screaming again. "Where are you, good-for-naught?" he raved. "Jane George! I know she's not far off," he added for the constable's benefit, "for 'tis but ten minutes since I let her in—and none leaves this place without my knowledge. Come, woman, if you've a mind to keep a whole skin! Ay, I thought that would fetch you," he added with satisfaction as Mrs. George came running, wiping her red hands in her apron, her miserable-looking face seamed in lines of fear and worry. "Take this young woman to the female side and lock her in," the jailer commanded.

"And give her a mattress, and a fire," Carver prompted.

"As the constable says. Chaff, mind. And a jug of water—and you can have her kerchief off her for it," he added with another sullen appraising glance at me.

"Which cell, Charlie?" Mrs. George asked anxiously. Her sunken eyes seemed so intent on catching her husband's meaning before he had cause to cuff her that she had not even looked at me.

"A dry one, if there is one—and on her own." Mr. George turned his brutish face towards me again. "Now see here, young miss, I know your sort—all airs and graces and ideas above your station. You've no money so you'll accept what we give you and be grateful for it. Any shelter is better than none on a cold night. And when Squire asks if you've any complaint of your treatment here, be very careful how you answer him. I've been a smith by trade, and I'm no weakling as you see—" He turned a little sideways and flexed the muscles of a mighty arm. "I've not had a complaint laid against

40

this jail yet, and I don't intend as there should be one." He grinned suddenly, exposing rotting teeth. "You should have a little talk with my wife. She will tell you what to expect if you cross me, see?"

"I will then, Charlie," whispered Mrs. George. "She'll do as she is bid, never you mind. Come then, miss." She drew a ring of keys from her pocket, selected one and taking a surprisingly strong grip on my arm began to drag me across the yard.

"No, oh no!" I heard myself cry out, too weak to resist. I twisted my head to look imploringly at the constable. "Oh, pray, sir, take a message to Sir Abraham for me—Sir Abraham Prendergast of Pheasant's Hall!"

"Sir Abraham?" growled the jailer, stiffening. "What have you to say to Sir Abraham, then, miss?"

"Why, he is my uncle and responsible for me," I cried, heartened by the fact that the name evidently meant something to him. But to my horror he threw back his head and gave a great laugh which mingled horribly with the renewed screams of the poor maniac and the thin titter of the constable.

"Your uncle, miss! That's rich!" Then, sobering suddenly, the jailer shook his brawny fist beneath my nose. "Don't you try it, sweetheart," he warned me. "Just don't try it. I'm not a very even-tempered man, am I, Janey? And when a pert miss tells me such a corking lie—"

"But he is," I cried desperately. "Sir Abraham is my uncle by marriage—ask him!"

"Now, miss," said the constable soothingly, "just you go to your room and have a nice sleep. You're in a delirium, you see, and can't know what you're saying."

Mrs. George said uneasily, "I suppose there couldn't be no truth in it, Mr. Carver?"

41

The constable shook his head. "No truth in the world, Mrs. George. As you could see, did you look at the form I gave to your husband just now, Sir Abraham Prendergast is the very magistrate who committed her to jail!"

I sank to the damp cobbles. "That was Sir Abraham?" I cried incredulously.

The jailer dragged me to my feet. "Ay, that was Squire, as well you know, miss. Now are you going to come quietly?"

"One moment, George," cried the constable. "I'll thank you, miss, for that frieze coat."

Between them they pulled it off me and then Mrs. George put her sinewy arm about me and half-carried me to a cell. She lit a rush dip, which made a good deal of smoke and smell but cast little light, and I stood shivering and looking about me while she left me for a moment, but there was little to see but a naked-looking iron bedstead and a rickety spinning wheel in one corner.

Mrs. George returned with a shovelful of glowing coals which she thrust into the grate, and under the other arm, a thin mattress and a couple of coarse grey blankets.

"There's water in the jug," she said, and slammed the door.

With some difficulty, for my hands were shaking, I wrapped the blankets about me and sank down on the lumpy bed. Where now was the fine fur rug Aunt Layton had given me? I remembered her smile as she stroked it. Warmth, she had insisted, was so important when travelling . . . tears of weakness filled my eyes and made it seem as if flames were dancing in the sulky fire. Oh, Uncle Prendergast, I cried out in my mind, how could you commit me to this place? And what should I do now, for he was the very man on whom I had been depending to release me? He had been drunk, of course; he had no head for names; he had not connected me with the visitor his wife was expecting. Tomorrow, perhaps, he would realize and then, no doubt, I would be freed. Despite this thought, however, I sighed deeply. In the next cell, as if in sympathy, the madwoman began to croon and sing.

I must have slept sooner than I had expected for in my dreams Mad Maudie's tuneless droning became the postilion's mournful dirge:

"O, the hangman waits for you and me,
Alas!
O, the hangman waits for you and me,
Alas!
He waits for us by Tyburn Tree—"

and then I dreamed of people dancing about the gallows, people masked and dressed in black. There was a building, too, a cold and dripping ruin, through which the dance swayed in and out; and a man's voice that told me harshly that this was a coven of witches: the witches of All Saints.

I woke and slept and dreamed and woke again, now hot, now cold, now seeming to be at home in Essex with my dying mother and kindly grandparents, now in the stuffy overfurnished house at Kensington hearing my aunt telling me strange and wonderful tales of Admiral Layton's adventures in other lands; and again travelling in a chaise drawn by headless horses towards some inescapable doom.

It was almost a relief to see dawn lightening my barred window at last, though I felt so ill and wretched I wondered if I could have succumbed so soon to jail fever. Then came the grating of a key in the lock and the door was flung open by Mrs. George.

"Time to get up and sweep out your cell," she called, not

looking at me as she threw a twig broom into the corner. "Quick about it, mind, for your bread will be coming soon from the oven."

She went away, leaving the door open and the cold air rushing in. Next door I could hear the mad woman groaning horribly as Mrs. George shook her awake; then the jailer's wife returned to me.

"What, miss, not stirring yet? Here's a slug-a-bed! You'd best get up afore George finds you and drags you to the pump, for he don't know when to stop, and that's a fact—he'll drown someone one of these days, I fear. And I'll have that kerchief while I think of it," she added, pulling it from my shoulders with a red, swollen hand incongruously embellished with a curious plaited golden ring, which had also, no doubt, once been wrested from a reluctant prisoner.

"Oh please—I beg you!" I cried, as she ripped out the pin and shook out my handkerchief with an air of triumph. "It is not so much the cold but my gown is so low-cut—it was made to be worn with a handkerchief—"

"You should have thought of that before you lost your purse. Now, up with you!"

I shivered. "I think I can't get up—"

"Ho! We'll soon see about that. George!"

"No, wait—I will try." I put my feet to the floor and clutched the bed as the room seemed to spin about me.

She regarded me mercilessly. "Up—and sweep!"

"May I not wash first?"

"My!" she exclaimed. "We've a fine lady here, and no mistake! No, miss, you may not . . . you'll be asking me for a lady's maid next, I suppose," she muttered as she turned to leave. "Oh, and your door is open that you may sweep the dust through it," she added. "Don't think of stepping outside, for you're a prisoner now, you know."

44

I forced myself to stand in order to shake out my mattress and sweep the floor. Then I splashed my face with water from the jug and, not daring to return to the bed, sat down on the three-legged stool before the spinning wheel and wondered how I should pass the long hours till nightfall. I did not even dare to spin, for the previous occupant of the cell had left a fine even thread upon the spindle that I could not hope to emulate. If only I had listened to Grandmama when she had told me that every girl should be able to weave and spin, to card and dye.

"Here's bread and a mug of water for you," cried Mrs. George from the doorway. "Eat up, and then you can scrub, for 'tis Sunday, you know, and we must have all in order for the chaplain, when he comes to pray over you."

I pulled a piece off the loaf. It smelled good but I could not eat it.

"That's all you will get, girl, till your midday broth," said Mrs. George, as I pushed it away. "Put it in your pocket for if you're too proud to eat it now, you'll come to it later and 'twould be a pity to let the rats have it."

"Rats?" I looked about me fearfully.

"Ay, terrible plagued with 'em, we are. Did you not hear them in the night, scuttling all about you? Well, gossiping here won't get the work done, and here's Sairey with your bucket." She stepped aside as a slatternly girl set down a wooden pail and a box of sand and ashes. "Scrub into the corners, mind, for Chaplain's terrible set on cleanliness."

The problem of how to occupy myself was solved, at all events, I told myself as I dropped to my knees and picked up the scrubbing brush. If only I did not feel so weak! But I set my lips firmly and began to scrub.

After a few minutes I was taken with a fit of sneezing and shivering and when it had passed strange images began to

45

fill my mind. Somehow I thought that I was in Hell and that as I scrubbed, the fires were being stoked ever higher until even the once-icy water became boiling hot. At any moment the pitchfork would reach in to cast me on the flames . . . and then a man's shadow darkened the doorway and I shrank back in terror.

"The Devil!" I whispered, while some shred of sanity assured me that it might, on the contrary, be the chaplain. But the man was dressed for riding and though his back was to the light I could see that his eyebrows at least were decidedly satanic.

He inclined his head. "You do me too much honour, Miss Tremayne."

"But—you know my name!" I cried, hardly aware of what I was saying.

"I have come to take you away," he continued evenly, looking me up and down.

"No!"

He seemed to smile. "Why, do you like it here so much? But I fear my stepmother knows nothing of your odd tastes and requested me to lose no time in bringing you home to her."

I rose slowly and shook my head, but far from clearing it, the mists about me seemed to thicken. I would have fallen but that with one stride my visitor crossed the cell to catch me by the arm and hold me upright.

"Leave me," I said faintly. "Oh sir, please let go of me!"

"What, and have you swooning on the floor? I hardly think any useful purpose would be served by that."

I would never have believed I should have been so pleased to see Mrs. George, who appeared in the doorway just then, resplendent in a newly ironed apron, crackling with starch.

"Oh, you have found her then, sir," she exclaimed rather

breathlessly. "I am sorry I had to put her to scrub, but 'tis the rule, you see—"

"I daresay it will not have harmed her," the man declared indifferently. "Let us have her out into the light, for I am curious to see her properly."

"Very well, sir," said Mrs. George, plainly relieved that she was not to be taken to task for ill-treating me. "Come then, miss."

I struggled feebly. "I won't go with him!"

"No, no, miss—with me!" Mrs. George drew me to the doorway, adding to the stranger, "She is a little out of her mind, I think. It often takes them so at first. And then she may have caught a chill—though George and me was careful to let her have a bit of a fire and a mattress, even though she'd not a penny on her to pay for the privilege. . . ."

I heard the chink of coins as my visitor took the hint.

"Thank you kindly, sir; ay, that will cover it. Turn round now, miss, and let the gentleman have a look at you."

I found myself staring up into the critical eyes of a man not many years older than myself: a hard man, I thought. Healthy, alert—but intolerably remote. My face burned under his comprehensive look, and I lifted my hands defensively to my low neckline.

He raised a twisted eyebrow and remarked that I was not quite what he had expected.

"No, she don't look like a jailbird, sir," Mrs. George agreed sycophantically. "She has a pretty little face and her hair would be like silk if it were brushed—and she has given us no trouble, that I must say. Did I hear George mention that the charge against her has been removed?"

"You may have done. I gave your husband an order for Miss Tremayne's release. It seems that her purse has been found and so there are no longer grounds for a charge of

47

vagrancy." He stared at me and then turned to glance into the cell. "Had Miss Tremayne anything with her when she came or do I take her just as she is?"

I clung to Mrs. George. The stranger looked impatient. "Don't be so foolish, Miss Tremayne. I can't assure you that I am your friend, but I shan't eat you, you know."

But, I thought confusedly, why did he want me to go with him, if he did not like me?

He took my arm in a forceful grip. I struggled, and Mrs. George offered to fetch her husband.

"No need for that," said my abductor firmly, and to me, "You do not wish me to carry you, I suppose? Come, then."

I submitted, for he was certainly extremely strong, and we proceeded to the outer court and thence to the great door beside which the blacksmith was standing, rubbing his cold red hands and looking quite regretful to be seeing the last of me.

"You have her safe then, sir?" he cried, opening the door. "She's your responsibility now, Captain—and my compliments to your father, sir."

Outside a curricle waited, with a ragged boy at the horses' heads. The prison doors clanged shut behind me, but I was in no mood to savour my freedom.

"At least tell me where you are taking me!" I begged, as my new captor threw me up on the seat of the open carriage. "Tell me who you are, and by what right you take me from that place?"

He did not answer immediately, handing me a rug and calling out to the boy to stand away from the horses, taking the reins, flinging the lad a coin, and turning the carriage in a practiced movement.

"Who am I, Miss Tremayne?" he said at last. "Why, I am

48

your cousin, ma'am. Your step-cousin, if you like it better—Captain Prendergast."

"Oh! But then—was that truly my uncle last night? How could he! And my name—surely he must have known my name?"

"My father was too drunk to have recognized one of his own horses last night and names mean nothing to him at the best of times—but this morning, when the mists had cleared a trifle from his brain and he was able to pay heed to the wailings of my stepmother about her missing niece—'such a sweet child,'" he quoted with a sarcastic intonation, "'so pretty, the very image of her mother, so dutiful and kind—and now with a fortune all her own!'" He broke off and favoured me with a hard stare. "Was that why you were so dutiful and kind, perhaps? Were you vastly surprised when you learned Mrs. Layton had left her fortune to you? Now, why do you look so reproachful? Tears, too? Is it possible that I do you an injustice and that you are what your face proclaims you to be? Well, time will tell, but the evidence so far prompts me not to forget for an instant to regard you with suspicion."

"Why?" I cried out. "Can you really believe that I killed that girl?"

He twirled his whip. "As to that, I do not know. But that you are capable of murder, I am sure."

"What! How can you say so?"

"Very easily, Miss Tremayne, since only a few hours ago you tried to put a bullet through my heart."

I gasped and released the rail to clasp my hands together. "Oh God! It *was* you—I thought I recognized your voice—"

"I thought you must have recognized something about me by the way you greeted me, but I hardly expected you to

49

admit it. Well, at least we know that there is a charge against you that can be made to stick, if you cause us any trouble while you are at Pheasant's."

"But I did not—I swear I did not shoot to kill you! I aimed to miss!"

"And are you much in the habit of firing on strangers, whether to miss or to kill?"

"Of course not! It was only that I had the gun in my hand—and I had seen that horrid dance, and you were masked and shouted at me—anyone would have fired on you in the circumstances. Besides," I added more indignantly, "you do not seem to have been harmed. I don't understand why you should be so cross and—and hateful to me over such a trifling incident."

"You call it trifling, do you, to have a gun fired off at me at point-blank range without so much as a warning—and when I am on leave supposedly free from the constant expectation of being shot? I am strongly tempted, Miss Tremayne, to use you for target practice—not with the intention of doing you the least permanent harm, of course, but merely to discover how you enjoy it."

"Well—well, I do see it was not very pleasant for you—but have I not been punished sufficiently?"

"I don't know. Have you, Miss Tremayne?"

I stared at his stern profile. "You can't seriously believe me to—be capable of murder."

"Why not? From your face one could not, perhaps. But I have learned that faces can mislead. Circumstances are more significant—and you must own that in this case they are suspicious. You were found at All Saints, alone with the body; and when your postilion arrived, instead of shedding light upon your presence there, he proved to know little of you but that you possessed a dagger—the very instrument of murder, Miss Tremayne—a dagger that by then was mysteriously missing."

I pressed a hand to my aching head. "But—but has my dagger not been found, with my reticule?"

"It has, fortunately for you, and seems not to fit the wounds, or else you would not now be going free—but that is the opinion of one medical man only and others may be found to swear differently. Is that the whole burden of your defense?"

I drew the rug close about me. "What motive could I have for killing a girl unknown to me?"

"What motive did you have for firing upon a man unknown to you? Whether or not you meant to kill me, the fact remains you might easily have done so. Perhaps your motive was no more than fear—perhaps Polly Holford frightened you in much the same way; only then, instead of a pistol, you had a dagger in your hand."

"But I had lost the dagger earlier! Besides, her body was upon the altar."

He shot another penetrating glance at me. "How do I know in what strange ways your mind may run? You were spying last night on a ritual that did not concern you. The fact that you stayed, that you actually went back to the church, suggests that you did not find the witches so alarming as you pretended. Perhaps you are secretly in sympathy with them—"

"But you were there, and masked," I protested, breathlessly. "You are just as likely—more so, indeed—"

"Precisely, Miss Tremayne. And that is why I begged my father to allow me the privilege of conveying you to Pheasant's Hall this morning."

"I—don't understand you, sir."

"I needed a chance to talk to you alone, Miss Tremayne. No one but you—and one other who will not speak of it—

knows that I was at All Saints last night; and no one but myself is aware that you attempted murder, or manslaughter, by shooting at me shortly before you were found with Polly's body in the church. I propose, therefore, that we both keep silent as to our meeting."

I was shivering, my hands clenched on the rail. It seemed unthinkable to compound such a bargain with such a man—one who, from his very desire for secrecy, might well be not merely a witch but a murderer also. But my brief sojourn in prison had left me prepared to go to some lengths to avoid returning there, and I could see that this additional evidence would blacken the case against me. Besides, I thought unhappily, nothing would be more certain to put my Prendergast relatives against me than the knowledge that I had fired upon the squire's son.

I bent my head. "Very well," I said in a low voice. "I will not speak of having met you at All Saints."

He cracked his whip suddenly about the leader's ears, a vicious slap of sound on the frosty air. "And I will not mention your attack on me, though God knows—but never mind. We are cousins, then, newly met today; and while I may be pardoned for regarding you with some suspicion, do not forget that others will expect you to look on me as a knight who has ridden to your rescue."

I sighed, acknowledging the truth of this, and shivered again.

"You had better take yourself in hand," he said coolly. "You have a moment only to compose your features, for we have already passed the gates."

I looked up to see that we were driving on a smooth carriageway through rolling parkland. A rambling sandstone house with brick chimneys was already visible through the trees, standing a little in front of a huddle of farm buildings.

The full contrast between the circumstances of my arrival as I had pictured it but yesterday, and as it actually was, struck me with force.

"My aunt!" I cried despairingly. "How much does she know? What will she think? Oh—I am not fit to be received by her—by anyone!"

"No, indeed," the captain agreed calmly. "Your hair is in a tangle, your clothes ruined, your face wet with tears. I shall not be suspected of bullying you, however, for no excuse is needed for your appearance but that you passed a wretched night in prison after what must have been a very shocking experience." I gave a moan, and he continued imperturbably, "Recollect, however, that it is my father who is to blame for your appearance, and my stepmother will know it by now, for she has a very relentless way of cross-examining one which does not always result to her advantage. . . ." He glanced at me again. "Well, Miss Tremayne, you are still a beauty, if you need my reassurance of it. I suppose it troubles you, that you have not had the opportunity to look into the glass for several hours? But you need not fear that your hair has turned white overnight, nor is your face sunken and lined by your experiences. Indeed, the wonder is that my father was not moved by your looks—though it is true that he was not in a state to notice much, at least by the time I encountered him last night," he added brusquely, reining in the horses before the front steps.

I turned to climb down, but the captain laid a restraining hand on mine. "Has it not occurred to you to enquire where I spent the evening, ma'am, while you were having your adventures?"

I stared at him like a dolt. "But you were there," I stammered. "You were at All Saints. I don't understand you, sir."

"Then your understanding is not great. I thought we were

agreed that you did not meet me in the churchyard? Indeed, you could hardly have done so, for I was playing piquet with Lord Knevett at the time of the murder—at the White Lion."

He swung himself down and went to the horses' heads.

"You—you were at the White Lion, sir?"

"Certainly I was—all yesterday afternoon and evening. Knevett will vouch for me. Now please oblige me by getting down. I don't want these horses to take cold from standing, and as you see, I cannot leave them to assist you."

Somehow I managed the descent. Then the front door opened and a servant came hurrying down the steps.

"Take Miss Tremayne's arm, Barclay," said Captain Prendergast, beginning to lead his horses away. "I fear the young lady is feeling a trifle faint."

FOUR

Some time later a knock aroused me. I woke slowly, delighting in the comfort in which I found myself, and looked about me in drowsy appreciation. I was in a white bed in a white room, and the glow of the firelight was mingling with the reflected carmine of a winter sunset on the white brocade. It was late afternoon, and I must have slept for hours.

The door opened and a woman stood there, dressed in black. I recognized Mrs. Slight, the housekeeper who had shown me to this room, and my heart sank.

"My—my aunt?" I asked, as the woman did not speak.

"I told you earlier, miss, that her ladyship is indisposed." Her voice was dry and cold, her hair dark and streaked with grey, her complexion sallow beneath the immaculate cap. But it was her eyes which held my attention. Who would have supposed that protuberant blue eyes could be so chilling?

"Sir Abraham sent me to enquire if you could see him, miss."

"Oh!" I clutched the sheet against me. "Why—yes, that is. Certainly."

She stepped back. In her indifferent voice she said, "You may come in, Sir Abraham."

A large red-faced man stepped past her into the room. He was undeniably the magistrate who had committed me to prison, my uncle by Aunt Margaret's second marriage, Sir Abraham Prendergast.

He had at least the grace to appear ill at ease. "Good day, good day," he said in a mumbling, embarrassed tone. "No need to look like that, my dear—you're among friends now. Friends and relatives, eh, Slight? Are you feeling better for your rest, Miss—er? Is there aught you need?"

"Good evening, sir. My—my aunt?" I ventured again.

"Ah, h'm. Your aunt, to be sure. . . ."

My heart sank. What had happened to her? Was she dead? Was I to be at the mercy of this drunkard and his hateful son? But surely Captain Prendergast had mentioned her, his stepmother?

"What ails Aunt Margaret?" I demanded, ignoring the discovery that my throat was very sore. "I trust she is not seriously indisposed?"

"No—not that precisely. She thought you would be happier to meet her when you had rested."

I blinked. That did not sound like my warm, impulsive aunt.

Sir Abraham noticed my surprise. "I fear you may find your aunt somewhat altered," he said gruffly. "But she will be in presently to see you, I daresay. Well, miss, I have an apology to make to you—but the circumstances were strange, very strange indeed—and if you had only made yourself known to me you need not have spent such a wretched night. I was sorry to hear from my son that they treated you badly at Hallchurch. I intend to make a complaint on your behalf."

I was torn between amazement that Captain Prendergast should have volunteered such an opinion, and cowardly terror that Mr. George the jailer might take his revenge on me for it. The latter emotion was the stronger.

"Oh sir, I beg you won't. I'm sure the Georges did the best they could."

"They set you to work—and on a Sunday, too."

"Only to scrub my cell—it was the rule, they said. Please, sir—I have caused trouble enough since I let those wretched horses go."

Sir Abraham gave me a shrewd look from his bloodshot blue eyes. "Has George been threatening you, eh?"

I said nothing, but my face flamed as I looked away.

"Ha! And Mrs. George—how did she treat you?"

"I think she is too frightened of her husband to spare much thought for others," I murmured, conscious of Mrs. Slight's enigmatic stare.

"Do you, indeed? Well, one needs a bully for a jailer, I suppose." He ruminated for a moment while I looked at him more closely.

"Excuse me, sir, but is that my reticule in your hand?"

He brought it from behind his back and stared at it as if he had never seen it before. "Ay, it is. My cursed memory— I came to tell you, miss, that our doctor does not think this dagger made the fatal wounds. The blade is too wide and Barton—Burton?—fancies something more like a stiletto was responsible." He dropped the bag upon the bed and I thanked him sincerely. "H'm—you're a tolerant child. I believe we'll deal together, for there's room for tolerance in this household, eh, Slight?"

The housekeeper started. She had been standing with her hands primly folded before her, staring blankly in my direc-

57

tion. She said almost at random, "Miss Tremayne looks poorly to me, sir. Do you not think the doctor should be sent for?"

It was true I felt quite exhausted and though I murmured that I did not think it necessary to trouble the doctor, I could not help being glad that Sir Abraham overruled me.

"We'll get Bolton—no, Burton—over tomorrow. I was going to put some questions to you, miss, but I see you're not fit for it."

He wandered over to the window and stood looking out. "A fine sunset. Pity you can't see it. We'll have good weather tomorrow. I've a mind to send a note to Curtis and take hounds to Lindenfold in the morning, where my hunt bounds with his." He turned. "Do you ride?"

"No, I fear I have never had the opportunity, sir."

"We'll change all that. You're an heiress now, I hear. My son shall teach you. Ay, the young dog! 'Tis time he found himself something to do other than shoot and hunt and game with that odd fellow Knevett, while he's on leave. Can't have Mark going back to the Peninsula with nothing more than that to think about, eh!"

I wondered vaguely what he meant but it was not until I was dining off my solitary tray a few minutes later that the answer occurred to me. The squire had mentioned my inheritance and his son in the same breath; he was thinking of allying the one with the other.

I stabbed a piece of chicken with determination. Sir Abraham could not force me to marry the intolerable Captain Prendergast, I told myself, and since the young man seemed to detest me I need not allow the thought of the squire's intention to worry me unduly. Indeed, I reflected, it carried the comforting implication that he, at least, was entirely convinced that I had not murdered the farmer's daughter.

The door opened; a lace-capped head looked round it.

"Tansy! May I come in?"

"Aunt Margaret!" I held out my arms, nearly upsetting the tray, but she merely sidled round the door and stood by it as if ready to flee. She had changed indeed, and not for the better. Her once-pretty plump figure was now far too thin, what I could see of her hair was a peppery grey, and her face, which used to be rather pert and amusing-looking, or complacent in repose, seemed now drawn and embittered. This was what the Prendergasts had done to her, I thought in dismay, remembering her as my mother's gayest, favourite relative, her youngest sister, who could not be forty yet.

"Poor child! What a terrible thing to have happened to you—" Even her voice sounded thin and strained, though perhaps embarrassment on account of my adventures was responsible for that. She had always been conventional under her light flirtatious manner. "I don't know what to say to you! When I heard what Prendergast had done—but we won't speak of that just now. You look pale. How do you feel?"

"Very happy to be here and to see you again," I assured her, busying myself in putting the tray upon the bedside table. "This is a lovely room. It belonged to your stepdaughter, I understand."

"Kitty, yes. I have two of them, you know, both married now. If only Mark would do likewise! He is the last of his line, and in a dangerous profession—but men go their own way, do they not?" she added bitterly.

"I—suppose they do. But since Grandfather's death I have scarcely spoken to a man, you know!"

At once she was all warm sympathy and I glimpsed the Aunt Margaret I had known in the old days in Essex. "My dear, I knew how it would be for you in Kensington—I felt dreadful, I assure you, at not taking you in earlier, but there was no one else to go to Dorothy when the Admiral died and since you needed a home at just that time, it seemed for the best."

"I was only joking, Aunt. I dearly loved Aunt Dorothy."

"Oh yes, anyone would—but she was not exactly lively, poor dear, and the last year must have been tedious beyond belief. But I mean to make it up to you, and shall see to it that you enjoy as much gaiety as is consistent with your mourning. I had not thought you would turn out such a beauty, I daresay young men will be swarming like bees to a honey-pot—once this dreadful affair is over and forgotten."

Her brief vitality left her, and she drooped again. I said quickly, "I was so relieved my reticule was found. Sir Abraham was good enough to bring it to me—"

"Pray don't mention his name to me," she interrupted. "I was so angry when I had succeeded in dragging the whole frightful tale from him that we are no longer on speaking terms. His only excuse is that he has no head for names— as if that could have blinded him to the sort of person you are!" She gave an exasperated sigh. "Such a dreadful night, too, so foggy and bitter cold. I was worried half to death over what could have delayed you, yet I never thought of anything so frightful as the truth. Well, no, perhaps that is not quite correct for I am sure I was imagining you dead, and worse, and if Mark had been here instead of playing those dreadful cards—the Devil's Book, do you remember your grandfather used to call them?—I should have sent him riding to Horsefield in search of you. But it is always so with men when you really need them—"

She broke off. "Even Browning," she muttered. "Even he, at the end—"

I stared at her aghast. Was it possible she had not forgiven her admirable first husband, Browning, the rich merchant,

60

for having allowed himself to be crushed by a barrel of his own merchandise?

"Well, poor man, at least he was a comfort to me while he lived," she owned. Then her expression again became aggrieved. "Your father, too. It was not until Ann became consumptive that he began to complain of the condition which killed him."

"You do not blame him for that, I hope?" She seemed obsessed on the subject and I wondered what had caused this illogical mistrust of men in a woman who had once preferred their company to that of her own sex.

My aunt shrugged. "He went so easily—without a struggle. And Ann was left almost penniless down there in Cornwall and had to make her way back to Essex with you when she should have been abed. But so it always is . . . men do as they please, and women pay the price."

I was angry. "You cannot say it pleased my father to die so young!"

But Aunt Margaret was fumbling with the door handle and paid no attention. "You had better stay in bed tomorrow," she said rather vaguely. "Or longer, if you wish. You can amuse yourself, I suppose? Mrs. Slight will bring you aught you need . . ." and then she was gone without so much as a good night, leaving me with nothing but my own thoughts for company. These, after dwelling for a while upon the change in my aunt, returned at last to the horrid scenes I had witnessed at All Saints.

Were they really witches whom I had seen dancing, as Captain Prendergast had said, or merely a party of high-spirited young people? And how involved was my courtesy-cousin in their affairs? Deeply so, I suspected, for had I not seen him dancing with the murdered girl shortly before I had fired on him? I sighed and picked up my reticule, rather grazed and torn by its adventures, and loosening the string, drew out my Indian dagger. The scabbard was a bright emerald green, intricately embroidered in gold thread, from which the heavily chased silver handle protruded. I slid my fingers round its satisfying curves and pulled. The blade slid out sweetly into the light and I stared at it as if seeing it for the first time. It was short and wide, tapering to a curved point at the tip, and had a sort of runnel down the length of the blade. I did not know of what metal it was made, but it gleamed dully gold in the firelight. It looked clean and unstained, innocent of murder.

I shivered and slid it back into the sheath. Nothing, I thought, would persuade me to use it as a weapon. Still, perhaps there were occasions, particularly in an area where there had recently been murder done, when the mere possession of a dagger might serve as a defense. I put it in another reticule, and transferred my handkerchief and purse to this more elegant bag, resolving to keep it by me in the future.

It was beginning to get dark. Tomorrow I would go downstairs, I told myself, getting out of bed. My legs felt a trifle weak after only a day of disuse, and it was time I began to exercise them. I made my way to the window and leaned against the sill. Outside, the sky was pink and grey, with one bright streak of pale gold far to the west, reflected in a sluggish river which was the same, I supposed, as the one that ran by the ruined church. Elms sketched their stark silhouette against the last of the sunset and everywhere starlings were noisily converging on their untidy nests. I noticed that the barns and outbuildings looked in good repair and that the fields, some flooded by the recent rains, perhaps would benefit from draining but were neatly fenced. The cattle, too, now being hurried in to be milked, looked strong and healthy in their rough winter coats. The squire, I deduced, was a responsible landowner, and I, I thought with a deprecating smile, for all my years in London, was still a country girl. If I were ever to make a good showing in society drawing rooms I must acquire a disdain for such things and cultivate a greater interest in the length of a train, the fall of a curl.

I heard a sound and turned, starting as I again recognized the housekeeper standing in the doorway, a black silent figure.

"Oh, Mrs. Slight—I did not hear you come in!"

She said nothing, but rested her blue protuberant eyes enigmatically upon me.

"I have got up," I babbled. "Tomorrow I will go downstairs."

Mrs. Slight inclined her head. Why had she come, I wondered, and how long had she been there? Could she be spying on me? Impatiently I dismissed this fanciful thought. Mrs. Slight was a quiet person of few words and I had no reason to suppose her to be my enemy. It was my place, moreover, to attempt to bridge the gap between us.

I said impulsively, "Mrs. Slight, I should not discuss this with you, perhaps—but I notice a great change in my aunt. Has she been ill?"

Mrs. Slight smoothed her hands over the folds of her black bombazine. "My lady suffers from the migraine and has to lie sometimes in a darkened room," she replied evasively.

"I recall that she used to suffer from such attacks occasionally—but she used to be plump and—and so gay," I burst out. "I was expecting her to have put on weight—"

"My lady was plump enough a year ago," admitted Mrs. Slight without expression. "Then . . . there was a change."

"A swift one, certainly. Can you account for it?"

The housekeeper turned away. She smoothed my bedcover,

63

picked up a china ornament from the chest and examined it minutely for traces of dust. "My lady has not been ill. I believe she worries a good deal." She set down the ornament carefully. "That is Dresden china, miss. Miss Kitty—Mrs. Beauregard, that is to say—sets a great deal of store by such things. This is her room, course."

"Beauregard," I repeated, diverted, as she had intended me to be. "Yes, I remember hearing that—Miss Kitty—married a Frenchman."

"Yes, miss. He is one of those emigrés—a gentleman, they say. It was a great sorrow to my master—and to my lady, I believe."

"So it might have been that which—affected my aunt?"

"No, miss," declared Mrs. Slight flatly, moving towards the door. "It was something nearer home than that." She bowed her head by way of farewell, and left the room.

What could she mean, I wondered. What could be nearer home than the marriage of a daughter, even a stepdaughter? But perhaps Mrs. Slight meant that my aunt was ill after all. Or it was possible that she had no notion why her mistress had changed but wished merely to hint that she did.

I shrugged away the problem for the time being, and went back to bed.

The next day I woke to find all trace of my cold had disappeared. I was startled but not surprised, therefore, when the doctor brusquely declared that it was wasting his time to visit me and furthermore that there was no medical reason why I should not attend the inquest which was to be held at ten o'clock upon the following day.

"It is your duty to do so," he informed me gruffly. "Apart from which I should say it would be decidedly in your interest to attend."

He might be right, I conceded, but it would also be an ordeal of, I feared, no mean order. There was nothing to be done about it, however, but to put the thought of the morrow out of my head as far as possible. I got up and found that my clothes were hanging freshly ironed in the cupboard, apparently unharmed by their adventures on the back of the post chaise. I dressed in a white-spotted black muslin with the help of Susan, a girl whose fingers were a good deal more nimble than was her tongue; and draped about my shoulders the carefully preserved silk Norwich shawl that had been my mother's. Then, pulling on my black gloves, I went out into a passage I could not recollect at all, and rather tentatively descended the stairs.

I could see myself in an oval gilded mirror as I hesitated on the last step, a girl who looked wan and large-eyed in her dark mourning. At least my hair had been skillfully dressed, I thought, brushed to gleaming pale gold and artfully arranged by Susan. The expression wanted altering, however; and I forced a smile, relieved to see my reflection lose its haunted look.

"Charming!" declared a sarcastic voice.

I gasped with shock, and clung to the banister. Mark Prendergast was lounging in a doorway opposite, staring me up and down as if he had a perfect right to do so; as if, indeed, he had just bought me in the marketplace and was wondering what work to set me to do.

"I am glad to see you are sufficiently recovered to take an interest in your appearance," he drawled while my colour returned in generous measure. "Indeed, it merits your approval, I think. You don't look to be quite so free with your favours as my first view of you suggested, but you are certainly more in keeping with my stepmother's drawing room."

"You—you—! Oh, you are unfair!"

"Not at all, only frank. Though I agree that it must be intolerable for you to be living under the same roof with one who knows too much about you."

I raised my chin. "If—if you are being so ungentlemanly as to refer to—to my state of undress in Hallchurch Gaol, allow me to inform you that Mrs. George had stolen my handkerchief."

"Really?" he said skeptically, raising a satanic eyebrow. "You did not complain of it to my father, I think."

"No—but that was because—"

"Never mind. Content yourself with knowing that you are beautiful, whether dressed or undressed. Knevett will be vastly pleased with you, I vow."

"Knevett?" I stammered, between rage and despair.

"My friend, and our neighbour. He rates himself a connoisseur in such matters and I wager he'll be over to inspect you the instant he hears you are up and about again. I have not hinted at your fortune to him, so you may accept his admiration at its face value."

"I wish people would not speak of my fortune," I said unhappily. "It is not large—not really large at all."

Captain Prendergast drew a gold half-hunter from his pocket and began to swing it on its chain, though his eyes never left my face. "But my stepmother also means to make you her heir, I believe. She has a good deal from her first marriage which there is no reason for her to leave to my father's family. Besides, Knevett's pockets are always to let. Any kind of heiress would be better than none, so far as he is concerned."

I pulled my eyes away from the gently swinging watch. "Where is my aunt?" I asked with dignity, wishing I were taller. I had drawn myself to my full height but even though

66

I still stood upon the bottom step, Captain Prendergast was taller than I.

He smiled mockingly. "In the drawing room. Lady Sinclair-Stewart has come to call. You do not know Lady Sinclair-Stewart so you will not appreciate what a signal honour this is. I wonder what could have brought her? Her son Francis is with her—quite the jester, Francis is. No doubt he will be reduced to incoherence by the sight of your beauty. I do not think I shall give myself the pleasure of witnessing the scene."

He made me an ironic bow and walking into a book-lined room, closed the door behind him.

I found my lips were trembling and pressed them together impatiently. Shaking open my fan, I took a moment to cool my cheeks. Then I closed it with a decisive snap and walked forward to the door which Captain Prendergast had indicated as belonging to the drawing room.

As I opened it, a disdainful voice was saying, "And then I simply cannot understand these persons who find pleasure in attending executions—many of them of good breeding, too—"

I stood still, my heart thumping. After all, the moment when I had feared that the hangman waited for me was not so far away. The speaker, a large and heavily powdered lady in a most elaborate hat, turned in her chair and raised her lorgnette at me. The slender young man who had been engaged in turning over some music which lay upon the piano looked round with much the expression of a startled rabbit.

"I say, Mother," he exclaimed, with something of a lisp followed by a high-pitched nervous laugh.

My aunt spoke from another chair. "Tansy!" She sounded rather breathless, as if I had startled her. "I was not expecting you down just yet. Lady Sinclair-Stewart, may I present my niece?"

But her ladyship did not wait for the introduction. She rose majestically. "Come, Francis, we must not keep the horses waiting. So good of you to entertain us, dear Lady Prendergast. Good afternoon."

I was only just in time to step out of her way as she swept towards me. She did not cut me, as I expected, but subjected me to a very hard brief stare before passing on into the hall. Francis, who on closer inspection looked even more like a rabbit, paused. "I say!" he murmured in an admiring tone, before bowing extremely gracefully and following his mother out of the room.

I closed the door and looked unhappily at my aunt, who was fanning herself.

"Oh dear!" she sighed, and added with an effort, "Come and sit by me, my dear. I am glad to find you so recovered."

"I am sorry to have disturbed your party, ma'am."

"Oh well . . . I am sure the Sinclair-Stewarts were about to leave in any case."

"I fear it was my entry which caused them to terminate their visit."

"Oh no, how could you suppose . . . ?"

I put my hand on hers. "Please, Aunt. Let us not deceive ourselves. I have been thoughtless, but it is obvious now that respectable people will not want to meet me. I have been in prison after all."

"It is all Abraham's fault!" she burst out. "How could he do this to me? But don't let it distress you, my dear. It will all be explained at the inquest. In time, no doubt, it will be forgotten."

I shook my head. "It is a stigma which cannot be removed so easily. I used to think people to blame for their troubles,

68

but luck has a good deal to say to it too, I now realize. I am sorry—" I broke off, regained my self-control and continued quietly, "I am truly sorry to have brought this embarrassment upon you."

"It is all so unfortunate," she agreed. "I had hoped to launch you into our county society, bring you out into the world. . . . I was so pleased when Lady Sinclair-Stewart was announced, but I soon realized she had only come in order to have something interesting to tattle to her neighbours. She was hoping, I am sure, for just such a glimpse of you as she unfortunately had, which enabled her to demonstrate her own impeccable respectability by sweeping out when you appeared. To think she will be boasting of her Christian charity in visiting me at such a time! I wish she had not seen you. If only Mark or Abraham had been in the hall, or if I had known of your intention to come down, you could have been warned to wait! But I hope everyone knows she is a very stupid and malicious woman. Not all our neighbours will follow her lead. Given time, no doubt, and a chance to become acquainted with you, they may recognize that things are not quite what they seem."

I bit my lip. The perfidy of Captain Prendergast I passed over for the moment; it was no more than I would have expected of him and I would have plenty of time to dwell on it later. The damage was done and I must try to assess how far it reached and whether anything lay within my power to mend it. With a pang, I recalled Aunt Dorothy saying affectionately of her sister that dear Margaret was such a stickler for high form, it should have been she who married the Admiral and Dorothy who wedded into trade; and when Aunt Margaret eventually married Sir Abraham, Aunt Dorothy had sighed with pleasure at the news. "Now Margaret is 'my lady' and as a country squiress may be happy at last," she had declared. "I always regretted her minute knowledge of social observance being wasted as a merchant's wife."

I said in a low voice, "Dear Aunt, I have brought nothing but trouble upon you. I think I had better look for some kind of situation, no matter where, so long as it be far from here."

"You must not think of it," she assured me. "People will forget. A respectable marriage, if it can be arranged, will do much to placate them. . . ."

"Marriage!" I exclaimed, feeling suddenly afraid. "I do not think of marriage, I assure you!"

"Nonsense!" she said, more briskly than I had yet heard her speak. "All young girls think of marriage."

"Well . . . in a dream-like way, perhaps."

She regarded me thoughtfully. "You are very young, perfectly innocent, I suppose. Have you ever been kissed?"

I shuddered. "Once. It was enough!"

"Indeed? Who was it?"

I looked away, and shook my head, but she insisted on an answer. "It will shock you, Aunt."

"I doubt it. Tell me, child."

"The doctor who attended Aunt Dorothy . . . he was quite old and smelt of snuff. He caught me behind the door. It was horrible!"

She smiled, with satisfaction, I thought to my surprise. "You must be married soon. It is much better so."

I stared at her. "I would want to be in love with my husband. It is too frightful to imagine otherwise!"

It was her turn to shake her head. "No, my dear. Better never to know passion . . . only duty and obedience. To be in love is to be vulnerable. Passion is evil!" She rose with decision. "You may leave it to me, my dear. I shall arrange everything."

"Aunt! How can I convince you—you will drive me to leave!"

"You have nowhere to go," she reminded me gently.

"I will advertise. I must leave in any case, I think—for your sake, if not for my own."

"You need not think of doing so. The shadow of this murder would hang over us at Pheasant's Hall even if you had not been involved."

I felt cold. "Pray, what do you mean?"

But she had drifted away in her elusive fashion, and I found myself alone.

FIVE

The piano had always been a solace to me, and on this occasion I felt in need of solace. I ran my fingers over the keys, noted the instrument was in tune and began to play with such absorption that I did not remark it when the door opened again, after half an hour or so.

"What a talented child it is!" said Captain Prendergast. My hands slipped down on a discord and I turned on the piano stool to see him strolling in with another man as tall as he but darker and more saturnine, a strangely handsome, almost foreign-looking man, whose black eyes glittered in the instant they met mine, before he bent his head in a polished bow.

"Here is the visitor I promised you," said the captain, smiling a little. "You have not met Lord Knevett, I think. Miss Tremayne, Knevett, of whom," he added cruelly to his friend, "you must certainly have heard."

Lord Knevett acknowledged the introduction while I murmured something, but I was disconcerted by the captain's knowing look, and also by the disturbing presence of the man who had given him a false alibi. I had not expected him to be so handsome nor to have such an air of power about him. I hardly knew what I said.

Captain Prendergast moved closer to me. "Don't look like that, Cousin," he murmured. "The sparks in your fine Spanish sherry eyes are quite becoming but out of place when one considers that I am to appear only your deliverer."

I looked away. In my agitation, I began to leaf through the pile of music, as Mr. Sinclair-Stewart had done not long before. To my amazement I suddenly noticed what appeared at first glance to be a scurrilous ballad written in a spiky upright hand, accompanied by an exceedingly bawdy cheap print. It must have been pushed into the pile somewhat hastily, for one corner was bent back and the broadsheet crumpled.

I stood up and began to excuse myself, my manner even more agitated by reason of my discovery.

"What is it, Miss Tremayne?" asked Lord Knevett, who had been watching me intently.

I shook my head in confusion and muttered that something had been put there by mistake.

"If Francis Sinclair-Stewart was anywhere near the piano, you can be sure he was responsible," remarked Captain Prendergast. I shot him a startled look. "Francis is a great joker," he explained. "Perhaps I had better have a look at it."

"Oh no! Pray don't—that is, I will dispose of it, Captain Prendergast."

He plucked the offending paper out of my hand, deaf to my protests. " 'Cousin Mark,' " he reminded me in a reproving tone. "Come, let me hear you say it."

"Please, Cousin Mark, don't look at it."

But of course he did so, smiling a little and raising an eyebrow at it. "Very apt," he said. "Quite witty in Francis, for once, though somewhat unfriendly to you, I fear. Did your sensibilities forbid you to read it through, dear Cousin? Briefly, it is an allegorical warning to those who nourish vipers in their bosoms. Are you a viper, angel-face?"

He did not wait for a reply but carried the paper to the fire and dropped it on the glowing coals.

"Pray excuse me," I said again in a low voice. "I—I should not be here—my aunt—"

"No need to remove yourself, Cousin. I have sent Barclay to instruct my stepmother to chaperon us—ah, here she is!"

Aunt Margaret entered on his words, as agitated as I. "Oh! Lord Knevett. Charming to see you," she remarked unconvincingly. She glanced at me. "Should you be up, Tansy? We will excuse you if you wish to rest."

"I hope you don't, Miss Tremayne," said Lord Knevett warmly. I was grateful for his intervention and moved towards my aunt. "I am quite better now," I told her. "If I might sit here, by you?"

"Very well. Lord Knevett, pray be seated." The words were correct enough but spoken with extreme coolness. Either my aunt disliked his lordship, or she did not want him here just now.

"And I shall sit next to my cousin," said the captain dropping down on the sofa at my side. "Smile!" he adjured me. I glared at him instead, and turned my shoulder. Instantly I felt his hand upon my hair. He gave one of my ringlets a vicious tug, at the same time remarking on the beauty of my colouring. "If it were not for those dark, concealing eyes one might suppose little Miss Tansy to be an angel, don't you agree?" he asked his friend.

My aunt said quickly, "Mark, as you see, is vastly taken

with his cousin. It is quite a novelty to him to have a young girl to tease—his sisters both being older than he. Of course," she added carefully, "Miss Tremayne is no blood relation of my stepson's."

I shot Lord Knevett a quick glance beneath my lashes to see what he made of this blatant declaration and was gratified to find him staring at me with an appearance of the keenest interest.

"Prendergast is extremely fortunate," he remarked in his deep vibrant voice. "I wish we had such a visitor at Abbot's Grove."

"Abbot's Grove?" I repeated, wondering why I should sound rather breathless.

"Our house," explained the baron, smiling a little. "It has been in our family upwards of four hundred years." He had good teeth, I noticed. Captain Prendergast's were somewhat uneven. No doubt my courtesy-cousin had been frequently punched in the face, for good reason. Indeed, a side glance convinced me that the captain's nose had been broken at one time.

"I should be enchanted," continued Lord Knevett, "to show you over the house, if Lady Prendergast can be persuaded to bring you to drink a dish of tea with us one of these days. My mother is not well enough to be paying calls," he added. "Her presence in the house will, however, make such an invitation eligible for you to accept, I hope."

He turned his sparkling eyes on Lady Prendergast, who looked at him without expression. Fanning herself slowly, she replied that it was possible, of course, but he would understand that, just at the moment. . . . Her voice died away but instead of murmuring some civility and leaving the subject, Lord Knevett took her up on it with gratifying sharpness.

"Just at the moment?" he repeated, leaning forward to look at her attentively. "Do you mean me to understand that Miss Tremayne is inundated with invitations? I had hoped that in view of her mourning . . . or perhaps," he added, turning back to me, "you have been too recently bereaved to wish to go visiting?"

I said steadily, "The death of my late aunt was long expected. I think perhaps Lady Prendergast was reminding you that because of my . . . unfortunate experience, Lady Knevett might not care to receive me. If you feel she would not object to my visiting your house, I would be most interested to do so."

"I am glad to hear it. My poor mother will certainly raise no objection."

Captain Prendergast jumped up impatiently and strode towards the door.

"Do you want to be talking forever, Knevett?" he asked in his blunt way. "Or are you game to try my grey? I've had him saddled ready and they are walking him in the yard—but I warn you he has never yet let any but a Prendergast settle in the saddle. What do you say?"

Lord Knevett had little alternative but to assure the captain that he was ready for anything, even an unridable horse, and they went off together after he had made his farewells with a punctiliousness which formed an agreeable contrast to the manner of Lady Sinclair-Stewart's departure.

"What do you think of Lord Knevett?" my aunt demanded a few minutes after the door had closed behind him.

I spread my fan upon my knee and regarded it thoughtfully. "I don't know him yet," I replied cautiously. "But I suppose no one could deny that Lord Knevett is an extremely charming man."

My aunt turned away her head, covering her face with a trembling hand.

"Lord Knevett is an extremely dangerous man," she said in a muffled tone.

I stared at her in amazement. A moment later she had regained her composure. "I should not have said that. Be so good as to disregard it."

She glanced at me repressively and the thought occurred to me that she did not really mean me to disregard her warning, merely not to comment on it.

She rose with a soft rustle of her black silk. "I had better show you over the house if you are fit for it."

"How good of you. I should like it of all things." I had supposed Mrs. Slight would be delegated to perform that task and was glad to find my aunt prepared to trouble with me to that extent, though I would have preferred to retire to my room and examine in peace the effect that Lord Knevett had had on my inexperienced heart.

A dangerous man! No doubt he was, especially where female susceptibilities were concerned. . . .

"This is Mark's sanctuary," declared Aunt Margaret, leading me across the hall and into a comfortable book-lined room. "Oh, you are here, Mrs. Slight!" she exclaimed as the housekeeper moved ˋsilently away from the writing table, made a small curtsy and passed into the hall without a word. Aunt Margaret looked after her, and bit her lip. Her hands were twisted together, I observed; but as if she felt my surprise, Aunt Margaret loosed them immediately and continued with a conscious smile, "This room is accessible to us all, of course; but we have an understanding that the desk is Mark's, while he is in residence here." She gestured towards the handsome table set in an alcove, littered with papers, quills, penknives, and ink in a silver standish. "Do you read a great deal?" she asked, seeing me looking at the bookshelves. "Your father's nose was never out of a book, as I recall, even when he was courting your mother—but then one expects that in an attorney."

"I must own that I am very fond of reading—"

"Indeed? I am sorry to hear it. A novel or two from the Circulating Library may be very well for a young lady but bookishness is precisely what does not appeal to gentlemen. You would do better to occupy your time in other ways. Are you fond of needlework?"

"I do enjoy it, on occasion. I learned a great deal from Aunt Dorothy's sewing woman and make my own clothes as a rule."

My aunt clicked her tongue. "That won't do either. The dress you are wearing is very pretty and the stitching is neat but still one can tell it is homemade. Your circumstances now are altered, you must remember; and even though you are in mourning there is no harm in recollecting what is due to your consequence. I will summon my own dressmaker to attend you when next she is in the district—Friday, I believe. This is the breakfast room, by the way—pleasant when the sun is shining. But I meant rather, embroidery and fine sewing, when I spoke of needlework."

"I have learned to do such work, but I have none in hand."

"I shall procure some for you." She smiled. "I have it! You shall embroider my stepson a pair of slippers."

I gazed at her in consternation. I could too well imagine Captain Prendergast's reaction when the time came for me to present him with the finished articles. Then, recalling that I was meant to be regarding my cousin in the light of a hero to whom I was beholden, I hastily adjusted my expression.

"If only I could be sure he would like them!" I said earnestly. "But somehow I cannot imagine him in slippers. Would not Sir Abraham prefer such a gift from me, ma'am?"

She went red and her hand closed tightly on the doorknob. "By no means! You owe nothing to Sir Abraham—"

"A home?" I suggested.

"Bah! When he has ruined your life? Or will have done, unless—" She broke off, to continue more coolly, "Mark is in boots all day and would, I am sure, be glad to wear slippers in his room. Besides, I made Sir Abraham a pair myself, not two years ago." She sighed, as if an unpleasant thought had occurred to her, and opened the door she was holding.

"This is the dining room. You will be down for dinner tomorrow, I hope; but for tonight you had better have a tray in your room."

There were several portraits on the walls. I stared at one over the mantel. "Is that the former Lady Prendergast?" But the young woman whose painted eyes met mine could only have been the captain's mother; it did not need my aunt's assurance to inform me of it. Her hair was a bright glossy brown, her eyes grey, not cold like his but indefinably sad, her eyebrows strongly marked. Her hands were lightly clasped about a spray of flowers and two children, a boy and a girl, nestled in her satin skirts, very secondary to the main figure.

"Yes, indeed. I never met her, of course, but I am told it is very like. Certainly one cannot mistake Kitty and Mark. Elizabeth had measles at the time, unfortunately. There is a miniature of her here, taken a little later."

I reflected that Elizabeth had a kinder face than Kitty, who looked a sharp, uncomfortable sort of girl, even at the age of seven or so. Her mother's grey eyes were, in her, set too close together, and she had her father's long enquiring nose and protuberant chin. The general effect, however, was one of somewhat aggressive handsomeness; and I wondered how this early promise had developed.

"Elizabeth married very well," my aunt was saying in a voice warm with approval. She passed me the miniature and looking more closely at the pink and white face and large, shyly smiling blue eyes of the squire's younger daughter, I thought she seemed just the girl to be approved by the kind of domineering mother-in-law who would have rejected Kitty at first sight.

"Her husband is Sir Humphrey Barton-Fowler. He is a good deal older than Elizabeth, of course, with a first family almost grown-up; but he is so kind and indulgent—and they have two pretty dears of their own already."

"And Miss Kitty married a French emigré, I understand?"

My aunt pursed her lips. "She threw herself away on the music master at her boarding school. Oh, Beauregard is very well-born, no doubt, but who cares for such things now, where the French are concerned? Times have changed, and a fine-sounding title is worth little if you have no estate to back it. Not that Beauregard has so much as a *de* to his name," she added scornfully. "He is a little mincing fellow with nothing at all, so far as I can see, to recommend him. But Abraham says that Kitty likes to be a puppet-master and must needs have a puppet for her mate. Well, well, I am very lucky in the others at least. Mark is a man of whom any parent might be proud, do not you agree?"

I thought of her stepson hooded in the graveyard, dancing in the ruined church, and suppressed a shiver. Somehow I managed to murmur that he was a well-built man and made, no doubt, a dashing soldier.

"Yes, indeed; he has several times been mentioned in dispatches—twice, at least—though he has so far come through without a scratch. But after some exploit of his while the regiment was behind the lines at Torres Vedras, he suffered from exposure and was ill enough to warrant being sent home for a few weeks. In any case, there won't be much more fighting until the spring, he tells us; the weather is so bad there at this time of year. The lull is a relief to us but Mark is the oddest creature and positively looks forward to battles and promotion. I am sure he will go far in his chosen profession, if he is not killed. He is very intelligent," she added thoughtfully, as if this were a side of him that she feared a little.

"What is it, my dear?" she suddenly demanded and I realized I must have shivered again. "Are you cold? Should you not return to bed? Come, I shall see you upstairs."

She linked her arm in mine and hurried me into the hall. I protested a little that I had only shivered at a passing thought.

"A thought, Tansy? But what thought could affect you so?"

I stared at her in surprise. "You have a short memory, Aunt, if you can recall nothing likely to disturb the tenor of my thoughts."

"Oh, that! But that is all over and done with now, dear child, but for the inquest. After tomorrow you need never think of it again."

"How can I help but think of it, when the mystery is not solved and is not likely to be solved even at the inquest, I suppose? Someone in these parts, and perhaps not far from here, is a murderer!"

"Hush, Tansy." Aunt Margaret's eyes looked very dark, staring from her white face.

I paused on the stairs. "But I am saying nothing that everybody does not know. I make no accusation. How could I, indeed? I know too well what it is to be falsely suspected.

But when I think of that wretched girl I cannot help wondering . . . and I shiver."

"It is better—a great deal better—to put the whole affair out of your mind, as the rest of us are endeavouring to do."

"But is that fair?" I murmured rebelliously. "Fair to her, I mean—to Polly Holford?"

My aunt's lips tightened. "Fair to that little—" She broke off, but her tone had been vicious enough to set my heart thumping. "Nothing you can think or do will help her now," she said in a controlled voice. "Besides, no doubt she came by her deserts."

"If you say so, Aunt. But what of the murderer? He has not come by his deserts. Is he to go free, unpunished—until the next time the mood takes him to kill—and perhaps kill again?"

Aunt Margaret almost pushed me into my room. "There was no murderer," she said flatly.

"What! Why, Aunt, what can you mean?"

"The girl was killed by several people, I understand."

I was shivering in earnest now. I pushed my back hard against the bedpost and stared at my aunt. "How do you know?"

"From the evidence which the doctor is to give at the inquest. I have heard that, from the angle of the wounds, at least two persons were concerned, and probably more. My husband discussed it with Pole-Carter, a neighbouring vicar with some experience in—in witchcraft. That is to say, he has read a great deal on the subject. In any event, Pole-Carter believes the girl's death to have been a ritual killing."

"A ritual killing?" I repeated blankly.

Aunt Margaret glanced over her shoulder, though we were patently alone. "It is a great deal better not to talk of such

82

matters, but if you will have it—yes, a ritual murder of a selected victim by the witches, to lend power to their rites."

"Oh God! How horrible!" Then, swift and unworthy came the thought I voiced, "It might have been me! I might as easily have been their victim."

Aunt Margaret turned her attention full upon me. "Tush, child, you are as white as a snowdrop. What nonsense you talk. Why should they murder you, may I ask? You were not one of them, I hope, as no doubt Polly was."

"You don't mean—she consented? No, it could not be. Besides, I wonder if she was a witch? Alone of them, she was not masked."

"What of it? Don't look to me to tell you more, Tansy. I only told you so much as a warning not to meddle. Let it alone, I pray. Thus in time it will all be forgotten, and we may feel—" She broke off and turned away, her hand upon the painted china doorknob.

I caught at her sleeve. "Please, Aunt, finish what you would say. We may feel—?"

She sighed and looked me up and down. "We may feel—safe, Tansy."

"But—do you mean—?"

She smiled faintly. "You are like the little hunt terrier that digs and digs for the fox when it goes to ground. Remember that sometimes he succeeds in unearthing his quarry, and gets badly bitten for his pains. I saw one such dog once which was dead when they dug him out at last."

I shook my head. "I know you would prefer me not to ask questions, or even to wonder . . . it is unladylike, no doubt. But in the circumstances—"

She turned away. "You are our guest, Tansy. We are very glad to have you here and hope you will become a close member of the family, as I have always thought of you. In return, perhaps you will consider my wishes in this matter?"

Without waiting for my reply, she closed the door gently behind her.

SIX

The following morning I dressed in my plain travelling gown, and having breakfasted lightly off a tray in my room, went downstairs conscious of a most dismal feeling of apprehension.

I was not relieved to find the captain waiting for me in the hall, where Mrs. Slight also stood, my heavy cloak in her hands.

"Ah, I was about to send for you, Miss Tansy," said my step-cousin. "I hope you have breakfasted, for we must leave at once if we are not to be late for the inquest."

I hesitated. "I am ready but—is not my aunt to accompany us?"

He smiled mockingly. "She is still abed, I fear. My father has already gone on, and asked me to escort you. Mrs. Slight comes with us, to lend you countenance."

There was nothing for it but to allow the housekeeper to settle the cloak over my shoulders and the captain to lead me outside to the waiting chaise. The postilion attracted my attention by the odd manner in which he was staring at me, his head quite twisted round upon his neck, his expression horrified, his eyes starting. Then his gaze shifted towards Mrs. Slight, following us down the steps, and the horses pranced as if they had been struck. The captain shouted a reprimand and positively bundled us inside. A moment later the door was shut and we set out at a brisk trot, retracing our steps, so far as I could tell, towards the prison.

"Ay, the inquest is at Hallchurch," said the captain, reading my thoughts. "They have taken the corpse to the Green Man, and the jury will be viewing it now."

After this agreeable announcement he said no more until we had entered the town, passed the jail, and pulled up before a bustling hostelry. "Here we are," he then remarked. "What a press of people, to be sure. But then the case is one of unusual interest."

"I wish I had a veil!" I cried, shrinking back into my corner.

"Too late!" said the captain grimly. "Dr. Radway will already be growing impatient, if my watch is right."

The door was opened by a servant from the inn. There was a murmur from the crowd as the captain helped me down the steps, followed by calls and shouts. I looked round at Mrs. Slight. She was staring straight before her, but her mouth was a little twisted in what might have been a tiny complacent smile. I clenched my teeth and marched into the inn, looking neither to right nor left.

A portly landlord, his face flushed with excitement, bowed us into a large scrubbed room quite full of people and set with long tables. One group seemed to be peering at me with particular interest.

"The jury," whispered the captain, his fingers tight about my arm as if he suspected me of intending to escape. "The foreman, Trimble, is a very fiery tailor from our village, who preaches sedition. He wants to rise in the world himself and lower those above him. You had better hang your head a trifle, and assume a humble manner, if you wish to please him. Ah, there is the coroner, Dr. Radway, talking to my father and the constable." He saw me seated, settled himself on the next chair, crossed his legs with all the ease in the world, and looked about him as carelessly as if he were at a social gathering. "I thought they might have called in the Bow Street Runners to assist," he remarked, "but I see none here. Time enough for that when a verdict has been reached, perhaps."

There was a sudden rapping for silence, everyone who was not seated hurried to find a place, and the coroner sat down and picked up his pen.

"The witnesses are all present," the captain informed me obligingly. "We are about to begin!"

The jury was duly sworn and the evidence began with the constable, looking extremely nervous as he described how he had come to discover the body, at what time, and where it had been found. Dr. Burton followed him with an odiously detailed description of the fatal wounds, and his opinion as to the approximate time of death. He also identified the body and owned that the girl had visited him a few days previously in connection with her pregnancy, which was in an early stage. I did not know where to look at this, but forgot my embarrassment in astonishment when Mrs. Slight seized my hand and held it tightly. Was she indicating sympathy for me, or was she in the grip of some excitement she wished to communicate? I then became aware that the foreman of the jury was staring at our hands, and hastily pulled mine away, only to return it in order to give the housekeeper a quick pat lest she take offense.

The postilion, Hodgkin, next came to the stand. There was some whispering at this point among the legal gentlemen, which, as the captain was kind enough to explain, was probably concerned with the propriety of my remaining in the room as, under the old Tudor statutes, a witness should not be allowed to hear evidence against himself. However, possibly due to the great press of people outside the room, I was allowed to stay. I felt more afraid at this juncture than I had been before, and rather wished I might have been excused from listening to evidence designed to incriminate me. I might then have been glad of Mrs. Slight's bony hand on mine, but hers were now primly folded in her lap and I was obliged to stare at the Parliament clock instead and tell myself that when it had ticked away another hour or so, this ordeal would be over.

I was unduly optimistic. The evidence had all to be recorded by the clerks, and signed by the witnesses. The coroner asked many questions rather to clarify matters for the jury, I thought, than himself. The procedure was very slow. At length, however, my own turn came to witness and I rose, conscious of whispering all about me and an increased movement of pens and rustling of paper on the part of some gentlemen who were, the captain had not omitted to inform me, reporters and artists from various daily and weekly newspapers.

Prompted by the coroner, I described the fog and how I happened to lose the chaise left in my charge. The court was very still as I related how the cracked bell had led me to the church. There was a concerted gasp when I came to the music I had heard and the leaping shadows I had seen—then utter silence again as I described the black forms dancing and the young girl near the window. I looked up at this

88

point and saw again the foreman of the jury watching me sardonically. He did not believe me, I thought, with a catch of the breath. He supposed I killed the girl and made up this tarradiddle to account for it! But then he pulled down the corners of his mouth, turned to the man at his side and nodded portentously, and I was no longer sure I had understood him correctly.

"As these—figures—with the one exception of Miss Holford, were all gowned or cloaked and masked there is not, I suppose, any likelihood of your recognizing them again?" the coroner asked.

I closed my eyes, reliving the moment when for an instant the fog had swirled away. The scene returned to me in vivid detail; I saw again the fair young girl, the tall man behind her, the hunchback, a fat woman, another female twisting her hands, a spry little fellow who lifted his skirts as he danced to reveal bowlegs. I pressed my hands against my eyes.

"I remember—certain things—" I began.

Someone dropped a pencil into the silence with a clatter. I looked up. Sir Abraham was staring at me aghast. Even the coroner seemed disconcerted. He had been leading me, I suddenly realized. For my own safety's sake, no doubt, he had shown me how to avoid the responsibility of identifying the witches. Swiftly I said what with one exception was true, that of course there was no way for me to recognize persons who must of necessity be strangers to me since I had never set foot in the county before the day in question. "Besides," I added, watching the scratching pens hurrying over the foolscap, "the fog—the uncertain light—the—as you said, sir, the disguise . . . it is true I did recognize the deceased when I saw the body but she has—had remarkable hair."

89

I felt suddenly faint and was grateful when someone held a glass of water to my lips.

Mindful of the captain's eyes upon me and endeavouring to forget the phrase of the awful oath I had sworn that enjoined me to tell "the whole truth," I continued my evidence by saying that I had run away and fired the gun to bring the postilion to me; that the—the persons in the church had fled at the alarm and that, having dropped the pistol due to the shock of the concussion, I had returned to the church and entered it for the sole purpose of ringing the bell, for the further guidance of Hodgkin. I told the rest just as it happened, did not falter under some sharp questioning, and returned to my seat feeling somewhat more confident than I had done all day. Once I had sat down, however, I began to tremble and this time it was the captain who gave my hand an encouraging squeeze, in gratitude, no doubt, for my not having betrayed him.

Further witnesses followed: Sir Abraham, Maggie Smith to describe how she had vainly searched me, the constable again to tell of his fruitless efforts to find the weapon, dragging the river and searching the churchyard. At this point the pistol was produced and a gunsmith witnessed that a shot had been fired from it, while Hodgkin, who had become rather excited on seeing his valued barker, was privately assured that it would soon be restored to him. Jem came to the stand to describe where he had found my reticule the following day, with the dagger in it. The dagger was required to be produced, the squire censored for not having entered it as evidence, and I pulled it from my bag to the accompaniment of a good deal of noise in court, which annoyed the coroner. Someone carried the dagger to the jury, who then departed with it and Dr. Burton, to another room in which the body had been laid; and Mrs. Holford, a poor, thin, distracted looking woman, fainted ungracefully across her husband's knees.

The jury returned and all at once, it seemed, the examination of witnesses was concluded and the coroner began his summing-up. Suicide, he declared, was clearly impossible, owing to the number and depth of wounds inflicted, and the fact that no weapon had been found by the body. Accident or manslaughter also seemed to be ruled out. If the death was caused by another person, or persons, with intent, then they must have been strong enough to raise the body to the altar, dead or alive, and to inflict the wounds to the depth which the jury had just observed. It was natural that any person found in the presence of a body that had violently expired must be regarded with suspicion, and the jury must ask themselves whether they believed the story they had heard to account for Miss Tremayne's presence in the church. They should also take into account the fact that far from making any attempt to escape, she had advertised her presence and sought help by ringing the bell; she had no means of knowing the dead woman, for it had been deposed not only by Miss Tremayne herself but by Sir Abraham also that Miss Tremayne had never before been in Sussex, and by Farmer Holford, that his daughter had never left the county. The jury should also consider the fact that Miss Tremayne had no weapon on her, no apparent motive, and a good deal less than the necessary strength. With regard to the wounds, he would remind the jury that Dr. Burton's opinion was that they had been inflicted by at least two hands, from the differing angles of the incisions.

With a heavy sound of boots on bare boards, the jury again left the room. There was a general feeling of temporary relief, much shuffling, and several persons left in search of refreshment. The captain offered to fetch lemonade, but Mrs. Slight shook her head.

"They'll be back in a moment, sir. The foreman will see to that."

"Mrs. Slight is always right," the captain observed. He stretched his legs and looked about. "All the world is here today. There's Knevett, of course—"

Of course, I echoed to myself. Lord Knevett had the sort of presence of which it was not possible to be unaware. I had known the instant he entered the room, soon after the inquest had begun.

"There is old Crofton looking more apoplectic than ever," the captain continued. "Colonel Horton—he's another of the Justices, of course. Curtis from Lindenfold—"

"Who is that woman who keeps staring at me?" I asked in a low voice. "The one opposite, next to the fat woman and with a footman on her other side?"

"Oh, that's—I can't recall the name, but you need not mind her. She is only the wife of the lodgekeeper at Lindenfold Hall—Mrs. Davies, I believe; and the other woman is the cook from Holy Mote. Don't pay any heed to them, Miss Tremayne. Let them stare their fill. It won't hurt you, and it gives them pleasure."

I gave an exasperated sigh—and at that moment the jury began to return. I stared at the foreman. He could easily be the nimble bowlegged dancer I had seen at All Saints, I thought wildly, just as the cook could have been the fat woman. Would the coroner have committed me to Bedlam if instead of denying any chance of recognizing the witches again, I had pointed at these two, and at the man by my side? I must be careful not to let the whole affair prey upon my mind too much, I decided, pinching my wrist sharply.

It would be too easy to see a witch behind every staring look, every chance resemblance of gait or figure. I returned my attention to Mr. Trimble, who was in the very act of announcing the verdict.

"Murder by person or persons unknown!"

"And is that the verdict of you all?"

"It is, your Honour."

It was all over. I had not been named a murderer—and neither had anyone else.

Confusion reigned. The writers and artists elbowed their way out and leapt into waiting post chaises, while ordinary folk followed, just as anxious to be first with the news.

I stood up and swayed. It was Sir Abraham who caught me.

"This has been too much for you, miss—get her home quickly, Mark. There's water on the table, Slight; fetch it, and—ah, Barton, just the man we need!"

"She'll do," replied Dr. Burton, eyeing me sharply. "A short rest, a bowl of broth is all she needs—the verdict should act as a tonic as soon as the reaction has worn off."

The captain had forced a passage to the side door and presently I was handed up into the chaise. A moment later Sir Abraham mounted his horse and we set off through the rapidly dispersing crowds. Mrs. Slight, seated opposite me, seemed to be concentrating her blue stare upon me. I twisted and turned my head to avoid it and was on the point of voicing a protest when I must have fallen asleep.

I woke as the chaise was pulling up outside the house. I felt refreshed and was able to take my broth in the breakfast room where my aunt was also partaking of a little luncheon. We discussed the inquest briefly, for all she wished to know was what verdict had been arrived at, and then I excused myself to walk in the shrubbery. She raised no objection, her thoughts apparently elsewhere, so I put on my cloak again and was just crossing the hall when the front door opened to admit my step-cousin and Lord Knevett.

"Ah, what a fortunate chance!" cried the captain. "Knevett, you are come just in time to escort my cousin about the garden. I know she needs some fresh air to blow away her memories of this morning, and you are the very companion for her."

Lord Knevett bowed, and looked agreeable, but I was angry and mortified by the captain's manner.

"Thank you!" I said stiffly. "But I think—that is, my aunt—"

"I will engage to tell her you have gone out," said the captain, with his mocking smile.

"But I must refuse! Or at the least have her permission," I added weakly, seeing to my gratified amazement that Lord Knevett actually looked disappointed.

"Surely you may safely entrust yourself to me?" the baron said persuasively. "Especially since I assume you always carry that lethal dagger with you?"

"I do, sir, but even so—"

"Pray don't hesitate a moment longer, as the sun will go in. You may safely leave your aunt to Prendergast, I am sure."

They exchanged glances and I remembered uneasily how close their understanding was—close enough to enable them to swear false alibis for each other. But if it gave me a pang to reflect that Lord Knevett was a man not always bound by his word, the possibility that he had compounded with Captain Prendergast for twenty minutes alone with me was thrilling enough to outweigh my qualms.

"Very well, sir; since you have been so kind as to offer to escort me."

"Capital!" Lord Knevett extended his arm and I slipped my black-gloved fingers lightly through it. Captain Prender-

gast gave a short, disconcerting laugh, and closed the side
door behind us.

Having been brought up to believe in the absolute necessity for chaperonage, I was half-prepared for Lord Knevett
to put me to the blush, either by his speech or manner; however, he showed no inclination to take advantage of the un-
conventional circumstances in which we found ourselves and
began to converse easily on the subject of his house, of which
he was obviously extremely proud. To my pleasure he informed me that he had brought a written invitation for my
aunt and myself to visit on the morrow.

"The older part dates from Norman times," he said, after
assuring himself of my interest in domestic architecture.
Assisting me down the stone steps, slippery with lichen, he
went on, "The main house, however, was restored by my
grandfather in the earlier part of this century. The chapel is
said to be extremely old and has medieval murals still in
quite good condition. I have been advised to cover them with
tapestries to preserve them for posterity; but how do I know
that posterity will appreciate them as I do, Miss Tremayne?
I intend to leave them as they are to decay in the fullness of
time, and meanwhile to be enjoyed by us."

I reflected that when he had children of his own, perhaps
Lord Knevett would change his views. Noticing that he was
expecting some comment from me, I said diplomatically, "I
expect your mother prefers to see them as she is accustomed
to do. What are her interests, sir?"

"She has none," he said with finality. After a moment he
added, "When I spoke in the plural just now, I meant my
chaplain and myself."

"Oh. You have a chaplain, then?" How I wished for inspiration to converse easily with charm and wit; instead, my
brain felt numb and even my feet moved clumsily upon the

gravel path. Being alone with such an attractive and dominating man was not the unmitigated bliss I had expected it to be, I was disappointed to find.

"Arbuthnot, yes—a poor fellow who was lecturing at Oxford when I was up. Increasing age drove him to look for something less demanding but he could not find a living to suit him, until I took pity on him when he eventually applied to me. He is some sort of company for my mother—and he amuses me." Lord Knevett broke off rather abruptly and held back a spray of some mist-beaded leafless shrub. "I was so sorry to hear of the distressing circumstances of your arrival in these parts," he continued, with a sudden change of subject. "Even more distressing than your prison experiences must have been your brief glimpse of—pagan rites, I assume."

"Yes," I said slowly. "That was horrendous. But the greatest shock of all was seeing the body, of course."

"Ah, the unfortunate Miss Holford. But will you—for a rather particular reason—gratify my curiosity and tell me what you actually saw in and about the church? Your cousin Prendergast for one, I understand," he added encouragingly, as I hesitated.

I was aware first of disappointment. Somehow I had hoped that Lord Knevett had given Captain Prendergast an alibi while remaining in ignorance of what he really was about. Next, I was conscious that he had put me in a difficult position. I drew my cloak a little more snugly about myself and said in a tone which I attempted to render expressionless, "Indeed? But I understood that Captain Prendergast was engaged with you at that time, my lord."

He said nothing for a moment but I knew he stared at me and I felt my colour rise.

"Very discreet," he said at last, and I was aware of having disappointed him in my turn. "There is no reason why I should have expected you to trust me, I suppose. Perhaps I had better inform you, if you are not already aware of it, that I am a brother Justice of your uncle's—a magistrate, Miss Tremayne—and that, having a peculiar horror of the practice of witchcraft, I asked Prendergast to spy on that particular sabbat for me."

My mouth fell open as I endeavoured to readjust all my ideas. Mark Prendergast on the side of the angels! But I did not think it was entirely prejudice which prevented me from believing it. There was something else, something which I was far too agitated at that moment to recall. . . .

"You sent him there?" I breathed. "But why did Captain Prendergast not explain to me . . . ?"

"Because, for his own sake, I had enjoined secrecy upon him. I did not want him endangered by his having seen what was never intended for an outsider's eyes. It would be a shocking thing if they—whoever they may be—were to revenge themselves upon your cousin as perhaps they revenged themselves upon Miss Holford."

"But should you not own to it now?" I blushed. "I mean, to Sir Abraham, perhaps?"

Lord Knevett struck with his cane at a twig in the path. "It is not quite so simple as you suppose, Miss Tremayne. It is not the first time that Prendergast and I have had this agreement with each other . . . for more frivolous reasons. We have gone to some trouble to perfect our arrangements, and so long as I know why he was at All Saints on Saturday, I see no object in exposing myself as a liar and jeopardizing such a convenient system."

"But then, why do you confide in me?"

He smiled. "You knew a little, and I felt it better for you to know more, than to mistrust me. Besides, I am sure you will respect our secret."

I said in a stifled tone, "I suppose you mean that I too

have something to hide. Captain Prendergast told you that I had shot at him, I collect?"

"Not immediately. I could see he was disturbed when he returned to the White Lion, but he said nothing of either the shooting or the murder at that time, and to me the fact that he had witnessed a witches' sabbat was more than sufficient explanation for his state. The next day, as soon as I heard of the murder, I rode over to discover why he had not told me of it. He denied having had any knowledge of it at that time, and then admitted that his state of shock had been due less to having seen the witches, whose dance he described as being something of a joke," said Lord Knevett incredulously and with a shudder, "than having been shot upon, and missed very narrowly by, as he put it, a pert slip of a girl who turned out to be his cousin, and whose baby-face would not save her from a beating if she ever gave him the opportunity to administer one. You may think it mischievous of me to retail his comments to you," he added, gazing at me earnestly, "but sometimes 'forewarned is forearmed,' you know."

I tried to look as if I did not care. "Well, if I had known the captain was upon the King's business," I said with a shrug. "As it is—supposing if someone else saw him there? Would it not be better for you to speak first?"

Lord Knevett sighed, looked doubtfully at a damp stone seat, and led me on. "I have already owned to having passed the afternoon in playing cards with him," he reminded me. "I am not eager to change my evidence, even in spite of the new gravity of the circumstances. Besides, Mark Prendergast is my friend—I have known him forever. We were at school and university together. I can't remove my support at just the time he needs it."

I stared at him in perplexity. "But, sir—if you sent him there—?"

He frowned. "I should not mention this, perhaps, but unfortunately I have heard some rumour of Mark's having had a particular acquaintance with young Polly Holford, and it might go ill with him if it becomes known that he was present at the fatal time, and in disguise. It would not only be from the witches that he would be in danger then."

I gazed at a dingy statue, its outline weathered and blurred. If there had indeed been something between Mark Prender-gast and Polly Holford—and I remembered now that I had thought it was he with whom she had danced—then there were at least two reasons for his apparent hatred of me. Either he had killed her, and feared my testimony; or he was inno-cent and genuinely suspected me of being implicated in the murder of his beloved. How could I discover which it was?

"Yes," Lord Knevett said reflectively. "I know Prendergast would never raise a hand against a woman. I shall stand by him."

I did not remind him that my cousin had promised to beat me if he could. Instead I remarked with concern that it seemed to me he was playing a dangerous game; and I re-peated that I thought the fact he had himself sent the captain to All Saints must surely clear my cousin of suspicion.

"Anything I say in Prendergast's favour is likely to be discounted once it is known that I lied about his movements that afternoon," he said grimly. "I am in a difficult situation, Miss Tremayne. In normal circumstances I would make a clean breast of the whole affair to Sir Abraham—indeed, if further facts come out, I may still be obliged to do so."

"Further facts?" I repeated. "Do you mean there is still some enquiry being pursued?"

"Certainly, ma'am. Sir Abraham is one of your British bull-dogs. Once he has his teeth into something he will not let go, and even if it occurred to him it would be better to do so, his reputation would make it seem suspicious if he were to abandon the case. No, the books are not closed upon that subject, nor will they be for some time, I believe."

I shivered, and he gripped my arm a little more tightly.

A moment passed in silence. "Well, Miss Tremayne," Lord Knevett said in an encouraging tone, "do not be afraid to speak! For I perceive you are engaged in some kind of a struggle with yourself."

I took a deep breath of the cold damp air. "I still think that if you, in your capacity as a magistrate, instructed Captain Prendergast to disguise himself and go to the church, it must clear him at least of—what is that phrase?—malice aforethought. You could explain the reason you had kept it secret, as you have done to me; and ask for further discretion in order to safeguard the captain."

"You are persistent, Miss Tremayne. You have yet to learn that very few matters are as simple as they may first appear to be. The fact is in this case that Prendergast and I met, as arranged, for purely frivolous reasons and only in the course of a game of piquet did the idea of spying on the witches occur to me, when one of us—him, I rather think, mentioned that it was the Feast of Candlemas. Indeed, if I were asked under oath, I believe I could not perfectly swear whether it was he or I who first made the suggestion. It has long been whispered, of course, that All Saints was a witches' meeting place. But you are cold," he said, observing me shiver again. "I had better take you inside."

"I—yes, I am cold."

He led me towards the house. "You are cleared of all suspicion, I understand. The doctor's evidence was in your favour. It would not harm you unduly, therefore, to own to having fired upon your cousin that evening, but I hope you will not do so, ma'am, when you reflect that such a confession would oblige me also to change my story, against my judgment."

Thus neatly did the baron remind me that I was in no position to criticize him. I said quietly that there seemed no point in my mentioning that episode. It was quite unlikely I should be questioned further, and even if I did eventually feel obliged to confess to it, I would still not be able to swear to the identity of the man who had accosted me, as he had worn a hood.

"Thank you," said Lord Knevett warmly. I blushed a little and turned as if to admire the prospect of blue-toned meadows fading into mist beyond the ha-ha; for it was indeed for his sake that I had determined not to ease my conscience by confessing the whole truth to Sir Abraham: it was to save Lord Knevett embarrassment and not Mark Prendergast from anything worse that I had agreed to keep silent.

When I felt sufficiently composed, I glanced again at Lord Knevett. He seemed preoccupied, and I was able to reflect that, after all, it was extraordinarily pleasant to be the sole companion of such a handsome young man, if only for a short time, and even more pleasant to have been asked a favour by him. Why then was there this feeling, faint but uneasy, that there might be something more behind his request than had yet appeared, something which I should be able to think out for myself—?

"Francis Sinclair-Stewart is predicting that you will become the toast of the county," Lord Knevett remarked abruptly. He seemed displeased, I thought, and I wondered for an intoxicating moment if he could be jealous.

"I hardly think so, sir," I assured him. "Mr. Sinclair-Stewart does not know me. Besides, as his mother demonstrated to me, I am in disgrace."

"Odious woman!" he declared, striking irritably at a fluted urn with his cane. "No doubt she was afraid of your effect upon her son—and with reason. But the disgrace, as you call it, will soon be forgotten."

"I fear I doubt it. In any case," I added more lightly, "the toast of the county would have to be famous for some lively skill, such as riding to hounds, and I am no Diana, I fear."

"No, you are a Persephone," he retorted swiftly, "tiptoeing into the underworld. I cannot tell you how affecting it seems to me that you, of all persons, should have stumbled upon those frightful proceedings at All Saints. However, you don't wish to talk of that, I see. I hope Lady Prendergast is kinder to you than was her friend, Lady Sinclair-Stewart. Your aunt seems rather averse to the idea of your having anything to do with me, I thought. Can it be that she hopes to marry you to Mark? I believed I saw something of that in her eye last time we met."

The presence of a chaperon at this moment would certainly have saved me embarrassment, I thought. "Really, sir," I stammered, "I hope you do not expect me to discuss my matrimonial prospects with you upon such a short acquaintance?"

"I should not, I know, for you are modest and shy—admirable! But I wanted, never mind why, to discover how the land lies. Do you find your cousin—who is not your cousin—agreeable? For that he must worship you is beyond question, I should suppose."

"You are extremely flattering, sir; but quite out in your supposition."

"What! How is this? You mean he does not worship you?"

"Captain Prendergast detests me," I said rashly.

"Impossible!"

"I assure you, sir, that so it is. From the very first—" I broke off, stifling a sigh. "I suppose he won't forgive me for shooting at him—I even think he does not yet believe me entirely cleared of complicity in the murder. At all events, he behaves as if he suspects me of deceit. But we are both, of course, endeavouring to keep our antipathy a secret."

"It is mutual, then?" He frowned at me. "Yes, it occurred to me earlier, and then I forgot it—but I believe I know why he mistrusts you."

"Oh, why?" I said eagerly. "Pray tell me, sir, even if it is unpleasant."

For a moment I thought he would not answer. Then he said slowly, "It is possible that you remind him of someone he has—had, I should say—good cause to hate. You have something of a look of her, though her eyes were blue, and the same innocent, impulsive air—deceptive indeed, in her case—"

"In whose case?" I whispered as he paused. "Of whom do you speak?"

He shook his head. "I must not tell you that, Miss Tremayne. No doubt time, and a closer acquaintance with you, will persuade him of his mistake. If that is the case"—he frowned again—"and I know one should not say this of a friend but you need counsel, I believe; if, I say, Prendergast decides to overcome his prejudice against you to oblige his parents, then be warned: he is not the husband I should choose for an innocent young girl—and he may have reason to want you in his power."

I stared at him. What could he mean? What secret knowledge did he have? I heard myself say in a cold clear voice, "You need have no fear of my taking Mark Prendergast for a husband, sir. I suppose he would be the last gentleman upon the planet with whom I would willingly ally myself!"

Lord Knevett's expression changed. He smiled a little ruefully as his gaze shifted. I turned, my pulses leaping with apprehension, to see that Captain Prendergast had come out of the house during our conversation, and was lounging on the stone steps behind us with a gleam in his cold eye which boded ill for me.

SEVEN

All the captain said, however, was that at his father's suggestion he proposed to give me some instruction in riding, so soon as I had changed my dress.

"You have a riding-habit, I suppose?" Captain Prendergast added, still regarding me with that cool, alert expression.

"No, sir, I have not," I returned hotly. "Nor does it matter, for I detest horses, and mean never to find myself upon one."

One of the captain's dark alarming eyebrows rose. "Are you afraid, Miss Tremayne?"

"I am not always afraid of those whom I detest," I assured him tartly if misleadingly.

He bowed slightly. "No doubt my stepmother will lend you something to wear—for since it is my father's desire that you should learn to ride you will agree, I hope, that your own feelings are somewhat irrelevant."

I felt Lord Knevett's hand stiffen on my arm. "Good heavens, Prendergast, you don't mean to force Miss Tremayne to learn when she so plainly does not want to?"

The captain regarded me closely. "Why not? She does not

know what she is missing. Besides, young ladies—properly brought-up young ladies—must do as their elders bid them."

"Look here, sir, I beg you won't consider putting Miss Tremayne upon a horse against her will."

"But I am considering it. It should be amusing, if a trifle undignified for her. She may even find she likes it."

"I shan't!" I cried passionately. "Please don't let him, Lord Knevett."

"No, no—even if I have to call him out to prevent him."

"You would be sorry for it if you were to do anything so ill-advised as to challenge me," said the captain very coolly, with another lift of his eyebrow.

"Very true," agreed Lord Knevett promptly. "I was forgetting you were the better shot. But I can't let you bully Miss Tremayne, you know."

The captain looked at me very directly. "Am I bullying you, Miss Tremayne?"

"Yes! Yes, you are. I should not be surprised at it if you tried to put me up on that horrid stallion of yours."

"Good God, you would not do that, I hope," cried Lord Knevett. "That horse is crazy, I believe. He got the better of me the last time I tried to mount him but I'll master the brute yet, or die in the attempt."

"The latter is the more likely," returned the captain. "But you are both letting your imaginations run away with you. My stepmother's gelding has been saddled for Miss Tremayne."

I stared. Why was the captain so insistent on teaching me to ride? A possible answer occurred to me and I shivered: a riding accident could so easily be arranged. I said firmly, "I absolutely refuse to ride," and turned with a look of appeal to Lord Knevett.

He smiled. "Bravo, Miss Tremayne. Shall I conduct you to your aunt—and sanctuary?"

I looked at Lord Knevett with gratitude. "If you would be so kind, sir."

He began to lead me up the steps. Captain Prendergast straightened himself, moving with elaborate politeness out of our way. "My stepmother has a visitor," he remarked.

"Indeed? Who is it? Anyone I know?"

"I imagine you might. It is Miss Crofton."

Lord Knevett halted. With a rather theatrical gesture, he struck a hand to his head. "I have just recalled a promise I made Sir Abraham, to visit him today. I must beg you to excuse me, Miss Tremayne. We have to discuss one or two lines of enquiry that he might possibly pursue."

Captain Prendergast looked quite expressionless. "If you wish to boot the sleeping dog, it's no affair of mine, I suppose. You will find my sire in his den."

"Very well. Your servant, ma'am. Yours, Prendergast."

Lord Knevett walked briskly up into the hall. I only realized I was gazing forlornly after him when my cousin said coldly, "Yes, he is a handsome fellow, is he not? And if one cannot call him rich, at least he has a good deal of property, and a very ancient name. You could do worse for yourself, Miss Tremayne."

"Thank you. I will bear your advice in mind, and when I have been in the district a few more days I may be able to repay the compliment and suggest a spouse for you."

The captain relaxed. He almost smiled. "I wish you would, Miss Tremayne. But am I correct in thinking it unlikely that you will suggest yourself?"

I gasped. "You know, if you are honest, that such a match would be as detestable to you as to me," I pointed out.

107

He laughed shortly. "Perhaps—perhaps not. How detestable would it be to you, may I ask?"

"No, you may not ask! This is a ridiculous conversation and I mean to go indoors this instant."

"Very proper—but I do not mean to let you."

"Oh! But I am cold."

"Curious, when you look so warm and rosy red. You hate me very much, I suppose?"

"Well—you have not exactly striven to endear yourself to me, sir."

"No, quite true. To begin with, little girls who devote themselves entirely to invalid relatives seem quite unnatural to me—until the relative dies and leaves them everything. Then one does begin to wonder if such young ladies are not rather farsighted than unselfish. And when they write to other relatives proposing themselves for more devoted service, and those relatives immediately also determine to change their wills, one cannot help being rather prejudiced. And when the same young lady, for now we come from the general to the particular, is discovered at a witches' revel watching over a murdered body—to say nothing of a certain shooting—when the circumstances are so suspicious that she is conveyed to jail—and when upon inspection she appears too sweet and innocent to be true even if one had encountered her in impeccable circumstances—then is it any wonder that a man vows he will not fall into the trap his own father blundered into, will not be misled by a charming face—"

"Is this some kind of an apology, sir?" I demanded, when I had recovered sufficient breath. "Because if so, allow me to tell you that I think nothing of it!"

"An apology?" he cried, seizing me by the shoulders. "No, curse it, it is no such thing! It is—it is—I do not know what it is!"

I gave a frightened little laugh, so ludicrous yet so alarming was his rage. Instantly he seemed to freeze. Then he raised one of his hands and, as I flinched, wound his fingers in my hair. He pulled my face closer to him. His eyes were grey and very cold as they stared into mine. Then their expression changed again, as stone mellows when sunlight strikes it, and with a sharp gasp I began to struggle to be free.

"All in good time," he murmured. "The question is, just what sort of a young lady are you?"

The next moment, incredibly, his lips were on mine. He did not kiss me—fleetingly I remembered the horror of the physician's snuff-spiced kiss as he spat and gobbled at me. Captain Prendergast just held me there against his smooth warm lips. My mouth trembled and he threw back his head.

"Ha!" he exclaimed, dropping his hands and dusting them together as if to sweep off contamination. "You gave yourself away then, I fancy."

I stared at him blankly, and then blushed painfully as I realized that the moment our mouths met I had ceased to struggle.

"A murderer, Miss Tansy?" the captain murmured. "No, I think not—but an adventuress? Yes, perhaps. At all events, I mean to keep the possibility in mind."

I gave a sob and turned to flee. Instantly his hand shot out and again detained me. "Not so fast, sweet Cousin. What, real tears? The truth hurts, then? I always thought the finest actresses had the greatest capacity for self-deception."

"Please—let me go!"

"Certainly not. If you will not obey my father's instructions and come riding with me, you can at least support your aunt in entertaining Miss Crofton. Now, will you precede me, or must I carry you?"

I stared at him reproachfully. He muttered an oath and

flung open the door. A moment later, while I was still struggling to unfasten my cloak, he pushed me into the drawing room and closed the door sharply behind me.

I made a great effort to compose myself. My aunt seemed mildly pleased to see me and introduced me to the visitor. Miss Crofton struck me at first sight as being the sort of dessicated spinster who collects string and candle-ends and rather more cats than she can properly control; but when she turned her very light-blue eyes on me I wondered if there might not be more to her than at first appeared. She for her part examined me with an interest even deeper than that which I should have supposed my experiences warranted. She stared as I talked, almost as if she hoped to catch me out. She had a nervous trick of passing her pointed tongue rapidly over her lips that made me think of snakes. I noticed her expression did not warm when she addressed herself to my aunt, but her speech, in contrast to her manner, was very mild and submissive.

"As I was saying, dear Lady Prendergast," she began with a little deprecating laugh, continuing the conversation my entrance had interrupted, "if it was in the newspaper, you must not expect me to have read it. Papa is so particular, you know. First the paper has to be ironed so that it is warm and smooth and the print is set; then no one else must touch it in case he wishes to refer to something, and as soon as he relinquishes it, it is used to clean the pans or light the fires. I believe much of the trouble in our family was caused by the fact that he could never cure poor dear Mama of tearing out paragraphs which interested her."

"And how is Colonel Crofton?" enquired my aunt, after a short pause.

"Oh, he is in good health, I am glad to say—in spite of the upset," she added, almost in a whisper, with a side glance at me.

"The upset? Oh, you mean—but why did that affect him?"

"Papa is so orderly: he likes everything just so. An affair of that sort—so shocking, so inexplicable—and still unsolved. . . ." She shook her mousy head. "It is enough to send him into one of his rages whenever he thinks of it." She sighed and looked out of the window. "I wish they could discover who was responsible—just so long as it was nobody one knew, of course—and then we could all forget it."

There was another uncomfortable pause. I began to suspect that the contrivance of such pauses was one of Miss Crofton's particular pleasures.

"Why, there is Lord Knevett!" she exclaimed suddenly, patches of colour appearing in her faded cheeks. "He is walking with Sir Abraham." She turned her pale eyes upon my aunt. "He calls here, then? Somehow I should have thought. . . ."

Aunt Margaret bent her head, but not before I had glimpsed a fleeting expression of fear cross her face. "He has matters to discuss with Sir Abraham, who is also on the Bench," she said coldly. "Also, of course, Lord Knevett is a particular friend of my stepson's."

"Ah yes, the gallant captain!" cried Miss Crofton in a high little voice. "Are we to have the pleasure of his company this afternoon?" She looked searchingly at me. "He is a very dashing gentleman, is he not? Quite the hero!"

She expected me to look self-conscious, so naturally I began to blush. Anger at her and myself only served to deepen my colour. Aunt Margaret noticed it at once and a distinct expression of triumph curved her lips. However, she was sensitive enough to make an attempt to divert Miss Crofton's attention from me.

"I daresay Mark is busy," she suggested quickly. "Gentlemen are not over-fond of drawing rooms, alas. But is it not fortunate that he is on leave just now? Young company is just what my niece requires, after nursing my poor sister for so long. By the way, Tansy, I have been meaning to ask you, what became of the ivory elephants the Admiral brought back from India?"

"Aunt Dorothy gave them to Chivers, her maid. She particularly admired them and had served Aunt Dorothy so long. . . ." My voice trailed away as I caught the disbelieving gleam in Miss Crofton's eye. She, I realized, was convinced I had sold them and pocketed the price. Had Mark Prendergast been spreading tales about me, or was I naturally an object of suspicion to this small community which perhaps had led an uneventful existence until my doomful appearance in their midst?

Miss Crofton looked at Aunt Margaret. "I have a grandmother, Lady Prendergast—no, you have never met her, she quarrelled dreadfully with Papa and has never visited us at Heron's Mere—but she requires a companion and it did occur to me that Miss Tremayne might be looking for some such post."

I gasped. It seemed that Miss Crofton had not misjudged me, after all.

"Oh no," my aunt said promptly. "There is no question of it, I am sure." She flushed a little at my look of gratitude, and frowned as some afterthought seemed to strike her. "Where does your grandmother live, Miss Crofton?"

"In Yorkshire, ma'am—the West Riding."

"Oh. So far? Well—but no, I am sure Tansy will stay to be a comfort to me for many years."

"She would suit Grandmama very well, I am sure," declared Miss Crofton, rising. "Her name is Mrs. William Crofton, and the address, Oak Dene, Near Harrogate, should you wish to correspond with her. I must be on my way now, ma'am. Papa will be quite put out if he does not find me at home when he returns."

Miss Crofton was tall and thin. She looked down on me with almost a pitying expression. "It was charming to make your acquaintance, Miss Tremayne. One hears so much nonsense. . . . What a shame that you are in mourning. You would put our country beauties in the shade, if you were to make a public appearance. Perhaps you had better give serious thought to the possibility of moving before those less fortunately endowed find cause to scratch your eyes out."

She left me wondering if she had intended to put a special emphasis into the words "fortunately endowed," and if her pleasantry had been meant to sound so much like a warning.

My next meeting with Captain Prendergast was at breakfast the following day. All the family were there when I came down aware of having overslept after a bad night. The servants had been dismissed from the room, as was customary, but no one seemed to be taking advantage of the opportunity to speak freely. The silence was gloomy and even my quiet greetings seemed to be resented.

"What is it?" I asked apprehensively, catching a stricken look from my aunt. "Has something happened?"

"It is certainly no concern of yours if it has, miss," said the captain grimly, setting down his coffee cup with a crash.

"It concerns us all," said Sir Abraham heavily. "Why not tell her, eh? 'Twill be all over the county by now, I'll wager."

"Well, I'll be damned if I stay here and listen to you discussing me with a baby-faced chit of a girl—"

"Mark!"

"Oh, very well, Stepmama. I'll go and then you may say what you will."

Ignoring me, he strode from the room. Aunt Margaret gave a distracted sob and put her napkin to her eyes. The door slammed and Sir Abraham took a long draught of ale. When he lowered the tankard, froth edged his upper lip like the moustaches of an earlier day.

I said in a hesitant voice, "I don't wish to pry but—this has all the appearance of a calamity." I put my arm about my aunt's shoulders. "Is there anything I can do, Aunt Margaret?"

She shook her head, dabbed at her eyes and looked up at me with an air almost of defiance. "It is nothing, my dear—some stupid prank, no more—it is merely that it seems—coming after the event in this way, it looks—"

"The fact of the matter is," said the squire, peering into the dregs of his ale suspiciously, "that young Jem—or Jim—no matter which, but a labourer who works for Holford, the father of the murdered wench, you know—young Jem has seen fit to come to us after this lapse of time, and swears he saw my son meeting poor Polly in—er—clandestine fashion."

I was silent a moment. Then I said slowly, "Has Captain Prendergast ever denied knowing the girl? What has he to say of the matter?"

"The young fool!" exploded the squire. "Oh, he admits it, right enough—or did when I put the question to him direct. But he has made up such a foolish tale to account for it, there is not a jury in the world would listen to it for a moment."

"I believe him," said Aunt Margaret staunchly.

"A jury?" I repeated faintly. "You think it might come to that? This new evidence is so important, then?"

"Damned if I know what to think," Sir Abraham groaned, pushing his tankard aside and resting his head in his hands. "The truth is, I'm too close to the matter to see it straight, I daresay. Lord! As if the other was not trouble enough, and now this! I'd say the young fool must be shielding someone, but no—Jim swears it was Mark he saw with Polly, and now it is my duty to look into the matter, stir it up, distress the

114

Holfords just when they are trying to turn their backs on the tragedy—"

"Perhaps Lord Knevett could be of assistance to you—"

"No!" exclaimed Aunt Margaret. She was very pale and shook her head helplessly at our enquiring expressions.

Sir Abraham sighed. "No," he echoed. " 'Tis damned unpleasant work and I must do it myself. Pull the bell, will you, Niece, and I'll send Barclay for my hat and stick."

"You—are going now?" faltered Aunt Margaret, looking at him with something like horror.

"Ay. Disagreeable tasks don't improve with keeping, my dear."

He left the room, apparently forgetting that I had rung for the butler, shuffling a little like an old man.

I looked down at my aunt's bowed head. What could I say to comfort her, knowing as I did that Captain Prendergast had first arranged an alibi, and secondly, compounded with me not to say that I had seen him in the churchyard?

I shivered, and tightened my arm about her. "Dear Aunt, if he is innocent, it must transpire. If not—"

"Ah!" she cried on a sudden fierce note. "Do you think if Mark is guilty then he deserves to be tried and hanged, and that it were better so for us all? Well, you are wrong, miss. The deed is done. If Mark were guilty of it, which of course I don't believe, would it not be better for it to be forgotten, and for him to go back to Spain and serve his country to the end? What good would it do to have him hanged—and us forever shamed? Will it bring back that foolish girl or comfort her parents if my husband is ruined? For that is what it would amount to: he would have to resign from the Bench and from his clubs—" Her voice broke. "Even his hunting— who would want to hunt with him after that? And what would my life be, socially shunned, and married to a broken man?

115

To say nothing of my stepdaughters and their children, some as yet unborn?"

"Do not distress yourself, ma'am. Remember that you believe Captain Prendergast to be innocent." I sighed. "Why is this story of his so unacceptable—his explanation for meeting the girl, I mean?"

"If only he had not said it was a hoax," she murmured, twisting her fingers together and staring blankly before her. "Any tale were better than that—even an admission that they were lovers—as likely enough they were."

I started. "Why do you say that?"

"Oh, she was comely enough, and pretty free with her favours, no doubt."

"But you said that you believed his story," I reminded her in some bewilderment.

"I don't believe he murdered the girl," she said stubbornly. "This tale of his is just what he might contrive to save the Holfords further pain. Parents can be blind—" She gave a bitter laugh. "God knows, love in any form is blind enough. I daresay they thought Polly a very model of maidenly virtue. In any event, what does talking signify? I have a migraine coming on and soon I shan't know what I am saying," she added abruptly, squeezing her eyes shut. "I go—am going—upstairs to my room to lie down. Pray don't disturb me."

"Dear Aunt! Do let me help you."

She did not dissuade me and seemed grateful for my arm. I delivered her to the care of Mitchell, her maid, who clicked her tongue and declared that the mistress was getting worse. Two migraines in a few days—she had not known of such a thing before. I left them and went downstairs, aware that the moment of a difficult decision was upon me.

I hesitated outside the library, and then, with thumping heart and shaking hands, boldly threw open the door.

Captain Prendergast was seated at the far side of the desk,

116

frowning at his clasped hands. He started at my entrance and half-rose to his feet. "What the Devil do you want?" he growled ungraciously.

I stared at him coldly. Polly Holford's lover? Yes, I could see him using her carelessly offered charms—but I was not so sure that I could imagine him closing forever that loose generous mouth of hers.

"I have come to warn you," I said firmly. "I told Lord Knevett I did not think I would refer to—to the incident of our first meeting, but matters are altered now."

He stared at me. I wondered if he had heard me properly, and stepped closer. "Surely you can see that the fact I met you by the church that night is now more serious than I thought it? I intend to tell your father—"

He flung up a hand, silencing me. "You are a very stupid little girl," he said coldly, his eyes like ice.

I gasped. I had expected him to bluster, to threaten me, to bargain—even perhaps to plead with me; but for this cool disdain I was totally unprepared.

"You mean—to warn you?" I stammered. "No—there are people within call—you cannot silence me here!"

His eyes narrowed. He seemed to be looking at my throat, where a pulse beat nervously. Was he measuring my neck, estimating, perhaps, the amount of strength it would need to squeeze it fatally? Defensively I put up a hand to it, and he smiled slightly. "What do you think of Knevett?" he asked in a conversational tone.

Again he had surprised me. "I don't see what that has to say to anything," I began.

"No, that is where your stupidity is apparent. It has not occurred to you, then, that an alibi provided only by one other person might serve as well for him? You think it was I who accosted you by the church—at whom you fired—but can you be certain it was not he?"

"You mean—? But of course it was you—you admitted it—and besides—" I grasped for support at the door handle behind me. "It was your voice," I concluded breathlessly.

His lids fell, hooding his eyes. "Our voices are very similar," he remarked. At once I realized the truth of this. It had not been obvious to me because the manner in which each addressed me was so different: one polite, admiring, the other cold and sneering—but there was no doubt, now that it had been pointed out to me, that their voices were alike.

"It is often so in boys who attend the same school," he continued quietly. "The person whom you saw was hooded—we are both of a similar build. I think you would be lying if you said you could swear positively to that person's identity."

"But—but—"

He disregarded my interruption. "I want you to consider seriously that in revealing all—you might be betraying him."

I found myself suddenly angry. "How can you throw suspicion on your lifelong friend? Lord Knevett cannot have been at All Saints—he has a horror of witchcraft—it was his idea to send you—"

"How much of a friend is he?" mused Mark Prendergast. "He was a strange boy. I have never really understood him. We were friends at school, for we were both far from home and at first knew no one else—but we were not close at Oxford, even though we were there together. Our interests, our circles at the university were entirely different. Afterwards, I saw little of him. It is only since I have been home on leave that we have resumed our closer acquaintance. He interests me but sometimes I have wondered—his parents were cousins and both eccentric, to say the least—"

"Really, sir!" I cried, forgetting my danger in my disgust

and advancing to stand before him. "I find your lack of loyalty repellent and, if you wish to know, I think his lordship charming. He has risked a great deal for you, giving you the alibi he did—and it was you in the churchyard, hooded or no—the horror I felt when you touched my shoulder could not have been inspired by anyone else! Besides," I finished triumphantly, "I saw your grey thoroughbred tethered to the hedge and it seems that no one but yourself can ride him."

During this speech the captain had stood up. Now he leaned across the writing table and grasped my wrist. "Are you sure of what you say?" he demanded tensely. "That it was my grey, I mean? You don't care for horses—it is not likely you know much about them."

"I know a grey from a chestnut, I suppose!"

"I don't have a monopoly on grey horses, miss."

"No, but—does Lord Knevett own a grey?"

He stared angrily at me. "No," he said at last.

"Well then, sir, if you will be so good as to release me, I think I had better be about my painful duty—of apprising your father—"

"Don't lie!" he snapped, hurting my wrist. "It won't be painful to you—far from it. I am sure it will amuse you to suppose you are betraying me. You are one of those sirens who like to see men suffer, or you would not have given yourself the pleasure of uttering this warning to my face. I can well imagine your delight, your demure smile, should the moment come for me to dance on air at Tyburn!"

I gazed at him in horror. Somehow I had contrived to lose sight of the fact that on the gallows was where it all might end. Fog seemed to swirl about the room. I could hear again the hoarse chanting of the postilion as he intoned his mournful dirge:

119

" 'O, the hangman waits for you and me,
Alas!
He waits for us by Tyburn Tree—' "

I shook my head to clear it of the memory. "That is nothing to the purpose," I managed to say quite steadily. "Merely, I think the time has come for all of us to tell all the truth. The fact that, as you say, Lord Knevett owns no grey horse—"

"He owns a roan," declared the captain harshly. "A blue roan, Miss Tremayne. I doubt if you could tell the difference —in a fog."

I felt my eyes widen. He stared at me, imposing his will on mine, his fingers cruelly tight about my wrist.

"You are very bold, Cousin Tansy," he said. "I don't want to have to threaten you, but don't you realize that the more you say, the more dangerous an enemy you are to me? You had better be careful, miss. Very careful—and very discreet."

There was a tiny sound. Instinctively we both looked down at his other hand which lay upon the table. Whether by chance or design, he had knocked his paper knife against the silver inkpot.

The knife was long and pointed—a stiletto of Italian craftsmanship. All along the blade there was a brownish stain.

I flung up my head. Captain Prendergast was still looking down. I snatched my hand from his suddenly slackened grip, took two backward steps—and fled.

EIGHT

I did not go to Sir Abraham. I escaped to my room. There
was no key in the door but there was a bright brass bolt
which I slid shut. Then, panting with terror but temporarily
secure, I leaned back against the door.

What should I do now?

Like a gleam of sunlight in a storm came the thought
of Lord Knevett. He had invited my aunt and myself to
take tea at Abbot's Grove today. If only she were recovered
in time to take me there, I should be able to find some opportunity to confide in him. He would know by now of Jem's
evidence, I supposed, and must already be wondering if the
moment had not come for him to own to his fellow magistrate
that he and the captain had not after all been together at
the fatal time. When he heard that I had seen what looked
very like the weapon of murder on the captain's desk his
duty would be clear.

But what a place to leave such incriminating evidence,
I reflected. It was almost a proof of the captain's innocence,

surely. But then, I thought, it might have been even more incriminating to have removed it. Supposing Sir Abraham had chanced to say, "The murder weapon must have been something very like that paper knife of yours, Mark, dear boy. You had better let me have another look at it. What, you have lost it? Damnably careless of you, sir!" That would have looked extremely black for Captain Prendergast, would it not?

But he might at least have wiped the blade.

I shivered and went to the fire. Perhaps he had tried to clean it, and found it stained. Lady Macbeth had also found it impossible to remove a similar stain. . . .

Mark Prendergast. Had his lips, that had pressed mine so warmly, also pressed on Polly's to distract and silence her in that last moment before she died?

The knife—I should have taken it before he found time to hide it but there had been no opportunity. Well, at least I knew about it. If it disappeared, I could bear witness that it had been there.

But my knowledge, as the captain himself had been good enough to inform me, was dangerous to me.

From this time forth, I determined, my aunt would find me a very close companion. And, after all, it could not be so very long before either the processes of the law or the resumption of the captain's military duties must rid me of his presence. But supposing he thought it unsafe to return to the field while I lived, and resigned his commission? Supposing he contrived to answer all charges and somehow succeeded in tricking me into marriage? Before that happened, I vowed, I would travel to Yorkshire and throw myself on the mercy of Miss Crofton's grandmother. Thanks to dear Aunt Dorothy, I was financially independent and not positively obliged to stay here in danger. Yet I knew that, foolhardy as it might seem, I did not want to leave.

A tap on the door startled me, but it was only Mitchell.

"My lady wants you, miss. I believe she is a little better."

Eagerly I hurried to my aunt's dark and overcrowded room. She called to me to come in and I moved cautiously towards her, avoiding little tables crowded with patch-boxes and snuffboxes, candlesticks and ring-stands. The bed was draped in some heavy material and in the center of it my aunt lay upon her face.

"Will you try drawing the curtain a little, Tansy?" she murmured against the pillow. "I think this is just a headache —not a true migraine, thank Heavens."

"I am so glad. We won't have to postpone our visit, then." I pulled back the window curtain and a pale gleam of sunlight stole into the room. The sky was heavy with swollen clouds, the river was wider than it had been, and everywhere little brooks were becoming broad streams, and meadows sinking into lakes.

Aunt Prendergast sighed. "What visit is that, dear child?"

"Why, to Abbot's Grove, Aunt. You know how I am longing to see the house."

She groaned and I hurried to place my hand on her forehead, which felt quite cool. "Don't you think it will do us good to get out for a little while?" I suggested hopefully.

"Oh dear. But it is true that you have been nowhere except to the inquest since you came. I suppose it is very dull for you here."

I caught my breath at an assumption so far from the truth. "No, indeed," I assured her. "It is merely that all I hear of Abbot's Grove makes me eager to explore it."

She reflected for a moment. "Very well, then: we will go—

and let us hope that one visit will be enough for you. But are you prepared to meet Lady Knevett, I wonder?"

"Why yes, ma'am—but she is ill, I understand?"

Aunt Margaret shuddered. "She is mad. But perhaps you will see for yourself though in general she keeps to her own rooms. Indeed it might be as well for you to meet her. Now why did I send for you? It was not to discuss the Knevetts, I am certain, for I had quite forgot the wretched invitation. What was it now? Oh, yes—Mark, to be sure." She grasped my hand and peered up at me. "Mark was so rude to you this morning," she said. "You have not quarrelled, I hope?"

My laugh, that was meant to be reassuring, sounded extremely strange. "I fear we are not friends, dear Aunt. Your stepson took me in aversion from the moment we met. It has been suggested to me that I bear some resemblance to a person who wronged him in some way."

"A person who wronged Mark?" she exclaimed, staring at me. Suddenly her eyes widened alarmingly. "My God!" she exclaimed, and actually recoiled from me. "I see it now! How could I not have noticed it before? It was always your mother whom I saw in you, I suppose—but, yes, there is a resemblance to another. Oh, is that accursed woman to ruin all our lives and go on and on doing so?" To my horror she burst into tears, great racking noisy sobs, while I, wondering and alarmed, could think of nothing better to do than pat her shoulder and murmur all the platitudes that came to mind, such as that time passed and life changed, and even, I remember, that "time and the hour run through the roughest day."

Gradually she quietened. "Oh, I am so ashamed," she said at last. She turned a wet imploring face upon me. "You will forget what I said?"

"I will try," I assured her, wishing I better understood

124

just what it was she had said. "Shall I send Mitchell to you now?"

"Oh no, I could not bear her to see me in this state. Won't you help me to dress?"

"Of course, dear Aunt. What do you propose to wear?"

I looked through her gowns while she was bathing her eyes. She had a well-filled wardrobe and many of her clothes were suitable to her half-mourning. I pulled out a pretty worked cambric in a flattering shade of grey, but she rejected it.

"Not that! I am sorry, my dear, but it is far too pretty. There is nobody I wish to impress at Abbot's Grove, I assure you."

"You really detest Lord Knevett, don't you, ma'am?" I said boldly. "I wish you will tell me what it is you have against him."

"Oh, nothing," she said too quickly. "Nothing in the world! Only that he has a way of saying one thing and meaning another. He is very charming, to be sure—but I would not trust him too far, if I were you."

Aware that I was about to place a good deal of trust in him, I turned to look at her. "But why not, Aunt? Charm alone should not condemn him. If he has a certain reputation, if you know anything in particular that he has done, I should be glad if you would tell me."

She stood very still, the hairbrush in her hand, staring at her reflection. "No," she said reluctantly. "I can't tell you anything positive against him, except that he has gambled half his estate away; but I feel—I am certain—that at heart he detests the female sex."

This opinion certainly startled me. "I feel sure you are wrong," I murmured, hiding my blushes among her gowns.

"Why? Because he flatters you, and bows low over your

125

hand? I think he has never forgiven his mother for shaming him, though I'm sure she can't help it, poor thing. But she has been a great embarrassment to him, not only here but at school when he was a boy, and—oh, everywhere he goes. But don't let us talk of him. We shall see him this afternoon in less than an hour, and that is bad enough. I expect his house will fascinate you, however," she added with a light laugh. "It is very dark and gloomy and alarming—positively Gothic, indeed. Come, that one will do—yes, the gown you are holding, little dreamer. We can pay a few visits in the village on the way home. I promised Sir Abraham I would see old Goody Clement; and Mother Latchington is sick too, and with a tribe of children to care for. We must see what we can do for them."

Somewhat abstractedly, I helped her into her gown and made a few attempts to subdue her hair. Impatiently, she dismissed me. "You are wondering what you will wear yourself," she accused me with some justice. "You had better send Mitchell to me after all. At least she keeps her mind upon the task."

Unlike Aunt Margaret, I was very sure there was someone at Abbot's Grove whom I wanted to impress. I pulled out half a dozen gowns and tried on three before I was satisfied, and then I could not decide whether to have my hair looped back or hanging forward. In the end I lost my patience with it and arranged it in a simple style, setting my prettiest bonnet on the top. Regarding my reflection, I decided that really it did not matter much: what made the improvement in my appearance was neither my gown nor my coiffeur but the air of anticipation which flushed my skin, reddened my lips and set a sparkle in my eyes. I felt a glow of confidence, as if I were easily capable of fencing with a murderer, comforting my aunt, avoiding my uncle's questions, and inter-

126

esting Lord Knevett. I was humming as I drew on my gloves and went in search of my aunt.

The chaise in which we drove out was fairly new, up-holstered in blue leather and fortunately reminiscent neither of the dank and gloomy one in which I had first entered this district nor the shabby open gig which had conveyed me to prison. As we settled ourselves into its corners, I noticed a steady rain had begun to lash the windows. The horses moved forward and soon were trotting briskly through it, sending up a fine muddy spray.

"If there is much more of this, we shall have floods," Aunt Margaret remarked. "I hope the ford may be passable. If I had thought of it before, I should have postponed our visit on that excuse."

I was glad it had not occurred to her, and followed the direction of her gaze. The chaise was descending a little hill between thick woods, contained on the left by a once-formidable wall now sagging in several places, and on the right by a straggling hedge through which could be clearly seen a hurtling stream hurrying to rendezvous with us at the bottom of the valley. When we reached the ford, the horses were reined in. Clearly, they were feeling uneasy at the prospect before them, for we could hear Sir Abraham's postilion arguing with them in soothing tones. With a slight struggle, Aunt Margaret let down the window and put out her head.

"How does it look, Thompson? If there is the least risk, pray don't go on."

"N-no, my lady," the postilion stammered. "Your la'ship ordered the chaise to—to Abbot's Grove and I'll d-drive it there. If your—your la'ship will be so good as to hold tight, I'll try a touch of the whip."

Aunt Margaret sank back into her corner as the chaise

leaped forward. There was a good deal of splashing, a suggestion of a struggle as the carriage lurched and swayed, and then we were emerging on the farther side with water streaming from the wheels. Aunt Margaret pulled up the window again, and sighed as she looked at the relentless rain.

"February Fill-Dyke," she murmured. "Do you remember that name from your country childhood? Ah, how I missed the country when I went to live in London—and how I loved coming back to stay with your mother or with my parents at my old home in Essex. Do you remember my visits, child?"

"Indeed I do, and looked forward to them for weeks. The very earliest times were best, before Mother was so ill and when Uncle Browning was alive."

"Did you like my former husband then, Tansy?"

"Oh yes, I thought he was wonderful, always bringing presents, and so kind and generous and full of jokes. He was very warm-hearted, was he not?"

"Yes," said my aunt, sighing a little. "That was what attracted me in him at first, that warm vitality of his—though it can be a little tiring, you know, living with it all the time. But then, when he died, I missed it so. I sometimes think he was more childish than he would have been if we had been blessed with children of our own." She rubbed her gloved fingers on the windowpane. "Here we are, these are the gates. It is quite a long way by road. There is a shortcut through the woods. . . . Yes, when I met your Uncle Prendergast it was the contrast that drew me to him, the comfortable sense of continuity, the knowledge that his family had lived in the same house for generations, that his life was bound up with the seasons, farming and shooting and fishing and hunting—nothing unpredictable about it—or so I thought," she added with that odd bitterness which had

128

had no part in the Aunt Margaret I remembered of those earlier times.

"There is the place," she announced a moment later. "Miserable, is it not? And just the weather for it, too."

Miserable was certainly not the word I would have chosen to describe Abbot's Grove, even on a wet day. It was extraordinarily gloomy but large and grand, with an intimidating portico of grey stone pillars which had been clapped on to the front of the original ancient building perhaps a hundred years before. The great fault in the place was that the trees had been allowed to crowd too near it, as if it were a woodcutter's hut rather than a great mansion.

A watch had been kept for us. As soon as the chaise drew to a halt the front door opened and two footmen ran out with umbrellas ready in their hands, though it was but two paces from the carriage to the steps, which were protected by that lofty roof.

A butler, dwarfed by the door he held, allowed us to enter a huge and draughty hall, in the enormous fireplace of which a small fire smouldered sulkily. I noticed some carved wooden screens, several over-varnished portraits, and a glimpse of two courtyards through narrow windows in the opposite wall. Then we were being shown into a darkly panelled drawing room—or perhaps it was a library. I was uncertain because it had some of the features of both, with a marble fireplace at one end, two sofas, a great many upright chairs, several bookcases, an extraordinary profusion of birdcages and some very white and naked-seeming statues and busts standing about haphazardly on columns of varying heights. I was also aware of a harp, and two unhappy-looking dogs with thin grey coats shivering before the fire.

"His lordship will be down directly," said the butler, with

a look of apprehension—or perhaps it was simply that his eyes were too large and bulged from their sockets so they were almost completely ringed in white.

"What a—curious room!" I whispered to Aunt Margaret as soon as he had gone.

"You don't like it?" she said, looking at me with approval.

"I—don't know. It is certainly original, but so strange. Why are there so many birdcages, and such large ones? And no birds?"

"Pretty bird," said a horrid croaking voice, frightening me almost out of my skin.

Aunt Margaret laughed in an odd way as if she might at any moment fall into hysterics. "There are birds, as you see, but they are not in the cages. Oh, don't look so alarmed, you silly child. Surely you realize that was a raven which spoke just now?"

"Good heavens. Where is it?" Then I saw it perched on the back of a chair, dark and sleek. I addressed it politely. "How do you do?"

"How do?" he responded instantly. "Good day, good day. Sit down, won't yer?"

I caught Aunt Margaret's eye. She shrugged and walked away towards the fire. Immediately, the door opened and Lord Knevett entered, seeming to fill the room with his powerful presence.

"Well, this is delightful," he cried, lightening the atmosphere by several degrees. "Do sit down. How was the ford? I feared you might not find it passable. You are quite comfortable in here, I trust? The fire does not smoke?"

He seemed nervous, though welcoming. Perhaps he did not often play the host, I thought, warming to him anew.

"Sit down, sit down," insisted the raven hospitably.

"Yes, do. Sit here, Lady Prendergast, by this table, and then you may do me the honour to pour the tea when they bring it in. And you, Miss Tremayne, over here—oh, never mind Corax. He will soon move, I dare say." The raven, as if it understood, immediately flapped its wings and alighted on Lord Knevett's shoulder. He brushed it aside with a quick repellent gesture and the raven, with an air of having taken great offense, removed itself to the laurelled head of a Roman emperor and began to preen its feathers.

When we were settled, Lord Knevett turned his dark eyes on me. "I am so very glad the weather did not prevent you from coming, Miss Tremayne. You look in good health, I am glad to see—quite recovered from your malaise."

"Oh—yes, indeed, I am." I began to feel infected by his nervousness and looked about me almost as apprehensively as the butler had done. "Are there more of them, sir—birds, that is to say?"

"There is a myna—over there by the bookcase."

I looked in vain. Rather diffidently I asked what sort of bird it was.

"It is a common starling in India, Miss Tremayne, but a great rarity in Sussex. It is also a talking bird, but I believe she is sulking today. She dislikes the rain."

"You must be very fond of birds," I began, but even as I spoke I remembered his expression when the raven had landed on him. On the other hand, he had sounded sympathetic with the myna.

"I detest them," he said thoughtfully. "I shoot all I can—but that is a secret in this house, of course."

I was still puzzling over this remark when he turned to Aunt Margaret in a decisive way. "This is a bad business I was hearing this morning," he began. "This tale of Mark and Polly Holford, I mean. Did you know anything of it? I shall ride over tomorrow and discuss it with Sir Abraham,

I think—and with Mark, of course. Is it true he says he was tricked into meeting the girl?"

My aunt inclined her head. "So he says. It seems he had a note from her asking him to meet her secretly—a matter of life and death—but when they met she claimed to know nothing of having asked him but insisted she had had a letter from him begging for an assignation."

The harp emitted a sudden plangent note. Now I could see the myna bird, which had landed on it and was clinging precariously to the strings.

Lord Knevett leaned forward. "Has Prendergast kept her letter? If it is in her writing, or in any but his own, he will be vindicated."

Aunt Margaret pressed her hands together. "He burnt it, as a postscript requested him to do."

"Ah. Unfortunate, ma'am. Most unfortunate. It is not that I disbelieve him, of course—but I wonder why he did not tell me of it at the time. In fact the only time I ever heard him speak of Polly Holford to me was on one occasion when he observed to me and another—Francis Sinclair-Stewart, I believe it was, that she had the prettiest ankle in the county. I hope Francis has not remembered that!"

"He would be a great fool if he placed any significance in such a typically masculine remark!" Aunt Margaret declared vigorously. "As for the assignation—I imagine Miss Holford was just the sort of girl who would not jib at initiating an adventure of that sort."

Lord Knevett frowned and gave a little shake of the head. He leaned back and placed his hand on the bellpull. "You will both feel the better for a cup of tea, I daresay. Then I propose to show you over the house, Miss Tremayne, since you have been good enough to express your interest in it. I won't presume to invite Lady Prendergast to accompany us,

132

for she knows it well and detests it heartily, she has told me."

I looked curiously at Aunt Margaret. It seemed strange that she should be so familiar with the house of a man she made no secret of disliking; strange also that one normally so socially correct should have told him of her feelings of antipathy towards his home. But then there was something about Abbot's Grove, I reflected, that might perhaps affect people and make them behave rather differently from their normal manner.

The door opened. I glanced towards it, expecting to see the tea tray being brought in, but it was a little old lady dressed in black who entered. She was very neatly attired with a fine lace cap and French gloves, and was obviously Lady Knevett.

I began to rise to make my curtsy, but hesitated at the look of embarrassment on Lord Knevett's face as his mother passed him, taking no more notice of any of us than if we had been a few more of the statues in which the room abounded. With an air of extreme calmness she reached out to open the door of a large ornamental birdcage in cast- and wrought-iron, and stepped inside.

"Don't be alarmed, Miss Tremayne," said Lord Knevett in a strangled tone. "My mother is not quite well. She suffers from the delusion that she is a bird."

NINE

The rain fell hissing down the chimney into the fire. The myna bird strummed a little upon the harp. My aunt gazed blankly at the raven, and Lady Knevett hoisted herself on to a narrow perch and sat whistling two notes and gently swinging her black-stockinged legs, which were very thin and indeed quite like a bird's.

I was sure that I had never been so disconcerted in my life. Had there been just the three of us it would have been no great matter. It was the presence of Lord Knevett, who looked as if he were quite willing to cast his mother upon the fire, which made the difference.

With a tremendous effort I said to him, "I do not think I can wait for tea, I am so eager to see the rest of your house."

Instantly he was at my side, gratefully assisting me to rise. "A capital idea! It will give us an appetite, for my chef makes a very good seed cake, you will find. What of you, Lady Prendergast? Will you join us after all?"

"No, I thank you," she said in a natural tone. "I shall stay and keep Lady Knevett company."

Instantly, as if the sound of her name had touched a spring, Lady Knevett spoke. "It is too bad, George," she declared in a high, rather monotonous voice. "I caught Pritchard—it is Pritchard, is it not, the head gardener?—going towards the apple orchard with a pruning knife in his hand. If he does not now understand that the trees must not be interfered with, then there is no hope of teaching him and he had better retire. There are few enough places to nest as it is, without him chopping off all the branches so one can be seen by every evil-doer—rats and squirrels and the like. You will speak to Pritchard, won't you, George? And about the nesting boxes— they must be made larger, indeed they must. I lost half my feathers climbing into one last night."

I risked a glance at Lady Knevett, while her son said in a proud tone that he would see to it. She had rather a sweet face, I thought, with her slight smile and large dark mournful eyes, and at a distance she must look like a little girl perched on a swing. I wondered if it would be possible to hold any kind of rational conversation with her; but there was no time to try it out, for Lord Knevett had his hand beneath my arm and was already hurrying me from the room.

I wondered whether I should make some sympathetic comment, or if it were better to remain silent on the subject of his mother. Lord Knevett, however, resolved my dilemma.

"You must be wondering why I did not prepare you—give you some warning," he said in a low voice. "The truth is that my mother seldom comes downstairs and I was as much surprised by her appearance today as were you."

"I was glad to meet her," I said gently. "I see now from whence you have those eyes—but in general, I suppose, you take after your father, sir?"

"In looks, I believe it is so. Not in manner, I hope," he added grimly. "Now, this is the Great Hall. This, and the

135

courtyards, are pretty much as they were in Norman times. The rest of the house is more modern, though in some parts it has been built on old foundations as may be seen by the thickness of the walls—here, for instance." He tapped against the wall of the corridor down which he was hurrying me. A powdered footman appeared, and shrank into an embrasure as if to have touched his lordship would have resulted in his execution.

"Now here," said Lord Knevett, throwing open a door into a delightful blue-hung sitting room, "is the room that was my grandmother's favourite."

"It is very pretty—the ceiling paintings are charming."

"I thought you would like it," he said, glancing at me with approval. "Now let me show you the gallery."

As we turned to walk back to the hall we encountered a woman in black with a pinched face who was, I thought, a housekeeper. She curtsied low and then hastily stepped aside as an elderly shambling figure emerged from another passage behind her—the chaplain, I realized, observing his clerical bands.

"Ah, Miss Tremayne, allow me to present Arbuthnot to you," said Lord Knevett while the housekeeper scuttled away like a nimble black beetle. "My chaplain, ma'am."

"Ah—ah yes, how do you do?" murmured Mr. Arbuthnot, feeling for his quizzing glass. "Ah, my lord, is that you? Tut, tut, my sight fails by the hour. What was that you said, your lordship? I am right in thinking you were making an introduction, am I not? A young lady, isn't it? Did I say how do you do?"

"You did, Arbuthnot," Lord Knevett reassured him genially. "And where have you been this afternoon, sir?"

"This afternoon, my lord? Dear me, is it afternoon already? Now, where have I—ah, yes, the muniment room, to be sure.

I find that with a good wax candle and a magnifying glass—these documents—some really most engrossing—the, ah, advowson—yes, that is what I have been pursuing this last month or two—the history of the advowson."

"Indeed? Well, we are on our way to the gallery. Perhaps you will join us presently in the drawing room for tea? You will find my mother there, and Lady Prendergast."

"Oh? In that case—most obliged to you, my lord. Those old parchments"—he shook his head—"monstrous dusty. Tea would be grateful, grateful indeed." Still shaking his head, he moved uncertainly away.

"Come, Miss Tremayne," said Lord Knevett with refreshing briskness. "Through here is the great stair—and on the gallery we may be private."

"I should be glad to have private conversation with you, my lord," I owned. "Your house, however, seems to be remarkably full of people."

"Ah, but when I am strolling on the gallery no one is allowed to approach me," he replied carelessly. "It is the only place where I can be sure of peace."

"I am honoured to be allowed to share it with you, then."

He paused, his hand on the carved banister. "The honour is mine, Miss Tremayne," he assured me. "It is unfortunate that today, at least, we have such matters to discuss as must remove a good deal of the pleasure from an occasion that will, I hope, often be repeated."

I murmured something and then stood dumb as we reached the head of the stair and the whole grandeur of the gallery became apparent. With such a place to call his own, Lord Knevett would hardly need another, I reflected. But did he not find those serried ranks of painted ancestors, all so curiously alike, rather oppressive? Or did they comfort him by confirming him in his pride? Then I recalled that he was used to repair to the White Lion at frequent intervals and thought it understandable enough that he should need a place to hide, to be himself, to forget for a little while that he was master of a house where the servants shrank from his presence in awe.

"Now, Miss Tremayne," he said, taking my hand and quite ignoring the noble prospect before us. "What do you think about young Jem, and his evidence against Prendergast?"

I shook my head. "I know no more than you, sir. It looks bad, you must own. Why did the captain keep silent until now?"

"Perhaps Prendergast guessed that I must tell the truth about that afternoon at the White Lion if I realized that there had been even that much between him and Polly Holford," he suggested grimly. "This puts a different complexion on the whole affair, no doubt of it. I suppose I shall have to make a clean breast of the alibi, after all; but I must warn him first of course." He dropped my hand and smote his palm with his other fist. "It is damnable! Damnable!"

I was silent a moment. "And what of Jem?" I said at last, when it seemed as if Lord Knevett would not speak again. "Why do you suppose he waited so long to tell of what he knew?"

Lord Knevett frowned. "Loyalty, in the first place, no doubt."

"And why does he confess it now? He must have realized the implications from the first."

"I rather doubt it. But I fear I may be somewhat to blame. In discussion with Sir Abraham, who, as I told you, is not disposed to let the affair be forgotten, I suggested he examine Jem particularly." He sighed. "It seems ironic now, but it was my hope that Jem would search his memory and couple Polly's name with some other lover—for that she had a lover cannot be in doubt—and now, alack, it seems that even her sister confirms that it was Prendergast." He frowned again, and then returned his attention to me as I stared at him.

"What is it that you wished to say to me? You wanted to speak privately with me, I understand?"

I looked away. I had wanted, almost passionately, to tell him of the dagger on Mark Prendergast's writing table, its slender blade, the ominous stain; but suddenly it seemed to me that the evidence was too much weighted against my cousin. Was it my place to speak? Would not the truth, whatever it might be, surely emerge in time without my playing the informer?

Lord Knevett took my arm. "Well?" he said gently. "What is it, ma'am?"

I made up my mind. "It—it was only that—" What should I say? A sudden memory inspired me. "It is merely that Captain Prendergast pointed out that you might be endangered by changing your story—"

"He did! The Devil! This sounds a little like a threat, Miss Tremayne."

"No, no—he meant it—objectively, I think. He merely observed that the alibi which had protected him had served to protect you as well. He—Captain Prendergast pointed out that it could as well have been you whom I saw cloaked and hooded at the church, you at whom I fired, your horse—a blue roan and not a grey—that I saw tethered by the hedge—" We stared at each other but I could not tell what thoughts were racing through his brain.

After a moment I went on, "Did not a waiter serve you, at the inn? Can no one vouch to your presence there while the captain was gone?"

Immediately, he avoided my eyes. Turning on his heel, he

139

strolled to the fireplace, carved in stone, and ran his finger over the petal of a petrified rose. "What—what is it?" I stammered.

He sighed. "What is it?" he repeated with a trace of bitterness. "Why, it is that there is rather more to this business of the alibi than you know—certainly rather more than I wish to make public—particularly now," he added in a softer tone, which I found as mystifying as the speech which had preceded it.

"Are you—in trouble of some sort?" I asked softly, expecting to be told to mind my own business in his curtest manner.

He looked round and smiled. "Good God, no—it is something quite different."

I found I was limp with relief.

"It is still difficult enough," he went on, with another sigh. "Perhaps, however, it will seem easier if I make my confession first to you. Are you in a tolerant humour? Will you remember that then I had not met you—incredible as it now seems that there was such a time," he murmured abstractedly.

My heart beat faster. I clasped my hands. "Pray go on."

"I am not sure I should."

"After this, you must!"

He turned his head and for one instant gave me such a haughty look that I was almost undone. Then he seemed to recollect that I was Miss Tremayne, a young lady whom he perhaps admired, and not some menial who had dared to command him.

"You are very right," he said, and I let out my breath. He waved to a carved upright chair, with a velvet seat. "You had better sit down." He began to stroll about the gallery, his hands clasped beneath the tails of his well-cut coat. "The fact of the matter is, as you will no doubt have guessed by now, that a lady is concerned in this."

140

I felt hot, cold, miserable, elated that he was confessing himself to me, impatient to hear the rest.

"I had a reason for wanting Prendergast out of the way that afternoon. That was why I sent him on the business of which I told you—why I was so eager to take up his suggestion, that I cannot now recall from which of us it came. Only if he had not made the move, I would have done so myself. I had to see —a lady, whose family is against our friendship. It was our last meeting. It is all over and done with, now. I do not want to draw this person into further trouble, but she can vouch that she was with me at the White Lion. The real difficulty is that I was so careful of her reputation that no one saw us there together."

"But—but she saw you," I said carefully, determined he should not guess how his revelation had dismayed me. "At least there is one who knows you innocent. I think you must ask her to make a statement, and trust to Sir Abraham to respect the secret of her identity."

"Yes, it sounds easy enough," he said with something of a groan, "but if it should get out—it would go hard with her. Well, I shall have to see what I can do, I suppose. But yet I can't believe Mark guilty, and unless that seems a serious possibility, what good would be served by adding to the evidence against him, as well as compromising another?"

I thought again of the stained dagger. Should I tell him of it? I said hesitantly, "If Captain Prendergast is guilty, I suppose I am in danger."

He turned quickly. "Why, how is that? Because you saw him at All Saints, you mean?"

"Yes, and his horse, which I did not mention in my statement but which might now incriminate him."

He took my hands in a tight, comforting grasp. "We must cling to the fact that Mark—Mark, of all people!—cannot possibly be guilty. The wretched girl was killed as some part of the witches' revel, I am sure of it."

I tried to pull away my hands, but he tightened his grip.

"What is it, Miss Tremayne? Don't you like me to touch you?"

I shook my head. "It is not that—"

"Dare I hope that you did not like my story of a clandestine meeting with another? But—well, it is dashed unchivalrous of me to say so, no doubt, but say it I will—the pursuit was more upon her side than mine, I vow." He released me with an air of reluctance. "Look, the sun has come out. Will you risk wet feet and take a turn with me about the garden?"

"Yes," I said rather breathlessly. "I should like it of all things." Then I wondered if my eager acceptance put me among the ranks of those who pursued him—and with his height, his handsome, somber face, his dark brooding eyes, there must be more than one who had done so in the past even if he were temporarily free of such encumbrances. "But perhaps we had better go back to my aunt," I added hastily. Something flickered in his eyes. Annoyance at my timidity? Disappointment? Amusement? Or, I thought hopefully, might it not have been admiration at my ladylike behaviour? At all events, he made no objection, did not attempt to dissuade me from the proper course but stood back immediately to allow me to precede him down the stairs.

In the drawing room, all was quiet. My aunt was sipping thoughtfully at a fragrant tea from a shallow Chinese cup. Lady Knevett had poured hers into a saucer and was nuzzling at it delicately. The chaplain sat, seemingly abstracted, sucking at the head of his cane. "Oh!" he exclaimed when he saw us, and scrambled to his feet. "A visitor!"

"You have already met Miss Tremayne, Arbuthnot. Lady Prendergast, be so good as to pour some tea for your niece.

No, not for me, I thank you." Lord Knevett strolled to the window and stood looking out at the watery sunlight, his fingers tapping impatiently upon the sill.

To break the silence, I asked Mr. Arbuthnot if he was a native of the district.

"Oh no!" he cried. "That is, not precisely. I am a native of Hampshire, ma'am. I was born in the Forest—" this had such an inappropriate sound to it that I could not forbear to smile but he was too shortsighted to remark it and continued in his breathless fashion, "but I have spent so many years at Oxford that I have come to feel that city is properly my home —and now Abbot's Grove, of course, yes, indeed." He took a noisy gulp of tea, choked, and pulled out an enormous silk handkerchief with which to wipe his mouth. I politely looked the other way, to see Lady Knevett throw back her head and swallow a few drops of tea before again burying her face in her saucer. I glanced at Aunt Margaret but she was staring into the distorted reflections of the fluted silver Queen Anne teapot as if it were a crystal ball.

Lord Knevett turned sharply. "Lady Prendergast, may I escort your niece into the garden?"

"Oh—why—is it not very wet?"

"The rain has stopped."

"I really think we had better be going before the ford rises any higher. . . ."

"The sun has come out. The ford is more likely to go down if you wait a while."

"Miss Tremayne has been indisposed—I should not like her feet to get wet."

"My mother will lend her a pair of pattens. We will walk on the paths and engage not to be long."

"Tansy, dear, do not you think—?"

But Lord Knevett had impatiently removed the cup from

my hand and replaced it on the tray. He smiled down at me. "We had better hurry, before it rains again." He put his hand beneath my arm and helped me from the room before I had even found the breath to excuse myself. Outside, we looked at each other and smiled.

"Confess that you longed for escape," he commanded.

"The tea was delicious, sir."

"Nevertheless, the company was not enlivening. Come, let us hurry before they come after us." He took my hand and we began to hasten across the hall to a side door that led on to the courtyard.

"But sir—the pattens!"

"Never mind the pattens. I can carry you if you are afraid of wet feet."

I did not want to seem spinsterish, so I shook my head though I noticed that despite the rain having stopped, the flagstones were very wet. Fortunately we were able to walk down a cloister between severe columns, setting our feet in stone paths that had been worn away over the centuries. An archway, pointed at the top, joined the two courtyards, and here I hesitated for I could see, on the farther side, steps leading down to a rain-soaked lawn. But Lord Knevett drew me on inexorably and soon I was beginning to feel rather uncomfortable as the damp began to soak through the thin leather, to say nothing of probably leaving water stains on one of my best pairs of slippers. But it would be impossible to take cold, I assured myself, while Lord Knevett held my hand in his. A rosy glow seemed to wrap me about with comfort and everything else, from murders to damp feet, was for the time being easily ignored.

We passed into the wood, along a mossy path that looked silvery until our feet imprinted green footsteps, and stopped before a little hollow where a low stone building seemed to crouch below the trees. "Here is the chapel," Lord Knevett announced. I realized he was awaiting some comment from me, and could only think of remarking that it must be inconvenient having the chapel so far from the house.

"I wonder why it was built here?" I added.

"There were other buildings here once," he explained, kicking at part of a fallen column that lay half-buried in earth and grass. I wondered why the chapel had survived while the rest had fallen, and looking at the great cracks that ran through the masonry, decided it would not be long before it too was a ruin in the grass. That, then, and not selfishness, was probably the reason he had determined to enjoy the murals while they lasted instead of preserving them for a problematical future. But perhaps he did not want to admit aloud that the chapel was in such a bad state of repair, I thought, remembering his pride, so I contented myself with agreeing that it had probably once been the logical place to build.

"But nowadays," I added, "why don't you consecrate a room in the house for the purpose?"

"Why should I? This chapel is a very notable survival of its kind and my family has worshipped here for centuries. And if you are worrying about our exposing ourselves to the elements," he added, opening the door to reveal the dark interior, "there is an underground passage to the chapel from the house."

"Good Heavens! How—romantic."

"I did not think I would expose you to that ordeal just now, however. It is kept swept but it has a dank graveyard smell and spiders seem to build there very rapidly. I think the servants don't like to go through it for some reason and are therefore not as constant in their attentions to it as they might be. Well, are you not coming in?"

145

"Why—yes, I thank you." I wondered why I was so reluctant to do so. I am rather fond of sacred buildings as a rule, and in London used quite often to seek out new churches and cemeteries to visit.

"Is it too dark for you?" asked Lord Knevett, very close behind me.

"No-no. That is, have you any means of light?"

"I believe there is a tinderbox somewhere about. Yes, here it is. Now wait a minute while I see if it is not too damp to strike a spark." It was not, and presently the comforting light of an oil lamp began to spread. Lord Knevett turned to smile at me. "Why, Miss Tremayne, you are quite pale," he exclaimed, and then as I flushed and turned my head away, he added quickly, "Pray don't be angry with me! You have remedied the fault already—if fault it was."

I smiled reluctantly and he reached out and squeezed my hand. Then, turning up the flame of the lamp, he began to lead me round the chapel.

"It is a pity it is such a dark day," he observed, holding up the light. "You cannot properly see the murals. Later on—at midsummer—one can appreciate them better." He went on, pointing out the features of the place, but I was beginning to be seriously distracted by the feel of his strong fingers about my hand, by the thought that we were out of calling distance from the house, by the possibility that he might even try to embrace me. And while I was still trying to determine whether this thrilling, if remote, possibility would be more alarming or delightful, he recalled my attention with a start by setting down the lamp and pulling me towards him.

"I don't believe you have heard a word of it," he declared, between exasperation and amusement. "Where are your thoughts wandering, Miss Tremayne? Or is it merely that

146

you are regretting your temerity in coming here with me alone and have chosen this way of punishing me for suggesting it?"

"Oh, please don't tease me," I said breathlessly, trying to pull free.

Instantly, and it must be admitted, rather to my disappointment, he released me. "Very well," he said coolly. "We have seen enough of this place, I believe. Will you go to the door while I turn out the lamp?"

Outside, dim though the light was, for the sun had gone in again, I blinked. I felt very dispirited and wondered how I could make him understand that I had not meant to rebuff or hurt him. With such a mother as his, he must have known many rebuffs in his time, I thought. It was understandable that he should be on the lookout for them. He was over-sensitive, perhaps.

I turned imploringly towards him as he emerged from the chapel. "Will you show me the maze?" I asked. And then, as he seemed to hesitate, I added quickly, "You did say there was a yew maze, did you not? I should so like to see it— should like," I amended carefully, "you to show it to me."

His eyes blazed briefly with understanding but his voice was still cool as he assured me he would be happy to do so.

"I don't think I have ever been in a maze," I admitted.

"It is a puzzle, merely. You have to find the center—and then discover your way out again. Simple enough when you know the trick of it. Here, we take this path, and now to the right under this archway. This is the beginning of it."

"This is the maze? What high hedges. Even you, my lord, cannot see over them, I think?"

"That is the object of it, Miss Tremayne."

We walked in silence for a while, turning this way and that through openings in the hedges, all of which looked exactly alike to me. There was the soft sound of dripping twigs, a bird sang a snatch of song and was silent. I began to feel rather cold, though here at least the wind was cut off.

"We are nearly at the center," said Lord Knevett. I thought his voice sounded rather odd, but when I turned to look at him he was staring straight ahead. Then our eyes met, he gave me a warm smile and stood back by the last opening.

In the center of the maze was a little seat, too wet to take advantage of, and facing it a piece of sculpture of two lovers entwined in a classical pose, from which I hastened to avert my eyes. The next moment I realized that Lord Knevett had disappeared.

"Where are you?" I cried in a panic fright.

There was no answer. It seemed that I was all alone in this alien world—alone, with wet feet, in an impenetrable maze to which I had not the key and, to make matters worse, with an evening mist beginning to come up.

"Please, sir," I called, "come back!"

There was no response, and I summoned pride to my aid. This, no doubt, was his punishment for my having failed to appreciate his chapel—for having asked him not to tease me. Hateful man! How could I have been so stupid as to suppose a handsome face must hide a handsome nature? I began to hurry through the paths, turning now left, now right, ever and again pausing to listen for the rustle of a footstep, the crackle of a twig. I could hear nothing, and seemed to be arriving nowhere.

In a deeper panic now I turned and tried to retrace my steps, thinking that if only I had stayed in the center of the maze, Lord Knevett would have known where to find me when the time came for him to relent at last, as I supposed he intended to do. I was very near to tears by this time, and found it hard not to imagine myself wandering between these horrid hedges until I died of terror and exposure. All too easily could I visualize future visitors being told the story in hushed tones, Lord Knevett's part in the affair being omitted, of course: "And here is the very spot where her skeleton was found, long months after she disappeared. No one had thought to look for her in the maze, of course; no one had supposed she would choose to wander there on such an inclement day as that ill-fated one—"

"Boo!" said Lord Knevett, appearing suddenly before me. I gave a little shriek and collapsed into his arms.

"Why," he exclaimed on a note of surprise, "I did not really frighten you, did I?"

"No, oh no!" I muttered, burrowing closer into his embrace.

"I believe you were afraid," he murmured, and I knew that in another moment he would kiss me. I closed my eyes in anticipation, all his villainy forgotten.

"Miss Tremayne!" called a voice in exasperated commanding tones. "Where are you? Answer me at once!"

It was, I realized as I leapt guiltily away, inevitably the odious Captain Prendergast.

TEN

I emerged from the maze breathless and dishevelled, with no very clear idea of how we had reached the entrance; and was disconcerted anew to find the captain standing slapping his gloves across his palm with every appearance of impatience and disapproval.

"What—what is it, sir?" I stammered defensively. "Is there something amiss at Pheasant's?"

He shrugged. "A letter from my sister Beauregard has been delayed. It seems she arrives to stay with us tonight and my father is anxious that proper preparations should be made to welcome her."

I was repelled by the apparent indifference with which he regarded a visit from his sister; but Lord Knevett was more sympathetic to him.

"Lord yes," he said easily, taking the captain's arm. "Lady Prendergast will never hear the end of it if all is not just to Madame's taste. I only hope I do not run into Kitty during the next few days, for you won't have forgotten that she and I were always at daggers drawn?"

"No indeed. Come, Miss Tremayne, your aunt is awaiting us. No, there are few enough with whom Kitty has remained on terms, I fear. Miss Crofton, perhaps; Caroline Horton—"

"I should have supposed you would have discouraged that connection," remarked Lord Knevett lazily.

The flash in the captain's eyes was like a drawn blade. "What do you mean?" he demanded swiftly.

Lord Knevett shrugged. "Nothing in the world, my dear fellow. Ah, there is Lady Prendergast, I see, ready to leave at a moment's notice." He turned to me. "I hope I shall be able to persuade you to come again to Abbot's Grove in the not too distant future, Miss Tremayne—when this visit of Madame Beauregard's is concluded."

I felt thoroughly upset for one reason and another, in no mood for the innuendos with which both the captain and Lord Knevett seemed pleased to spice their speech. I was glad to murmur my thanks for his Lordship's hospitality and fly to my aunt's side. She took my hand in a grasp which felt warm and protective but which also seemed to convey a slight reproach.

"You were a great deal too long!" she scolded.

"Well—I am here now, Aunt. This is—exciting news," I added placatingly.

Her eyes searched my face. Then, as if satisfied by what she read there, she nodded. "Yes, indeed. Only, I am afraid we shall have to move you from your room—it is properly Kitty's, you know, and she is jealous about such things. Come, there is no time to waste."

"You will not be calling at Abbotsgate, then, ma'am?"

She looked startled and concerned. "Oh, great Heavens, if I had not quite forgot! I sent word I was coming—I do not like to disappoint—what shall I do?"

"Perhaps I could visit in your stead," I suggested diffidently. "I could not do what you would have done, of course —but would just explain, so that no slight would be felt."

Her face cleared. She squeezed my hand. "That is the very thing! What a dear child you are. Mark shall escort you. The chaise can take me to Pheasant's and then carry you on to Abbotsgate, with Mark riding beside you—it is only to visit the Clements and the Latchingtons, Mark, if you will. Pray excuse us, Lord Knevett."

We were soon in the chaise, with Captain Prendergast trotting ahead on his intractable grey. The rain began to set in again and I caught a glimpse of him turning up his collar against the elements with the practiced ease of an old campaigner. He looked very well on a horse and I could imagine that in uniform he would make a dashing figure indeed—quite a catch for Polly Holford, I reflected, thinking that it was certainly not beyond the bounds of possibility that she had laid a trap to compromise him, as Aunt Margaret had suggested.

A sudden commotion returned me brusquely to the present.

Aunt Margaret uttered an alarmed cry and I pressed my face to the window. The horses were plunging in the currents of the swollen ford, the water was already hub-high about the wheels, but on my side at least the foreground was filled with a more alarming sight, the grey horse rearing high, pawing the air while the clear bubbling stream swirled about his hocks.

Then Captain Prendergast brought down his hunting-crop in what seemed to me a vicious gesture, just behind his horse's ears, and as the grey dropped on to all four feet again, my cousin leaned forward and took the reins of the leading carriage horse and began to urge him forward across the water. For one perilous moment the body of the chaise

152

actually floated; then, just as water began to seep in through the crack at the bottom of the door, the wheels grounded, and with a plunge and a rush we were out of it and Captain Prendergast fully occupied with his own horse again who was now bucking as if he had a hornet beneath the saddle.

Aunt Margaret and I sat back with sighs of relief. "Thank God Mark was with us," she cried. "We might so easily have overturned. I have never known the current so strong. It was Mark who led us out of it, was it not?"

"The captain did all that was required," I said ungraciously. "I imagine he is used to such things in Spain."

Aunt Margaret gave me a reproving look, and I flushed. She loved her stepson, I reminded myself, and while I did not want to deceive her with regard to my own feelings for him, there was no need to hurt her unnecessarily with too obvious a parade of my dislike. I turned the conversation to the house we had just visited, in an attempt to distract her from my tactlessness, and then we went on to discuss the forthcoming visit of her stepdaughter, until Aunt Margaret was set down at Pheasant's.

It was a tedious wet journey to Abbotsgate, alone in the chaise, and I was glad when the village was reached and the carriage halted under the shelter of a spreading oak. I peered through the rain-splashed window and saw that Captain Prendergast had dismounted and was tying his horse to the back of the chaise. That done, he loosened the girth, ran the stirrups up the leathers, and came round to open the door for me.

"The Latchingtons' cottage is just across the road," he explained, gesturing towards a low stone dwelling with a sagging roof, rising out of a litter of pigsties, hen-coops, and rotting sheds. "I'll come in with you, for Latchington is an unpleasant fellow when he's had a drink or two."

I could not hide my surprise at the uncharacteristic nobility of this offer, and was almost relieved when the captain added more brusquely, "Come, don't let us linger here all day. If you run you should not get too wet, or are you afraid of spoiling your clothes?"

I ignored the hand he offered and jumped down, straight into a puddle. Catching up my dripping skirts, I swept furiously across the road.

"Don't hold your head so high, or you will strike it on the lintel," the captain advised me, tapping on the door. I gave him a withering glance and on being invited to enter by half a dozen voices, moved forward proudly, only to stumble down an unexpected step. I would have fallen if the captain had not caught me by the arm. "Easy does it, Miss Tremayne. These cottages have sunk through the centuries—that is why the lintels are so low."

I caught my breath sharply, stepped carefully down, and was relieved of the necessity of taking any further notice of him by the children who immediately surrounded us—a charming tribe though they were dressed in little better than rags, had eyes too large for their heads, and for the most part, were plagued with running noses or hacking coughs. It did not take me long to discover that fortunately their father was out.

"He's at the inn, very likely," Mrs. Latchington told me, adding with a sigh, "Not that we ever know for certain where he is, save when he's singing in the choir—Sundays, of course, and practice nights. Sings like an angel, does Latchington—but for the rest"—she shrugged her thin shoulders—"he's one who drinks deep and keeps his own counsel—except when his temper is roused. No, he's not the sort you can dare question, if you take my meaning, miss."

154

I murmured an expression of sympathy but felt it wiser not to say too much. From the look of Mrs. Latchington, she would not be troubled by her husband's vagaries much longer, for I feared she was dying, as my mother had, of tuberculosis, very bravely. I decided also that the children, shunned no doubt because of their father's temper as much from fear of contracting the disease that was probably rife among them, were in need of friendship quite as much as food, and determined to visit them again.

When we left, I told Captain Prendergast what I had discovered. He looked angry. "Good God! Why did you not leave at once? This must be looked into. Some of them may have the consumption too, you think?"

"Yes, but—don't fear I shall bring it into your family. I nursed my mother and did not contract it; besides, I am strong and healthy and well-fed—more likely victims are not far to seek."

He gave me a strange look, as if I puzzled him. A moment later we had arrived at Mrs. Clement's cottage. He knocked, opened the door, and almost pushed me over the threshold. This time I was prepared for the step and stood well clear of the captain as he announced me, trying to accustom my eyes to the near-darkness. I could see a bed which took up a good part of the tiny room, and could dimly make out a figure in it, that of an aged crone with knitting in her lap and a crumpled cap crooked on her head.

"That's very good of you, Captain Prendergast, sir, to visit an old woman—and to bring the young lady, too—" she cackled, her bright eyes oddly at variance with her humble tone, even in that murky light.

"Well, Goody, how are you?" he asked. "I stay but a moment to introduce my cousin to you: Miss Tremayne, who is visiting you in her ladyship's place." To me he added, "I will soon return; but I must make sure the horses are not catching cold."

He was gone and at once I missed him. In the silence that followed the captain's departure I became aware of the steady ticking of a grandfather clock.

"Clement made that," said his widow. "Powerful clever with his hands, was Clement. Constable comes in once a week and winds that for me and puts it right, for that gains a few minutes here and there, but that ain't never stopped yet."

I admired the clock, and then turned with a prick of conscience to my task. "Have you oil for your lamp and fuel for your fire, ma'am? Lady Prendergast desired me to discover what you needed."

"Pray don't 'ma'am' me, young mistress. Goody is what they call me here, and I like what I'm accustomed to. Eh, well—Barney keeps us in oil and fuel, after a fashion. 'Tis company I miss more than anything, since Clement died. That Maggie Smith comes in to see me sometimes . . . but Barney keeps most of 'em away. Talk of the Devil!" she added with an odd cackle of laughter. "Here is my Barney now."

I looked round. Filling an inner doorway was a large young man with head held askew, light eyes squinting uneasily in his vacant face. In one enormous hand he held a cat by the tail, apparently oblivious to the scratches it was inflicting upon him as it struggled to be free.

"Now you leave that cat go, Barney," said his mother firmly. "That ain't yourn. That belongs to Constable, and he'll be after you for stealing if he catches you—hang you by the neck, he will, for that."

Barney giggled and opened his hand. The cat, a large

156

ginger tom, flattened itself against the worn stone floor and streaked away into the farther room.

"Out, now, Barney," Mrs. Clement went on. "Don't you see as I've a visitor, then? Go and fetch me a pail of water from the pump, there's a good boy."

He grinned and turned obediently away.

"Yes, that's my Barney," sighed Mrs. Clement. "He was a dear little boy, you wouldn't believe. Sit for hours, he would, as good as gold. But now—well, miss, the best I can do is warn you to keep out of his way, for there's no telling what he'll do now when one of his moods takes him."

I suppressed a shiver and stood up. I found myself looking through the door Barney had left open, into a kitchen full of unwashed dishes, with a bowl of blood on the floor beside a half-dismembered rabbit, and what looked like a tidemark of potato peelings, soot and cinders and rat droppings.

From the front door, Captain Prendergast spoke my thoughts. "I believe you could do with some help about the house, Goody. I'll ask Lady Prendergast to send someone down to you."

He hurried me out into the street, leaving the old woman chuckling and stabbing at her knitting. "What is wrong with you, Cousin?" he demanded. "Why do you look so shocked? Have you never seen a dirty untidy room before? To my mind it is a wonder it is not worse, when you consider how far it is to the pump."

"It is not that," I gasped as he half-flung me up the steps of the chaise.

"What is it, then?"

I glanced nervously towards the postilion, hunched and unhappy on the near-side horse, and shook my head.

Captain Prendergast gave an impatient exclamation. He looked at his horse's rein, buckled about the spring, spoke to the postilion, and followed me into the carriage. "Now we are private," he said, as the chaise lurched forward. "What frightened you in there? Was it Barney?"

"I—yes, it was." I fancied I saw scorn in his look, and hurried on. "I have seen him before—I knew him at once. The way his head lolls, his hunched shoulder. He was there that dreadful night. Barney Clement is one of the witches of All Saints."

It seemed a long time before the captain spoke. When he did so it was to say slowly, "So you know that much. You grow more dangerous by the minute, Cousin Tansy—and I begin to doubt the likelihood of your reaching an advanced old age."

I caught my breath. "You knew it also, sir, by your lack of surprise; so I must assume that you were at All Saints that night and saw at least as much as I." I should not have been so bold if I had not been aware of the dagger in my reticule and the postilion within call, but even so I repented of my rashness the instant the captain turned his cold eyes on me.

"You had better keep a still tongue in your head—for your own sake," was all he said; but it was enough to chill my blood and send me shrinking into my corner long after he had sat back, folded his arms, and addressed his somber gaze to the rain-drenched landscape.

I felt immeasurably relieved when the chaise drew up before the house. Lights blazed from every window, a footman was carrying in a pair of bandboxes, there was a glimpse of bustle in the hall, and a hired chaise was turning in the drive before us. Plainly Madame Beauregard had just arrived.

I hurried up to my room, hoping to give vent in private

to some of the mingled emotions that threatened otherwise to consume me. But I found my room full of an alien presence, scented with lavender-water, littered with a mantle, a muff, a shapeless bonnet, a bulging reticule lying upon the bed and a bandbox on the floor. Too late I recalled that this chamber was not mine after all, but had reverted to its original owner.

"Well—so you are my Cousin Tansy!" cried a rather shrill voice in a satirical tone. Madame Beauregard, still very similar to her portrait, stood in the doorway, surveying me with a mingled air of surprise and distaste which made me feel wretched indeed. She was not very like her brother, but there was a good deal that I recognized in her expression at that moment. "May I ask," she continued haughtily, "what you are doing in my room?" Eyebrows raised to ludicrous height, her glance went past me to her reticule lying carelessly on the bed. The implication was plain that she thought I might have been prying and I blushed as if I were guilty indeed.

"Good afternoon, Cousin," I said with an air, I hoped, of dignity. "I must beg your pardon—but this is the room in which I have been sleeping since I came to Pheasant's and I don't yet know what other has been allocated to me."

"Well, one has, I hope—for I don't intend to share my bed with you," she cried, ringing the bell with a savage jerk at the rope.

I looked at her in amazement. "Did you have a pleasant journey, ma'am?" I enquired, wondering if perhaps there was some reason for her being particularly out of temper.

"Pleasant!" she retorted, dragging off her gloves and hurrying to the china cabinet, "I should just say so! A damp carriage, lame horses, an idiot postilion and a rainy day is just what I like when travelling, I do assure you—and my condition made it all the more enjoyable, since you are so kind as to ask."

Her condition was not yet apparent, but I remembered that it might be the more uncomfortable for that, and strove to control my indignation at her unreasonable attitude.

"I am sorry it was so disagreeable," I said as calmly as I could, and began to open one of the drawers in the chest. "If you will excuse me while I remove my things, I can soon leave you in peace." But the drawer was empty and a quick glance showed me that nothing of mine had been left in the room. With a hotter twinge of guilt I realized that it had probably been Aunt Margaret's vain intention to conceal the fact that I had ever occupied it. I went towards the door.

"Stop," said Madame Beauregard, swinging on her heel to face me accusingly. "My Dresden shepherdess—where is it?"

"Why—I fear I do not know."

"Very likely! Have you taken it?"

"Is that what you are looking for, madame—there on the mantelshelf?"

"Where? Oh. Yes, it is, but I think it rather officious of you to rearrange my things. I made this collection, you know, and so soon as we have our own house I mean to remove them. Ah, Susan," she added as the maid hurried in, "you took your time in answering. Pray don't be so slow again. Ask Mrs. Slight where Miss Tremayne is to sleep, and lose no time about it. Then bring me hot water and inform my lady that I propose to lie down for a while. Well, don't stand there, girl."

I felt as if I had been buffeted by a storm and scarcely took

160

account of which passage it was that the maid presently led me down. Only when we passed an open door disclosing a room full of such masculine litter as foxes' masks, fishing rods, a purple brocade dressing gown thrown across the bed, and walls hung with maps, did I become alive to my surroundings.

"Whose room is that, Susan?" I asked, as she opened the door of the room beyond.

"That is Master Mark's—the captain's, I should say," she replied, with a smirk and a sideways look.

I was amazed. "Are you sure Lady Prendergast intended this room for me?"

"Mrs. Slight said the Green Room, and this is it. Truth to tell, there ain't no other for the bed in Miss Elizabeth's had the worm in it and hasn't been replaced."

There was nothing to be done but to put as good a face on it as possible. I looked about the room, hung in dark green, at the great shadowed bed behind its looped curtains, the latticed windows and the large stone fireplace. "This must be the older part of the house," I reminded myself aloud.

Susan looked blank. "I couldn't say, miss, I'm sure. You had better ask Mrs. Slight, miss." When she had hurried off to fetch up some water, I looked into the cupboards and drawers and found that Madame Kitty was quite correct, all my effects had been put away in here, presumably with Aunt Margaret's sanction.

A brief inspection of the door showed me that it was innocent of any bolt and though there was a lock, the key could only be used from the outside. A moment's reflection served to persuade me, however, that even Captain Prendergast would hardly murder me beneath his father's roof—and if he attempted anything of the sort there was a bell and a pair of fire irons, to say nothing of my Indian dagger with which to repulse him.

The evening passed off better than I had hoped, for Kitty stayed in her room and Captain Prendergast was engaged with friends elsewhere. Sir Abraham, apparently delighted to have his unpleasant daughter restored to him for a while, drank a great deal and contriving to forget the shadow that hung over Pheasant's and his son, became very jovial and full of lengthy anecdotes of Bench and hunting-field. Aunt Margaret, who had perhaps already felt the lash of Kitty's tongue and was not so cheerful, toyed with her food and contributed little to the conversation.

I retired early, but could not sleep. I had a good deal to think about, from Lord Knevett and his extraordinary but interesting home, to the captain and his grim warning; thence to the glimpse I had had of Barney Clement and my certainty that I had seen him dancing hooded in the ruined church, to end again with Mark Prendergast and his prediction that I should not reach an advanced old age.

I shivered, turned up my lamp, found an extra blanket in a cupboard, made up the fire, and stayed a moment looking from the window at the flooded meadows, white in the moonlight. It was very cold now the rain had stopped. The sky was clear, the stars sparkled remotely, the air was still. We were in for a sharp frost, I observed, and drew the curtains firmly with a rattle of the rings along the pole, before returning to my bed.

A good deal later, I heard Captain Prendergast return. He was certainly drunk, I thought, as I listened to the clatter of first one boot and then the other, followed by some unintelligible command, and then the crash of broken glass.

At last, silence settled on the house, and I slept.

162

ELEVEN

The bright frosty morning light mercilessly illuminated the faces at the breakfast table. Kitty looked sallow and drawn, shuddering at everything she was offered and consenting only to a nibble of dry toast and a cup of tea. Her father had the same liverish look, for other reasons, though he was making some effort for his daughter's sake to be cheerful. Aunt Margaret was quiet and I feared she had another headache coming on by the way in which she pressed her forehead and shaded her eyes with her hand every time the sun broke through the thin high cloud. Captain Prendergast however seemed quite unaffected by his excesses of the previous night.

"Well, my dear Kitty," said the squire as soon as the servants had been dismissed, "we must see that you are not dull now you have been so good as to pay us a visit. I believe if this frost keeps up we shall have skating soon, on the flooded meadows—but of course I suppose skating is not just the thing for you at this time—"

"Brisk walks are all I shall require, I thank you, Father. As for excitement, on the one hand I did not expect to find it in a house of mourning, and on the other I should have supposed you would have had enough of that to last you for a lifetime, if half what I hear is true."

"It probably is not," the captain suggested dryly.

His sister gave him a sharp glance. "I daresay you hope it is not, Mark. The story is all over the county, you know, and not likely to be merely a nine days' wonder; and I heard some gossip which looks black for you when we stopped for the last change at the Nine Bells."

"Listening to gossip, Kitty?" he said carelessly, but I thought he looked somewhat wary. "Well, we cannot stop idle talk, I suppose, but I'm dashed if we have to listen to it." He poured himself some coffee and offered the pot to Sir Abraham, who shook his head and leaned towards his daughter.

"What was this gossip, Kitty?"

Madame Beauregard tossed her head. "It was something I heard from a groom, Father. A groom from the White Lion —yes, I thought that would interest you," she added complacently. "It seems the fellow was working in the stables that Saturday—the day that slut was killed."

"Kitty, pray—" expostulated Aunt Margaret, as a matter of form.

"Well, if you don't know what manner of chit Polly was, Stepmama, you must be unique."

"Cut the cackle, Kitty," begged her father. "What did this fellow have to say?"

"Do you want me to begin at the beginning, sir?" she said mischievously. "Why then I saw a huddle of men in the yard at the Nine Bells while our fresh horses were being brought out—and one of the men began pointing at me,

164

and there were whispers and mutterings. I didn't like the look of it and asked my postilion what was amiss. He knew, well enough, but wouldn't tell me. However, I made him do so in the end, and it seems this groom, a rough, red-headed fellow, was working at the White Lion as I told you—yes, Father, I am coming to it now—and he swears Mark's grey stallion was stabled there for half an hour, on Saturday, and then was saddled up by a stable lad, whom it seems the gallant captain subsequently bribed to keep his mouth shut—"

"Mark!" exclaimed Aunt Margaret in horror. "Did you leave the inn? Did you bribe the boy?"

"I bribed the lad—but not for the reason you think," the captain owned. He caught my eye and shrugged, as if to say that he had expected the truth to emerge and there was no further point in concealing anything.

It was now the squire's turn to hide his eyes behind his hand. When he looked up again his forehead was red with the pressure he had been exerting. "Did this groom—I believe I know him, his name is Brent—did he know for how long the horse was gone?" he demanded unevenly of his daughter.

"A little more sugar, if you please, Stepmama. I thank you. Yes, he thinks—but he is a dolt and I believe might falter under cross-examination—that it was for precisely the fatal period—the time, that is, of the witches' revel and the murder. It only gradually occurred to the groom that this evidence might be of importance and when the stable lad refused to support him he came to discuss the matter with his friends at the next posting-house. Then one of them recognized me for your sister, Mark—and I may say I do not thank you for making me an object of notoriety—"

"That will do, Kitty," said her father, in a firm voice. He raised his head and stared at his son. "I may have to resign from the Bench, Mark; but before I do and before I pass on the case to my fellow Justices, I propose to have some sort of an informal enquiry here at Pheasant's. I take it I can count on your cooperation in this—your utmost cooperation?"

"I hope you may," replied the captain rather abstractedly.

Aunt Margaret said suddenly, "Then—then Knevett was lying! He swore you were with him all the afternoon—I told you that man was not to be trusted, Abraham!"

The squire groaned. "If he lied, I know not what to think. Lord, what a coil it is!"

Kitty said coldly, "Well, I hope one of you will have the goodness to enlighten me a trifle. I am quite as ready to detest Lord Knevett as you, dear Stepmama—rather more so, indeed, for did you not formerly defend him? But what are you suggesting he has done now? And what have you done, Mark? Can anyone seriously believe that it was you who sent Polly Holford to her Maker?"

"Oh no—" It was Aunt Margaret who spoke, in little more than a whisper. "Mark was not at the church—were you, Mark? Wherever you went when you left the White Lion, it was not there?"

The captain looked round the table, until his glance came to rest on me. "Damnation, yes," he owned at last. "There seems no further point in prevarication. I did go to All Saints that Saturday."

There was a sort of combined sigh. Kitty was the first to speak. "Lord, Mark," she cried on a high giggle, "never say you are a witch!"

"Were you there?" hoarsely demanded his father; and then, "Did anyone see you—to recognize you?"

"Mark," whispered Aunt Margaret, as pale as dough.

166

"So you were there—but where was Knevett during your absence?"

"Knevett had some sort of an assignation. I left him to enjoy it and went at his suggestion to spy on a meeting of the witches at All Saints. He gave me a hood and a loose domino to wear over my clothes, to protect my identity. The intention was that I should try to discover who these witches are—for Knevett is mad to put a stop to their frolics but hates them too much to be able to bring himself to spy on them—"

"He is too cowardly to do so, you mean," declared Kitty viciously.

"Knevett is no coward!"

"Very well for you to say so, Mark, but you were not there the day I was chased by his bull. Did he help, or try to rescue me? No, indeed—"

"Why should he, when you had been the trial of his life since you could walk? Besides, he must have seen that you had time to get through the fence before the bull could harm you, since that is what happened, in fact."

"Cease this foolish squabbling! Continue with your tale, my son."

"Why, there was this damnable fog. I reached the church meadow and tethered Thunder to the fence—it was turnip-headed of me to have taken a horse that everybody knows instead of going by the footpath, but I am only a simple soldier, after all, and not trained in the ways of spying—and arrived in the churchyard just as some madman began to toll the bell. Indeed, it probably was a madman," he continued reflectively, tilting back his chair on two legs and gazing at the ceiling, "for it is my belief that Barney Clement was among those present—"

"You saw others, then?"

"I had a glimpse of dancing. The only person there unmasked was Polly. . . . "

"Good God!" The squire's eyes were bulging, and beads of sweat stood on his forehead. "You were there—you saw it all—and never spoke till now!"

"It is an exaggeration to say I saw it all," Mark corrected him sternly.

"If it hadn't been for me none of this would have come out now," Kitty observed smugly.

"Good God, girl, don't you understand what danger your brother is in?"

"What, you do not really suspect him? Oh, this is too much —Mark, Mark of all people, stabbing that silly girl!"

"Kitty, be quiet!" thundered her father. The door opened and Barclay entered rather timidly. "Out!" cried Sir Abraham. The butler hurriedly withdrew and the door closed again. "If I hear one more word from you, Kitty, you must leave us. What did you see, then, Mark?"

"Precious little, for the fog was thick down there in the valley bottom. There was the cracked bell tolling, someone playing a flute—"

"A flute!" cried Kitty irrepressibly. "Papa, that could only be Dick Carver."

"It sounds like it—but the constable's brother! Well, go on."

"Everyone there was dressed in black, as I was myself, hooded and cloaked or in dominoes—but for Polly. She looked—strange, I thought. Half-mad—or as though she had been drugged with some vile potion."

"Ay, it could be so—they brew their herbs—God knows what discoveries they make. Perhaps it helped her at the end, poor child."

"I was afraid of being seen," the captain went on. "I was dressed like them but wanted no part of their damnable ritual—and even their disguise is probably more to protect them from outsiders than from each other. It is only just at first that it confuses recognition in most cases, I think. After one glimpse I stepped back and began to make a *reconnaissance,* as the French soldiers say—a search of the churchyard to see if they had put sentries out—I should have done it earlier but in the fog I was upon the church before I knew it. It was twilight by that time, as well. Suddenly I blundered into a figure. It was too late to avoid it and I essayed a bluff. I cried out some challenge—and was fired upon!"

I gasped. Somehow I had thought he would not have betrayed me, but of course I should have known my enemy better than that. Aunt Margaret screamed; even Kitty gave a little cry.

"Fired upon?" said the squire, his brow creased as he gazed steadily at Mark. "There was no previous mention of firearms in this affair."

I stood up. The captain let down his chair until it stood steadily on four legs again, and regarded me without expression. "Yes, there was," I said, in a voice which trembled slightly. "The postilion, Hodgkin, lent me his pistol and I told you I had fired it to guide him to me, if you remember. I was lying. I fired it at—your son."

There was an awed hush. The squire's face darkened. "By God," he said at last, with increasing wrath. "There has been a conspiracy between you, eh? I don't like the sound of this. You—fired at him—and later pretended you had met for the first time in the prison?"

"In prison?" cried Kitty ecstatically. "Did you say—Miss Tremayne in prison?"

169

Aunt Margaret looked at her. "Your father," she said bitterly, "committed my niece to prison that night on a charge of—vagrancy, I believe it was."

"I did what seemed best at the time. Well, sit down, girl, we are not finished with you yet. You fired at him—but you did not hit him, eh?"

"No—I did not intend to fire at all, but he startled me so."

"And you decided to say nothing of it—why?"

I looked down at my hands. "In the first instance, I lied from cowardice," I owned in a low voice. "It was bad enough being found in the church with the body—and the talk of my dagger—"

"Your dagger?" squeaked Madame Beauregard.

"Be quiet, Kitty. Go on, miss."

"And then—" I glanced helplessly at Captain Prendergast. "There seemed no object in mentioning it afterwards," I said feebly.

"Miss Tansy means that I threatened and bullied her into keeping her mouth shut," Mark supplied carelessly. "It was I who brought home to her that it would not help her to admit that she had already attempted to kill one person that night—for whatever she may say, that bullet passed devilish close—I felt the wind of its passing, hooded as I was. In return for my silence, I bought hers."

"But why?" demanded Aunt Margaret, looking from one of us to the other. "You were not thinking of her safety—were you?"

"Good God, no—I thought she was quite probably guilty of witchcraft, murder, anything you please. I was thinking of myself. That coven of witches had reasons for not wanting to be spied on even before Polly was killed. After it, I did not suppose they would stop short of silencing anyone who might be able to give evidence against them—and they were

170

not to know how much or how little I had seen of them. As it was, I was able to get away before the shot brought them all out of the church and hoped they would merely assume the girl to have been firing at random."

"You—abandoned me—to them!" I cried. "They might have killed me!"

"I did not know then about Polly," he pointed out. "Besides, you seemed to me very well able to take care of yourself and, for all I knew, you might have been a witch."

"You were thinking of Knevett," said Sir Abraham heavily. "You had to get back to the White Lion and tell him what you knew. Then, after he had lied to protect you, you did not feel able to expose him by telling the truth. You were wrong, Mark, but one must honour you for it."

"Thank you, sir—but Cousin Tansy does not honour me for it, I think?"

"I am still digesting the knowledge of your—your perfidy in leaving me in the churchyard," I said indignantly. "As long as I thought you were one of them, your behaviour did not seem so strange—indeed, I think I assumed I had left you stunned when I ran away—"

"Ah," he said softly, "so it was you, Miss Tansy, who abandoned me."

"Well, yes, perhaps it was," I stammered, confused by his look. "If I had wounded you, I agree that my behaviour would have looked very bad—"

"Not only looked so, little witch—but was."

"You call her a witch," cried Kitty, her eyes shining with excitement. "You thought she might have had a hand in the murder—how does it come about that this—this person is sitting here with us, enjoying Prendergast hospitality—"

"Kitty!"

"Hush, Abraham," said Aunt Margaret with dignity, "I

will deal with this. Tansy is my niece, Kitty, my dearly loved sister's child. The dagger that dispatched Polly was discovered not to have been hers. Her presence in the church was satisfactorily accounted for. Tansy has now no stain on her character, if she ever did. I should like you to apologize to her."

"I should be happy to do so if her presence in the churchyard could be satisfactorily accounted for to me," declared Madame Beauregard, unabashed.

"My niece does not have to account to you." Aunt Margaret turned to her husband. "What is much more important is that we have now discovered Lord Knevett to have no alibi for the fatal hours—and furthermore that he is now proven to be a liar."

"Margaret, my dear, I am sure that Knevett—"

But the squire's deprecating tone was overridden by a deeper one just as I half-turned with a sense of premonition. "Do I hear my name?" asked Lord Knevett pleasantly, from his position by the open door.

"Very apposite," murmured Captain Prendergast, with no sign of embarrassment, while my heart gave a great thump and I flushed scarlet on Aunt Margaret's behalf. "I am glad you are here, Knevett," the captain went on. "I have been obliged to own to our deceit, I am afraid, and had no time to warn you of it."

Lord Knevett bowed. "I had inferred as much." He looked about the room, at the squire, belatedly rising, at Kitty, staring at him in distaste, at Aunt Margaret who went first red then white but maintained her unusual air of determination. "I must apologize for entering unannounced," he went on, "but your butler refused to perform that office for me and as I had news of what seemed to me to be the most urgent nature I was obliged to force my own way in. But it seems now," he added frowning, "that my news may have preceded me?"

The squire found his voice. "You have saved me the trouble of sending for you, sir," he said stiffly. "The fact of the matter is that my son has just confessed to having lied to me about your alibi."

"It was the groom at the White Lion who gave me away," Captain Prendergast coolly explained. "He saw my horse saddled and only now has come to think it his business to inform the world—"

"And not only the world," supplied Lord Knevett, "but the authorities too, I fear. Brent came to me, feeling in the circumstances that it might be a little delicate bearing tales to Sir Abraham, but it appears now that he need not have been so tactful. I suppose you will not believe me, Sir Abraham, when I say that I am come expressly to make the true details of that afternoon known to you?"

The squire shook his head in bewilderment. "You are a member of the Bench," he said in a protesting voice.

My aunt said cuttingly, "You should know that is not necessarily enough to make him a man of his word, Abraham."

"Well, this is vastly interesting," Kitty declared, tossing her head. "If Mark was at All Saints, what were you doing at the White Lion, may one ask, Lord Knevett? Drinking alone?"

He gave her a quelling look, and drew a paper from his pocket. "I have here a statement from a person who can vouch that I was with her there," he informed the squire. "I have put a wafer over her signature; I would rather not remove it, but if you cannot place any dependence in an anonymous statement, I have the lady's permission to reveal her name, reluctant as I would be to do so."

The squire raised his eyebrows. He glanced down the paper

swiftly and his colour rose. "By God, I believe I recognize the hand," he exclaimed.

"Then there is no need for you to see who wrote it," Lord Knevett swiftly interposed. "You understand now, no doubt, the reason for secrecy—"

"Indeed I do—but an assignation, eh? I can scarce believe it even yet." He frowned at the paper again. "If she had not written to me just the other day upon some parish matter—"

"Hush, sir, I beg you. It is she who will suffer if her indiscretion becomes known."

"Ay, very true. But—it is very strange—why did you meet at the White Lion?"

"She dared not come to my house—I certainly could not go to hers. The—opposition to our meeting, sir, would have been terrible indeed had we aroused it. I can assure you a hint of it some weeks before was enough for us."

"Well, bless me," said the squire, savouring the scandal for a moment, "I had no notion anything of the sort was going on—should not have thought the lady to your taste. She is a trifle old for you, what?"

Lord Knevett was not disconcerted. He said smoothly, "I used to prefer older women." His dark eyes slid sideways until they met mine. "They say it is a dangerous sign when a man changes in that."

I felt myself grow hot, then cold. Meeting Mark Prendergast's satirical glance did not help me to regain my composure.

The squire handed back the letter. All at once he seemed to recall the gravity of the occasion. He said heavily, "So you were indeed at All Saints that afternoon, my son."

"If Knevett says so, then I must have been," admitted the captain carelessly, as if he had not already owned as much but was just now being unfairly accused of it. I gasped, and Lord Knevett narrowed his eyes suddenly.

I rushed into speech. "You were there, Cousin," I cried breathlessly. Two could play at this game of betrayal, I found, and he could not expect me to keep silent under the circumstances. Besides, I wanted to hurt him, and found a sort of pleasure in it. "I saw you dancing—hooded as you were. You saw me through the window—do not deny it. You stared at me—"

His fist clenched on the table. "You lie! I never set foot inside the church."

"You did! You were dancing with Polly—and a nasty dance it was—"

"I did not dance with her."

"I saw you there."

"You cannot swear to it," he said with conviction. I remembered his remarks earlier on the subject, and glanced from him to Lord Knevett who was watching me now with something like amusement.

"No—you wore a hood," I admitted. "But I heard your voice later, when you called out to me. Besides, when you were bringing me back from—that place, the next day, you spoke of the war as the reason for your particular shock at being fired upon—who else would think of such a thing? Oh, it was you—I felt it with every inch of me when next we met."

He raised one of those twisted eyebrows. "Did you, indeed?" he said softly.

"Mark has admitted to being there," put in the squire. He looked at me without friendship. "And if I had known what had passed between you it would have been for attempted manslaughter and not for vagrancy that I should have committed you."

"Don't you see," cried Aunt Margaret, "that that was why she could not tell you of it?"

"Really," exclaimed Kitty Beauregard, fanning herself, " 'tis vastly like a play!"

"Forgive me," said Lord Knevett coolly. "But does it matter very much that Mark was at All Saints? He had good reason for it and his presence can have nothing to do with the murder. For that, the witches must be responsible—and you cannot seriously believe your son to make one of the coven, sir? I have taken the liberty of discussing the whole affair with Pole-Carter," he went on. "He is an acknowledged expert on such matters, as you know, for he told me he had discussed with you his conviction that this was a ritual murder. I was also glad to hear from him that you intend to take his advice in appearing to be satisfied with the verdict and then, on the next sabbat—which it seems is not far off—to watch the church and apprehend the coven when they have gathered there. This seems to me a logical plan, though I hope you won't call on me to help in the execution of it, for I find something peculiarly distasteful in the notion of such gatherings."

"I should not object to being a witness, I can tell you," Madame Beauregard quickly declared.

"Be quiet, Kitty. Well, Knevett, I am not so hopeful of the outcome as Pole-Carter supposes. It is true I agreed to his suggestion, but I fear I doubt very much if this—coven, as you call it, will choose to meet again at All Saints after what has occurred. Surely they will expect the place to be watched after this?"

Lord Knevett shrugged. "It is a chance—but a good one, I think. Pole-Carter believes they are a dedicated group, strengthened by some others from Lindenfold, and that this churchyard of All Saints and the altar are important to their rites." He gave a scarcely perceptible shiver. "Pole-Carter says that they will reason that the dates of their meetings will be unknown to us and so long as they do not ring the bell they will expect to be safe—"

176

"Ring the bell?" cried Kitty. "Do you mean they have the temerity to ring the church bell to call the witches to their meetings?"

"It seems—Pole-Carter says—that they do not generally do so but that some of their festivals are more important to them than others—Candlemas was such a one, and this particular Candlemas above all, one assumes, if murder was to form a part of the rites."

After a short silence the squire said, "Well, and what do you suggest we do if they are meeting there, sir?"

"Why, you arrest them."

"It could be difficult."

Lord Knevett looked impatient. "We have a constable, do we not?"

The squire shook his head. "I have a notion Sim Carver would turn and run at the first suggestion of arresting witches. Besides, if his brother is one of them—"

"Well then, sir, you must find persons who are not afraid of them, or of their vengeance. Persons like your son—"

"Now there," said Mark Prendergast gravely, "I think you presuppose too much. I believe I am also afraid of witches—especially the witches of All Saints. You had better lock me up here that night, just to ensure that I do not slip out to join the coven—as I can see my dear sister thinks I have it in mind to do."

"Oh Mark, how could you? I am sure this is not a matter for jest. But since you mentioned Pole-Carter and his opinion, has Stepmama told you, Father, what he told her the other day? His reasons for supposing the murder to be a ritual one?"

The squire looked at Aunt Margaret. "You said nothing of it, my dear?"

"No." Aunt Margaret twisted the napkin in her hands and then laid it carefully beside her plate. "I thought the less the whole thing was discussed, the better. But now, perhaps. . . ."

There were thirteen wounds, it seems, which look as if they were the work of different hands by their positions—and though the—the throat was not marked as sometimes happens in such cases, the fact that the body was on the altar must itself point to the conclusion that everyone, including the jury, has drawn."

I looked at Mark Prendergast. He was staring down at his hands and suddenly the thought occurred to me that the dagger could have been used by one person in his left and right hands alternately to suggest precisely what had been concluded. The discovery seemed momentous to me. I wished to think about it alone and felt I could not bear to stay another instant in that room.

I rose with a murmured excuse and began to move away. As I closed the door I could hear Kitty's sharp voice saying, "And when is this sabbat as you call it, Father?" and paused long enough to hear his low reply, "It is for Sunday night."

In the hall I paused, pressing my hands together. Could Mark Prendergast have planned and executed such a murder? Why had not Polly Holford simply been pushed into the river and left to drown on such a cold foggy night?

Suddenly it occurred to me that I had a chance to act in privacy, as well as to think, now that everyone was gathered in the breakfast parlour. I hastened to the bookroom. First I must secure the dagger and discover if it were in fact the weapon of murder. I would show it to Sir Abraham and insist on his consulting Dr. Burton about it. I hurried to the desk but, not entirely to my surprise, the stiletto was no longer there. Another letter-opener lay in its place, silver, blunt, and innocent of any stain.

Hastily, with shaking hands, I opened the drawers of the rent table. There was no sign of it, of course. Captain Prendergast must have hidden it, for a dagger, however incriminating, was not so easy to destroy—but where?

His room, I thought—and felt myself grow cold. Dare I go up and begin a search in his room while the captain was actually in the house? But I might not get another chance, and despite what Aunt Margaret had said, I felt it of the first importance to discover once and for all, if I could, whether or no her stepson were guilty of murder.

I hurried up the stairs before I could have time to change my mind. At least I had excuse to be in the old wing, I thought thankfully, as I paused before the captain's door. I bent my ear to it, the old polished wood cool beneath my cheek. There was no sound of movement within. His valet would be at breakfast, very likely, and from my own observation I knew that the maids left this wing till last to clean. I raised the old-fashioned latch, paused again to assure myself the room was really empty, and stepped inside.

I closed the door and leaned back against it with racing heart.

After a moment I realized that I was wasting precious time, and opened my eyes. It was, I saw, an attractive chamber in its old-fashioned way. There was a good fire in the hearth—a luxury which I had not been offered today—and the leaping flames were reflected in all the polished oaken surfaces and in the blue-glazed chinaware. A certain untidiness prevailed: the bed was unmade and the clothes the captain had worn the previous evening were still in evidence, and this disorder would not facilitate my search, I feared. However, I must begin somewhere, and I decided to start by looking about the bed. I supposed the captain would not have left the dagger under his pillow for a chambermaid to find, but it was possible the bedposts were hollow.

After several minutes of twisting and tapping I abandoned

179

the four-poster and turned my attention to the cupboards. These were far too tidy for anything to be hidden in them, I soon decided. A drawer revealed only handkerchiefs and cravats, impeccably starched and ironed. What hiding place could there be that was safe from the eyes of maids and valets? Staring desperately about, I saw a bookshelf and hurried to pull out the books and look behind them. They were an interesting selection, from Hudibras to Clarissa, but I had no time to linger on them. I satisfied myself that no dagger lay behind them, and pushed them roughly back. Where else? Suddenly I spied a door in a shadowed corner, its top angled to fit beneath the sloping roof. A powder closet, no doubt, disused since powder tax came in—and since officers had been allowed to wear short unpowdered hair.

I looked eagerly into the closet, but it was very dark. I could make out only the shapes of coats hanging in it, boots standing below. I dropped hurriedly to my knees and began to grope behind those polished boots, somehow so reminiscent of their owner.

All at once my fingers touched something unexpectedly soft. I leaned forward, half-suffocated among the coats, and managed to secure a grip on a fold of material, an untidy bundle stuffed behind the wide beam that edged the floor. I dragged it quickly from its hiding place, and realized at once it was not what I sought. I spread out the fusty folds and peered at my discovery in the dim light. It was an enveloping cloth—the domino, no doubt, which Captain Prendergast had already owned to wearing at All Saints, and wrapped within it was the black hood with slits for eyes.

I backed into the bedroom, wondering why even now these vestments should have the power to frighten me. As the light fell on the larger one I noticed it was not black as I had

180

thought, but mottled brown, as if it had been daubed with rust.

I do not know how long I stood there, gaping at the domino. I was powerless to move even when I heard footsteps in the passage; and when the door opened to disclose the owner of the room, I could only lift my head and stare at him dumbly, the bloodstained garment crumpled in my hands.

TWELVE

The colour surged into the captain's face.

"Well, Cousin," he said softly, dangerously. "May I ask what you are doing here?"

"It was you—after all," I murmured stupidly.

He frowned. "It was I? What the Devil do you mean? And what have you got there? What is that—thing you are holding?"

But he knew what it was, I thought. I could see the knowledge in his eyes.

"It is the domino you wore that evening at All Saints." I thrust it towards him. "There are bloodstains on it—as well you know!"

His eyes narrowed and he stood very still, staring at the cloth. Gradually an ugly expression began to twist his face. I felt a shiver of fear, suddenly fully aware of my own danger. What would he do now? Would he tell me some tale of his horse having been cut, or some such thing, in an attempt to account for the blood—or would he silence me once and for all?

Somehow I found my voice. I said very quickly, "Don't touch me, sir, for I assure you I will scream."

Perhaps he had not thought of that. At all events his expression changed. He met my frightened gaze with a satirical look. Aware that there was no escape, yet I took a backward step. Immediately, the captain advanced a pace.

With a gasp of terror, I dropped the domino and dragged the Indian dagger out of my reticule and out of its sheath in the same movement.

The captain raised one of his satanic eyebrows. Then his gaze dropped to where the domino now lay, an evil dark pool about my feet.

"You have been reading too many romances," he said calmly. "Those are not bloodstains, Cousin. It was damp that day, if you remember, and I bundled the thing in the closet—it has grown mouldy, and the rest is in your disordered imagination."

He sounded so plausible—a jury might believe him, I thought.

"Your paper knife was bloodstained," I reminded him foolishly. "And so is this domino—"

"You have a very low opinion of my intelligence if you suppose that I would bring them home with me, if what you suggest were true."

"I am sure you intended to destroy them both at the first opportunity—but unfortunately for you, I saw them before you could do so."

He looked at me consideringly. "Are you not a little reckless, Miss Tremayne, to bandy words with me like this, if you truly believe me to be a murderer?"

"I—I have my dagger," I stammered.

He smiled a little, as though I amused him against his will. Suddenly he threw out his hands as if to seize me but before

183

he could complete the movement my dagger had flashed through the air and pierced his skin. He recoiled, and I stared aghast at the widening red ribbon about his wrist.

"You little vixen," he said, straightening and letting his hands fall. An instant later he added grimly, "What are your bloodstains worth now, may I ask?"

I looked down and saw the bright drops falling from his wrist to splash down on the domino and be absorbed among its rusty folds. Had he deliberately provoked me to bring this about? It seemed unlikely, and yet—at that moment, the captain plucked the dagger out of my slackened grip and held its curved point to my throat.

"Now," he said in an indescribably menacing tone. "Now, Cousin Tansy, can I persuade you to forget what you have seen, to be a little less impulsive, foolhardy—brave, if you will —and a little more the demure young lady you pretended so hard to be earlier in our acquaintance? Or," and he seemed to grow in height and width as he added this, "will you force me to use stronger measures?"

I gave an involuntary gasp and burst into tears. The captain muttered something and with a violent gesture sent the dagger spinning over his shoulder. It fell with a clatter to the floor, while I hid my face in my hands.

"Do you really think I would kill you here?" demanded the captain in an exasperated tone. "It would be tantamount to my committing suicide, I should suppose."

I suppressed my tears and risked a glance at him. He sounded normal now, but he had not done so earlier, and in a fit of madness considerations of personal safety could not be expected to weigh with him. But what was I to do now? If he were mad there was no knowing when the next attack would take him. He was between me and the door, however, so there seemed nothing for it but to attempt to escape by the window.

"Excuse me!" I murmured. "I feel faint." I tottered to the casement, while he leaned back against the door and folded his arms. I struggled with the latch and threw open the window. The captain made no move to prevent me, and a moment later I knew why, for there was nothing below but a nasty drop to a wide paved stone walk, with which I had no desire to make a closer acquaintance just then.

I turned slowly, to find the captain staring at me in that odd intent way of his.

"I am glad you did not try it," he remarked. "It would have been such a waste."

"What shall I do?" I said, and only realized I had spoken aloud in my agitation, when he smiled.

"Why, I shall let you go in a moment, miss. But first, just tell me, did you know Polly Holford to speak to at all?"

I stared back at him. "How could I, sir? I only came into Sussex for the first time on the day she died."

He shrugged. "I am disposed to believe you, but one hears so many rumours—and now, as I reflect, it seems that you have not answered my question, after all."

I glared at him. "I did not know Miss Holford," I said coldly. "I never met her—never spoke to her. I only saw her dancing, leaning her head against your shoulder."

His gaze flickered and he looked away. His eye fell on the dagger and he picked it up. "Take it," he said brusquely, offering it to me by the hilt, "and get out of here."

I shall never know why I did not immediately obey him, why I risked driving him into the dark abyss. At all events, I paused when I should have run, and faltered, "But—the domino—?"

He looked annoyed, no more.

185

"Do you think I will allow you to take that with you?" he demanded. "I daresay you put it there yourself, in the hope of proving—"

"But you owned to me that you put it in the closet," I reminded him, staring.

He shrugged. "So I did—or another exactly similar. But as you no doubt appreciate, it is hard to gain access to this room except by the door, so if someone substituted a bloodstained domino for my own, then it was probably you."

"So you—deny that one is yours?"

"If those are bloodstains, then most certainly I do. Furthermore, by the time you have told my father of its existence I assure you it will have been destroyed."

I looked again at the roaring fire, at the logs stacked neatly by the hearth. "But I have seen it," I reminded him rashly. "Is my evidence worth nothing?"

"Nothing, if you can be discredited," he said brutally. "Does it not occur to you that a clever lawyer might be able to throw enough doubt on your integrity to make a jury mistrust your word—jailbird that you are? Oh, go on," he cried roughly, as I flinched. "Leave, for God's sake, before worse befall—and if you value your safety, keep a still tongue in your head, for though to inform will avail you nothing, it will certainly run you into danger."

He flung open the door and almost pushed me through it. I stumbled into the passage, clutching my dagger and nearly tripping over my skirts. Somehow I reached my room and sank down on the bed, but my hands were shaking as I pushed the dagger back into its sheath, and my thoughts were equally ineffective. I could not decide what I should do—tell someone, yes, of course, I must do so. It were madness equal to the captain's to keep silent in the face of such evidence as I had to bear. But whom to tell? The captain's father? Or his friends?

186

It should be Lord Knevett, I supposed; and this time I must find the resolution to go through with it. It was not enough to hope that on Sunday the whole mystery might be resolved, for the captain at least was aware of the plan to catch the coven, and would no doubt take steps to warn the rest.

A sudden knock fell on the door. I made some sound, and Madame Beauregard entered, looking highly excited and rather wicked.

"Here!" she cried, just as if we were girls at school together. "Where do you suppose I have been just now?"

"I really can't imagine."

"Come, dullard, think over that conversation at breakfast and see if you cannot find the answer there?"

I stared at her. She flung down her muff upon my bed and began to loosen the strings of her bonnet.

"Oh, never mind then, if you won't. But I'll tell you, and see how you look then! I had out the chaise and drove to Lindenfold!"

"I trust you had a pleasant drive."

She narrowed her eyes at me. "You are a tease, miss, but you will soon be laughing on the other side of your face. I called at the vicarage, on Mr. Pole-Carter."

"Oh," I said, enlightened. "The authority on witchcraft?"

"Precisely so. And I discovered a thing or two, I can tell you. I mean to unravel the whole mystery, you know, and I shan't be long about it. What day is it?"

"Thursday," I said blankly.

"Oho! And you don't know that Thursday is ruled by Jupiter, I suppose?"

"No, I must confess I was quite ignorant on that point."

"Of course you would say so. You would not know either that Jupiter is most powerful in conferring invisibility—or

187

that the moon is also invaluable in such enterprises, as well as in grave-robbing, or raising spirits, I daresay? Or that one hour after sunset, on a Thursday, is her most powerful time?"

I shook my head, beginning to feel rather afraid of the excitement in Kitty's eyes.

She paused in front of the looking glass and eyed her figure sideways. "Beauregard won't like it, I know—but it's not as if I were an unmarried girl—and it is my duty, I think. Besides, you will be there to chaperon me."

"Where?" I demanded, rather hastily.

"Why, in the churchyard of All Saints, of course, at one hour after sunset. We will go by boat, and there is a convenient wall to lurk behind—"

"Madame, I assure you nothing is further from my intentions!"

"Ah, but you must do it, or own yourself a witch," she said triumphantly. "There are thirteen in the coven, Pole-Carter says. He says they need power now, to protect their identity. The best way they can acquire power, he thinks, is by desecrating the graveyard—All Saints is the most convenient one, being no longer used; Thursday must be the day. and the hour, in order to invoke the moon, one after sunset. Therefore, I propose, with your assistance, dear Miss Tremayne, to go secretly to the place of rendezvous—and count those who gather there. If only twelve do so, then I shall know what to think, shall I not?"

"Why, you might suppose that one has been detained," I said lightly, but of course I could see what she wanted to prove and began to fear she really meant to carry out her wild intention.

"None will be detained, unless it is you!" she cried. "This meeting is for the witches' own protection—it is essential that all attend."

"It seems to me very unlikely that any will. Surely they will keep away from All Saints at least for a month or two,"

"You may be right," she owned, "but Pole-Carter thinks they will gather there tonight—and again on Sunday, which is the day, he believes, of their weekly meeting, as Papa said. So prepare yourself, miss, for an adventure."

"A perfectly horrid one, in which I refuse to participate."

"You refuse?" she cried incredulously. "Well, I am very loath to think the worst of you, but upon my word!"

"You had better take your father with you," I pointed out. "Then, if *any* witches come, he will know how to act."

Kitty pouted. "But I want to catch them all—and I want to know soon. I can't wait for Sunday night, even if he can. Then, if you are not one yourself, you may recognize some of them, and so might I. Imagine the triumph of telling him! And a further consideration is that if they do gather at All Saints tonight, then they are positive to do so on Sunday."

"Assuming that I will not give them warning," I suggestly demurely. She looked a little taken aback.

"I can't really believe it of you . . . besides, I shall keep a close watch on you between now and then. Now, have you some paper? A commonplace book," she answered herself, seizing it from the bedside table and ripping out the center pages, to my annoyance. "A pen? Here it is. Now, look—I am going to make a list."

She sat on the bed and dipped her pen in the ink. I sat beside her, still somewhat vexed but curious to see what she would write. She headed her page boldly enough:

THE COVEN

and under it, she wrote 13.

"Well," she said to me with her customary impatience, "can't you think of the name of a single one? Did not my stepmother make mention of Dick Carver, the constable's brother?"

"I think this is a dangerous game you play, madame."

189

"Pooh! As if one should care for that! Now if there was a flute player it could only be he, for Dick is a poor cripple but plays the flute like Orpheus himself. So, we will put him down for number one. Now, number two—why, Barney Clement, to be sure. Come, this is famous! Who else did you see?"

"A fat woman," I said weakly.

"Very fat?"

"Enormous—but light on her feet."

"Mrs. Chivers, for a certainty. She is cook at Holy Mote and that house has always been a very hotbed of witchcraft, so I've heard. Mrs. Chivers, three, then. Number four?"

"A tall man—well built."

She looked exasperated. "That is not enough. Why, you might mean my father, or Colonel Horton, or—even Lord Knevett."

Or your brother, I thought, but did not say.

"There was a little nimble fellow, with bowlegs," I said quickly, to divert her. "You will think me mad, I daresay, but it did cross my mind to wonder, at the inquest—"

"Well, what?"

"Why, that it could have been the foreman of the jury—a tailor, it seems, though I don't recall his name."

"Can you mean Trimble? Ay, well it could be so. He has never been content with his station in life. It is power, you know, that these witches seek, so Pole-Carter says. They are likely to be people who have no influence in their own homes, who are kept down for some reason, or who long to change events by supernatural means, if not by natural. But then," she added reflectively, "does not everyone long for power?"

"No," I said without hesitation. "At least, I am sure I do not."

190

"How strange. And then it has an appeal, too, for the lonely, as well as for those whose natures are drawn to the darker side of things." She gave a little shiver. "We will put Trimble for four," she said firmly. "Tonight, you see, if we have only an idea of whom we seek, it might assist us in recognizing them in disguise. Five—well, we will say your tall man. Six?" She looked at me expectantly.

"Another woman."

Her eyes brightened. "Could it be Mrs. Slight?"

"Why, what in the world makes you say that? She is the very pattern of a witch, I am sure—but is that enough?"

"What is she doing here?" Kitty asked earnestly. "We had a good housekeeper, Gregson—she was a trifle elderly, perhaps, but not too old for the work; and she was positively devoted to the family—she had been here forever. Then suddenly she is retired to a little cottage outside Abbotsford—pleasant enough, I know—and this woman is appointed in her stead."

"Mrs. Slight seems most efficient," I suggested.

"Yes, I daresay, but no one could like her."

"So you think she appointed herself by witchcraft?"

Madame Beauregard took offense at my sarcastic tone, and pouted. "I don't know how she was appointed—I merely ask."

"Perhaps it was that my aunt felt she would prefer someone to take her orders who had *not* been here forever, in the time of her predecessor."

Kitty looked at me with the first sign of respect I had yet drawn from her. "You may be right. You are clever, aren't you? I shall have to be careful of you. Now, do you play backgammon?"

"Why do you ask?"

"Because we must amuse ourselves till dinnertime."

"You have finished with the list, then?"

"Yes, unless you can think of anyone else."

I shook my head. She stared at the paper a moment or two, then folded and returned it to its place in my book. True to her word, she stuck by me the rest of the day, and the squire was moved to remark at dinner that he was glad to see we had made friends, at which the captain and his sister exchanged a sardonic smile. It occurred to me that if Kitty had confided in me, so she might have in him, in which case there was little danger of our running into any witches that night or any other. But surely he would not allow us to set out on our own? No, I decided on second thought, it seemed that for once Madame Kitty must have been discreet.

"Come, Cousin," she cried, rising from the piano some time after we had retired to the drawing room. "Let us go up and finish our game."

"I must beg you to excuse me," I said, with an attempt to avoid her insistent eye. "I feel rather like conversation tonight, and would prefer to gossip with my aunt."

"No, dear," intervened Aunt Margaret, sighing. "I mean to go early to bed. Do go with Kitty. I like to think of you young people amusing each other."

Kitty smirked triumphantly, and I rose, perforce, and kissed my aunt good night.

"Quick," Kitty hissed, once the door had closed behind us. "Take your cloak and boots—they are ready in the cupboard—and come out by the side door. I have locked our bedrooms so they cannot look in and find us gone."

Still protesting, I found myself bundled out of the door, and there the very cold made me acquiesce in putting on my outdoor garments.

"It is absurd!" I complained. "If it is not absurd, it is foolhardy. Either one or the other."

"Oho! So you are afraid!" she taunted me, and then drawing me down the gravel path, "Well, it is very natural, I suppose—but have you no interest in discovering the truth?"

"I—don't know," I admitted unhappily. "The truth will mean more misery than perhaps you realize—"

"Cousin! Don't tell me you have forgotten that unhappy girl! If the witches are not found out, what is to stop them from choosing another victim, and another?"

"You are right, of course. But it is the folly of our venturing alone I question."

"Oh, pooh—I am to blame, if we are caught. I am a married woman, Sir Abraham's daughter. I think you will find I will not be censured."

"Or murdered either, let us trust."

"You are a miserable companion!" she declared, squeezing my arm. "Look about you—is it not a charming night? A gibbous moon, starry above, misty by the river—Beauregard would wax poetic over it, I can tell you. Now here we take to the road a trifle. Don't fret, we will soon be at the river and I made sure this morning that the boat was ready, hard by the bridge."

It was certainly a fine night, and it seemed I was committed to the adventure. I said no more but hurried down the road with my inexorable cousin until we reached the hump of the bridge.

"Hush, what's that?" she cried. "A horseman! Lord, let's get down quick!"

We slipped and scrambled down the path beside the bridge and ducked beneath the arch just as hooves began to ring above us on the ancient stones. The horse seemed to check, and then went on.

"It's well enough," Kitty assured me. "Even if he saw us, 'tis probably a gamekeeper or some such thing—it can't be one of *them*, for he's travelling in the wrong direction. Look, here's the punt, snug against the wall. My father keeps it for shooting waterfowl, and taught me how to use it, as a child."

We stepped in carefully. Kitty untied the rope and raised the pole. "I suppose you cannot do it?" she asked. "I enjoy punting, but it may not be quite the thing in my condition. However, the place is not far off, though it is upstream. Pooh, the water's cold, and it is hard to see. I hope I can remember where the banks lie, and how the currents run."

She fell silent, partly no doubt from her exertions, and partly also I fancied from a belated consciousness of the rashness of our expedition. She had avoided mentioning the name of the place where we were bound and had referred to "them" and not "the witches" almost as if she feared to invoke them by using proper names.

"We are drawing close," she whispered, startling me. "I shall pull in under the trees here."

She tethered the punt to a knotted willow. I stepped out and helped her ashore. We stood a moment listening, but all was silent and the light mist swirled about us as though we had been lent the very cloak of invisibility that the witches hoped to wrest from Jupiter tonight.

Kitty's hand slid into mine. She pulled me forward, stooping, through a sparse copse of ragged thorn. Then, putting her lips to my ear, she addressed me.

"There—do you see, through the mist? We will wait till it thickens, to cross the open space, and crouch by the wall. Be ready to run."

I gathered up my skirts in the other hand and peered through the damp and ghostly veil. Suddenly my heart jumped. There was the ruined tower, there the church, the tumbled wall, the tree, the gate—and then they were gone again.

194

"Now!" said Kitty, and began to run.

The ground was rutted under my feet, trodden by cows and grassed and frozen by turns. I stumbled after Kitty, unbalanced by the drag on my hand, and slid with her into an ungraceful attitude under the shelter of the wall.

My heart was thundering, my breathing loud. Kitty put her hand over my mouth. I shook it off. She nudged me, and very cautiously began to rise to her feet and peer through a cranny in the wall, while I followed her example.

At first I could see nothing, but then the wind began to die and the mist dropped to waist level, writhing over the neglected graves like spirits struggling to escape from their earthly bonds. I shivered, and stared at the dark windows of the unhallowed church.

"No one," Kitty whispered, "but perhaps we are early yet."

We waited. Soon I was cold and began to shiver. Then my teeth chattered and I clenched them tightly. There was a slight creak and we both started violently.

"Only the gate!" Kitty whispered. "See how it hangs ajar. It moved in the wind."

Nothing stirred except the mist. Then a twig snapped. We crouched, frozen with terror while the slow seconds passed away. I looked at Kitty, and she shrugged.

After some minutes longer, she said, "Shall we go in?"

"Ah, God, how could you think of it?"

"Well, I don't believe they will come now—it was only Pole-Carter's guess, after all. But I believe—I think—I would just like to see . . ." She sounded uncertain yet obstinate, if that were possible. She was determined to enter the graveyard, if not the church, I realized; and I stood up also, more afraid of being left alone than of going with her.

"Very well—but I can't conceive what object you hope—"

"Sh!"

She clutched my arm. For quite a second we both stood as if turned to stone. Then, gradually, she relaxed.

"I thought—I heard—"

"Oh, madame, pray let us go!"

"No, it was but one dead branch rubbing on another. There is no one about, you can see that. Indeed, I did not tell you earlier because I did not want to put you off, but it was more likely they would meet on Monday—the day of the moon, you know—and in the hour of Jupiter, rather than the other way about. Only I thought they would not dare to come back so soon after the murder, for fear of finding people here. But now it must be past the hour and there is no danger in our just making sure that they did come then—"

This time it was the harsh cry of a bird which alarmed us. The night was full of such noises, I tried to reassure myself, averting my eyes from the restless ground mist. Besides, even if there were ghosts here, they surely could not harm the living. And as for witches, they were but people that one knew, playing on the fringes of the supernatural, using the weapon of fear to enlarge themselves . . . but rational withal, and surely not so rash as to murder twice? Or were they, indeed, wholly rational? What of the authenticated cases of which one occasionally heard, of demoniacal possession?

"Come," said Kitty in a determined voice, drawing me along the wall to the old lych-gate.

I shivered as we passed beneath the ancient yew. "This is folly!" I exclaimed.

"No!" cried Kitty, clutching at me again. "Look there! Look at the gravestone!"

I pressed a hand to my heart and peered in the direction she indicated, close to the path. A very muddy headstone leaned precariously there.

"It is *upside down*," Kitty observed in a chilling whisper.

We stared, shaking. The grave had been disturbed, I noticed. The earth had been dug over, and then trampled again.

"The ring," Kitty hissed. "The magic circle!"

Almost at our feet, a dark line had been drawn about the grave. I stooped and put my finger in it. My glove was marked with black that smelt unmistakably of charcoal.

"And something has been newly buried here," Kitty announced. She seized a stick and began madly to dig, while I tried ineffectually to pull her away.

"Oh, faugh!" she exclaimed presently, in disgust. "It is a cat—or cats. Do you suppose they killed them?"

She held up one poor corpse on her stick. I shuddered. "Put it back, I beg of you."

"There are—other things here. What's this? Candles—black candles, burnt down! Pole-Carter should see this!"

"Kitty, I am going. I shall take the boat and drift downstream. You may come with me or not, as you please."

I strode away, and she ran after me. "Don't leave me! How could you?"

"You had better come with me, then. These sights are not for us. We came to prove identities, not to pry into the foul secrets of witchcraft. No good can come of it and I suggest you forget this night's work—if you can!"

"Oh, stay! That is, I want to come," Kitty panted indecisively. "Perhaps you are right, but the mist is almost gone—we might be seen!"

"There is no one to see us. The witches have done their work and I doubt if others choose to wander here."

I spoke boldly, but I was not so sure we were not overlooked. I seemed to be conscious of eyes piercing the darkness and the remaining skeins of mist, but the feeling only

197

lent purpose to my stride. The sooner we were gone from this hellish place the better.

Kitty, somewhat chastened by our discoveries, had no intention of being left behind. She stumbled at my heels as earlier I had stumbled at hers. I found the boat, cast off, and jumped into it, holding it by a branch until she had joined me. Then as she sank panting on the boards, I picked up the pole and let it float behind us, steering by this means as the seaward current floated us through the watermeadows to the bridge.

"Do you really think we should not speak of what we have seen?" Kitty asked, rising at length in time to help me steer the punt towards the mooring-ring.

"What object is there in it, but to lay ourselves open to some very severe criticism?"

"Perhaps you are right—but at least it means the church is still in use. They have not given it up despite the danger."

"Therefore Sir Abraham will catch them on Sunday—if that is truly their meeting-day." And if Mark Prendergast were not a witch and did not warn the coven, I added silently.

"Yes, I suppose you are right—Tansy, did you hear something then?"

"Only a stone falling. I thought you might have dislodged it with your shoe."

"Not I." She scrambled more energetically up the bank. "Do you think we have been followed?"

"By whom? Your brother?" It was a more alarming thought than she could have guessed.

"I—don't know. I only think—"

A wild shriek rent the air as a figure fell on us from above, where it had been concealed by the parapet of the bridge.

"Drab! Slut!" it screamed. "I have you now! So this is

198

why you make to leave me, the so dutiful squire's daughter! Where is the man? You, sir—put up your sword!"

"Beauregard!" cried Kitty, throwing herself between us. "Have you taken leave of your senses? What are you doing here?"

"Ha! You may ask that, faithless one. First I run him through, and then I beat you, do you hear?"

"You shall do no such thing!"

"Shall I not? I, Jacques Marie Dubois Beauregard, Master of Fence—"

"You shan't because you don't have a sword, and because my companion is my cousin, Miss Tremayne. This madman, Cousin, is my husband, the most jealous fellow in the world, I fear, on behalf of whom I apologize."

"*Miss* Tremayne?" the Frenchman cried suspiciously, peering at me more closely. "Is it true what you say there? A woman?"

I found my tongue. "Certainly I am a woman," I assured him. "But even in the moonlight, how did you know this lady was your wife?"

"Ah, my Kitty! My little, little Kitty!" He seized her hand and passionately kissed it. "How should I not know her, my spouse, my life?"

"He dotes on me, you see," remarked Kitty complacently.

"I see two figures in the dark," Monsieur explained by way of apology. "One look like her—aha! I say to myself, this is not far from the house where Kitty should be—what if it is her, and that she goes to make rendezvous? I see then the companion is female but I think they on their way to meet another. I ride on; so, they do not suspect me. I dismount, tie the horse, creep back and—*pouf!* My Kitty, she is gone. But I remember the boat, and as I run across the fields, I see it. I follow, I hide, I watch. The mist it comes and goes,

I am not sure if it is now the same woman with her, or a man. My eyes, they are red with the rage, you comprehend. I follow back, I reach the bridge, I lie in wait—"

"And give us the fright of our lives," his bride scolded mildly. "Why did you have to spring on me like that, though?"

"It is the element of surprise—very valuable in warfare. I am not knowing how big is this lover of yours—"

"Oh, really, Jack, you know very well. You have only to look in the mirror. He's just a little fellow, but a veritable fire-eater."

"Ah! So I am! But what were you doing, leaving your father's house at such a time?" he demanded fiercely, folding his arms. "It is not good behaviour, this. It does not look well. I am not satisfied. I demand an explanation."

"You are a silly boy," Kitty said fondly. "You are too impetuous by much."

"Why, what is this? I do not know what you mean."

"I mean, you foolish Jack, that it was Miss Tremayne who had the rendezvous, not I," she improvised calmly. "Only it was so cold and misty the—er, the person she hoped to meet did not arrive."

"The dastard! I run him through, eh?"

"No, dear, you need not. The truth is, she is tired of him and sought merely to persuade him, with my help, that such meetings were not at all the thing, and that this must be the last. The whole affair is now over, and you need say nothing of it to my stepmama."

"*Eh bien*, if you say so. But how are you, *mon amour*, with all this activity, surely it is not good for you to make the promenade at such time?"

"No, Jack," she agreed, leaning a little upon his arm,

though she was the taller. "I do not think it is at all good for me, and I want to go home."

"And so you shall, my cabbage. Perhaps you will lead the way, miss? I will bring Madame and the horse. But you must allow me, miss, to tell you that I do not think it at all *comme il faut* on your part to allow my wife to exert herself in such a fashion. Perhaps you are not aware of it but she is in a certain condition and requires to be tranquil—"

"Exactly as I supposed," I cried, goaded beyond endurance, yet loath to call Kitty a liar to her husband. "Only—you know your wife, monsieur—nothing would do for her but to accompany me. It was not my idea, I assure you."

"Very well, then," he said magnanimously. "We will say no more about it, eh?"

We proceeded, in silence on my part, and with gentle murmuring on theirs, while the horse docilely followed his master.

We arrived at Pheasant's in due course. Monsieur Beauregard refused to allow us to slip in by the side entrance, but beat upon the knocker until Barclay had unchained the front door and let us in.

"My dears, what is it?" cried my aunt, who chanced to be emerging from the drawing room on her way to bed. "Beauregard! What in the world are you doing here? That is, you are most welcome, I am sure—but Kitty—and Tansy—where have you been?"

"That makes no matter, my dear madame," said her son-in-law, bowing over her hand. "I send a note to Kitty," he improvised as fluently as his wife. "She comes a little way to meet me, Miss—er, her cousin accompany her, quite correct—it is so that lovers do, you must know. We cannot bear our meeting to be accompanied by ceremony. As for why I am here, I read such things in the newspaper, I cannot allow Kitty to be in such a place without protection, how could you suppose it? I come to keep her safe from harm, also to support you in your ordeal, madame."

"Extremely obliged!" murmured my aunt, looking as if she could have done without the obligation. "Now, the immediate question is, where are you to sleep?"

"Why, with me, Mama," said Kitty, opening her eyes. "My bed is large enough—and there is no other in the house just now."

"Yes, yes," her husband assented eagerly. "Let there be no ceremony, I beg! Has my saddlebag come in? Yes, there it is. Well, my dear *Belle-mère*, let me bid you good night. Kitty and I will retire immediately, for she is tired and we have much to say to one another. Good night, miss," he added, bowing slightly in my direction. "Come, my cabbage. I was so afraid," he went on as they began to climb the stairs, "that you would offer to share your bed with Miss, and allow me one to myself. I do not think she is at all a proper person for you to associate with."

"Hush, Jack, and I will tell you all presently." Their voices died as they crossed the landing and I turned smiling to my aunt.

She was not amused, however. "Why did he have to come just now?" she muttered wretchedly. "He is just the sort of blundering fool who might very well—" She became aware of my wondering glance and broke off abruptly. "Come, Tansy," she said immediately in a light artificial voice. "It is time you were abed as well. My sewing woman comes tomorrow, and you know how tiring it is to be standing still for hours at a time while pins are stuck into you—but I mean to have you very well turned out for church on Sunday."

202

She looked past me, and gave me a palpable start. I glanced round. Mrs. Slight was standing in the shadows, hands folded, staring steadily at Aunt Margaret.

"Oh—Mrs. Slight," cried my aunt. "You are put out because you were not told of Monsieur's coming. But believe me, I did not know of it myself until I saw him here just now."

Mrs. Slight said nothing, but turned away.

My aunt sighed and took me by the arm. She said something in a low despairing tone. I was not sure, but I thought she asked the question that had already once or twice occurred to me:

"Where, oh where will it all end?"

THIRTEEN

At breakfast Monsieur Beauregard revealed himself more fully as a sharp, sallow, tempestuous little man with a thin enquiring nose, somewhat twisted and with a red blob at the end. I guessed that his wife had been telling him her suspicions of me, because he directed a very piercing glance at me when I entered the room, bowed slightly, and thereafter ignored me.

"Your servant should take a tray to Kitty," he informed my aunt. "She should not rise in the morning. I was sorry to hear she had done so yesterday."

"I begged her to stay in bed, but she was afraid to miss our conversation," my aunt returned rather tartly. "No one, not even her father, can persuade Kitty against her own better judgment, as you, sir, should know."

"Ah, yes," he cried enthusiastically. "She know her own mind, my cabbage. That was what drew me to her so particularly. These other young girls, *pouf!* like thistledust—but Kitty has always her feet on the ground, her plan in her head." He drained his coffee with an expression of disgust, but passed his cup for more. "Well, madame," he demanded, "what do you do today? Are visitors expected? Do we pay calls? Shall I entertain you with my violin?"

"Lord," she cried in a distracted tone. "Did you bring it with you?"

"Always I bring it, unless the weather makes very wet. I know how you and Sir Abraham delight to hear it and it is to repay the hospitality, since you will not allow me to teach you the waltz or even the écossaise. When do you wish me to play?"

"Oh dear—that is, perhaps after dinner, if Sir Abraham has not fallen asleep. We are rather busy this morning. The sewing woman comes, and then—"

"The sewing woman? Ah, that is good. You have some elegant materials ready? Is she to make you an evening gown, or perhaps you had thought of something full for Kitty?"

"Well, sir, as it happens, I had intended Mrs. Fowler to sew some new curtains for my bedchamber but since my niece is come I thought she could benefit from some well-made mourning gowns. I always have some material put aside for such a purpose, of course."

"Mourning gowns? Ah, yes, Miss is in mourning, I perceive."

"As I am myself, and for the same reason."

"Your sister, yes, I recall it now. Well, if you wish my advice, madame, I am fancied to be quite an authority on such matters. You do not think this person will have time to sew for Kitty?"

"Not this time," my aunt assured him. "Perhaps later Mrs. Fowler can make something for the layette." She rose with determination. "Come, Tansy, we have much to decide.

Excuse us, monsieur, and order what you choose for Kitty's breakfast."

In the hall she shook her head wearily. "I don't know how it is, but I cannot endure that little man! As if I had not troubles enough just now without being obliged to—" She stopped herself. "Well, come upstairs, then. Mrs. Fowler will be here at any moment."

Even in the sewing room we were not free from Monsieur, however. He came in while Mrs. Fowler was draping black silk around me, and insisted on giving us the benefit of his opinion and suggestions, which, to my aunt's ill-concealed exasperation, were unfailingly sound. As soon as Mrs. Fowler had enough work in hand, therefore, I was easily able to persuade my aunt to accompany me to the village in order to call on the Latchington children.

"Abbotsford, m-my lady? Yes, certainly," said the wretched postilion, trembling as we entered the chaise.

"What is wrong with that man?" I asked, as the carriage sprang forward.

"Thompson? Poor fellow, he knows too much and not enough," my aunt replied abstractedly. "But I find him useful and I believe he will stay with us. He says that Sir Abraham has the best eye for a horse that ever he saw . . . and of course Thompson for his part is an excellent horse doctor, and a farrier too." She sighed and fell to thinking of something else, twisting her gloved fingers endlessly in her lap.

I had noticed that my aunt was pale and drawn but had forgotten that this visit would be a particular ordeal for her. It was not until after we had left the Latchingtons that I understood the extent of her courage and wished I had not persuaded her to come, for it was soon apparent once we had left the shelter of the cottage, that it was by now common knowledge that Lady Prendergast's stepson had been present at the church when Polly Holford was murdered. I found myself wondering as we moved along, forcing ourselves to smile at the knots of whispering gossips, bowing and looking into eyes which did not quite meet ours, how many of those whom we met had desecrated graves on Monday, the night of the moon—and how many were at that very moment planning to dare to risk another sabbat there two days from now.

It was a relief when a high voice accosted us in a pleasant tone. It was Miss Crofton, the sharp-tongued spinster whom I had not liked at our first meeting but who now appeared a little kinder, with her basket over her arm and a plump maid at her heels carrying a box of preserves.

"Are we on the same errand, Lady Prendergast?" Miss Crofton enquired. "I have been visiting Goody Clement and am now on my way to old Mother Sidney—the mother of poor Mrs. George, the jailer's wife, you know. The only thing is," she lowered her tone, "I see that dreadful man, Trimble the tailor, speaking to some people near her door. I am sure he is an Atheist! He is certainly a Radical. I greatly fear he will call me 'Lady Bountiful' in that sneering tone of his, and if that comes to Papa's ears he will be so angry, I am sure it will be wonderful if he is not carried off in an apoplexy!"

My aunt looked at her uncertainly. "Would you like us to accompany you, Miss Crofton?"

"Oh, by no means! I would not take you out of your way. Ah," she added in a tone of relief, "here comes Dick Carver, the very man I need." She beckoned to a little lame fellow just crossing the road. "You will spare me a moment, won't you, Dick? He is always so obliging," she added in a swift aside, "and plays the flute quite beautifully! Dick, would you

207

take these things to Mother Sidney for me, and tell her I will call on her two days from now? Thank you so much—and here is a groat for your trouble."

Dick Carver had an amiable if twisted grin. I found myself wondering if it concealed a hatred of his fellow men because they walked upright, or if he were indeed contented with his lot, in which case perhaps there was another flautist in the neighbourhood with darker tastes.

Miss Crofton had pressed a pot of her bramble jelly on Aunt Margaret and while they were engaged in discussing the hazards of preserving, I watched Dick Carver hobble towards Mrs. Sidney's cottage.

Trimble caught sight of him, and instantly changed the tenor of his speech. "The day will come, my friends," the tailor cried, his outstretched hand shaking with theatrical indignation, "when such men as these, unemployed through no fault of their own, will cease to be dependent on charity for their living needs—"

"Oh dear," exclaimed Miss Crofton, chancing to overhear him during a pause in her conversation. "Now Trimble thinks poor Dick is living on my charity! As a matter of fact, Papa frequently employs him, to chop firewood and the like. But Trimble is becoming very bold, is he not, Lady Prendergast? I am so glad Papa is not with us to witness it. But that reminds me, I must hurry home, for he is suffering sadly from the gout just now, and dislikes me to leave him at such times. First, though—" she paused, flicking her pointed tongue over her lips, and laid a thin hand on mine—"I must ask you, Miss Tremayne, if you have yet written to my grandmother? You have not? Well, I have taken the liberty of advising her of what a pearl you are, so you may be sure of a welcome in Yorkshire if ever the time comes for you to seek it. Enough! I must not tarry! Farewell, Lady Prendergast. *Adieu*, Miss Tremayne."

She bustled away with her maid hurrying behind. Aunt Margaret turned to me with an anxious look. "You won't go to Yorkshire, will you, Tansy? I confess that at one time I thought it might be wise, but now—I should miss you dreadfully."

I assured her I had made no plans to leave her, but for a good deal of our return journey to Pheasant's, I pondered on what she might have been going to say, and why she had changed her mind about the advisability of my leaving Sussex.

Kitty was very lively at dinner; the captain was silent, and the squire stayed awake until Monsieur was launched into his first piece, so matters might have been worse. I was tired and excused myself as early as was polite. I went to my room with the intention of studying the list Kitty had made out in my commonplace book, and adding to it in pencil some further names which might, I now thought, properly belong there: the names, for example, of Mark Prendergast, Thompson the coachman, and Mrs. Slight. But when I opened the book, the list had gone.

I turned, frowning, wondering if I had been mistaken in thinking that Kitty had returned the pages to their proper place, and started when I saw Mrs. Slight standing silent by the door, watching me.

"Have you lost something, miss?" she said, in her expressionless voice.

"No—well, only a paper that I had. It does not matter. Perhaps it blew into the fire."

"Perhaps it did, miss."

She moved forward with the faint creaking of whalebone that was almost the only sound she ever made. She bent and peered into the hearth. "Why, look, miss," she said, taking the poker and pulling something carefully from the flames. "I believe you are right. A paper has been burning here."

As I stared at it, the flame ran up the side of the charred paper, paused at the only thing legible upon it, number 13, and obliterated the ink mark with an audible hiss.

I shivered and looked round, but Mrs. Slight had gone.

On Saturday the Lindenfold Foxhounds met at Abbotsgate, at the White Lion. Kitty felt unwell, so my aunt and I drove out in the gig with Sir Abraham and the captain riding alongside. The air was cold, there was a pleasant clattering of hooves, jingling of bits and harness, blown vapour snorting from the horses' nostrils; and the fields were full of men pulling turnips before the frost could spoil them.

As we drew near the outskirts of the village we met other riders, and gentlemen in carriages attended by grooms leading their hunters, and others driving gigs with a cob tied on behind. The scene outside the inn was one of bustle and anticipation, perhaps having something in it of the excitement that precedes a battle, with the reflection that today glory might be won, or ignominy, or even death. Sir Abraham's father, so the squire told me, had been brought home on a hurdle after one such meet, with a broken neck; and though he lingered on for several weeks, he never moved or spoke again. This memory, I assumed, gave an added spice to every fence safely cleared by the squire.

A stirrup cup was handed, a spicy mulled wine, very appropriate on such a cold day. My aunt pointed out various local celebrities as we sat in the gig, sipping our tumblers of wine. There was the Earl of Mortmain, a dark, scarred gentleman on a fine grey stallion that required rigorous controlling; the red-faced Master, Colonel Curtis, on a peppery chestnut; Colonel Horton, one of the Horsefield Justices, riding a nervous black mare. A groom moved close to us, leading out a hireling horse. He was auburn-haired, with a sly look and a strong foxy smell. My aunt leaned towards me.

"That is Brent," she whispered. "The one Kitty—you know!"

I stared at the man, recalling that he had seen Mark Prendergast leave this inn at Candlemas and had only gradually realized the damning nature of the evidence he had to bear. Well, I did not like the look of him, but one must give him credit for having done his duty, unpopular though he must have felt himself to be. I looked from him to the captain, leaning from his saddle to speak to—Barney Clement! What could he have to say to him? As I watched, the captain straightened, looked about the crowd, and beckoned to another man, who approached him instantly with a light but bowlegged gait— the tailor, Mr. Trimble. They conversed for a few more minutes; then the man left abruptly to murmur in the ear of the fat woman who stood, legs apart and face agrin, and was, I recalled, the cook at Holy Mote, the place reputed to be a hotbed of witchcraft.

"Don't stare so, miss," begged a hoarse voice in my ear. I turned sharply and saw Thompson, the coachman, his face working, his eyes starting. "Don't stare at—them!"

My aunt, who had been talking to a mild-faced vicar, turned to lay a hand on my arm, and the coachman ducked back to his place at the horses' heads.

"Tansy, my dear," she exclaimed, her face flushed with animation which made her look more like the young attractive woman she had been not long ago. "This is Mr. Pole-Carter, the vicar, you know, of Lindenfold. My niece, sir, Miss Tremayne."

And he, I thought with a hammering heart, was the authority on witchcraft. Could he name any of the members of the coven as I had just now received a sort of proof that I might be able to do?

"Ah, Miss Tremayne, how do you do? We will see you in church tomorrow, I trust? Take particular care to observe the carvings, they are believed to be unique. Ah, excuse me, ma'am—my wife!"

He turned away to take the arm of a frail but exquisitely beautiful dark lady accompanied by a small excited lad, and led them to a secluded corner away from the trampling horses, just as hounds came round the bend of the road in a tide of white and lemon and tan at the huntsman's heels.

"The carvings," I heard myself saying at random to my aunt. "What is so particular about them?"

She gave me a strange, sidelong look and returned an evasive answer instantly arousing my curiosity, which had to be contained for the moment, as very soon hounds moved off to the first covert and my opportunity to question Mr. Pole-Carter was lost.

The next day, however, dressed elegantly in my new mourning gown, I was able to discover the carvings for myself. Set high in the roof of the old Norman church, they seemed to depict a most pagan selection of gods and devils and wicked men. I sat back in the low-walled pew and stared at them.

"My grandfather had the pew cut down," said Sir Abraham, believing he understood my air of astonishment, "when the bishop discontinued services at All Saints and we came here. Said he wanted to know what was going on about him—no chance of his falling asleep during the sermon, he would time it with an hourglass and the fellow had to ask his permission

212

to close. Not a word under two hours, it had to be in my grandfather's day—and he was happier if it went on for three. Now hear the great bell, Clap Hammer? Not another like it in the county, they say. Oh, the carvings? Pole-Carter says some come here to worship them—but better that than not at all, and one of his seeds might sprout on stony ground, he hopes. Ha!" With an explosive laugh the squire settled back with his chin firmly tucked inside his stock and, unlike his grandsire, fell at once into a gentle sleep.

I watched the choristers during the singing of the first hymn. One particularly took my eye. He was tall and strangely square, square head, square shoulders, as if he had been roughly hewn in stone; but it was more his treatment of the hymnbook that caught my eye, for he kept turning it about. There was but one book between two, and first he held it towards the boy at his side, then turned and studied it for himself for a few bars: but then he seemed furtively to turn the hymnbook upside down. I peeped between my fingers when we knelt in prayer, and sure enough the square-headed chorister was gazing upward, not towards the heavens but rather in the direction of the oaken satyr who leered down at him from the rafter end directly opposite.

I applied myself devoutly to my prayers, and listened with interest to the sermon, which enjoined us to put all our troubles on the shoulders of God, who cared for us; and act as He then directed us. This I would do, I vowed, and feeling my fear and fretting roll away from me, found myself during the next hymn quite calmly reviewing the list that Kitty had made and which Mrs. Slight, I was sure, had deliberately destroyed. I considered it, embellished it, and was even able to add a suggested name or two.

One: Dick Carver—perhaps?

213

Two: Barney Clement.

Three: the cook—Mrs. Chivers (I had not seen or heard of anyone else locally who was so fat).

Four: a tall man—Mark Prendergast.

Five: Mr. Trimble, the foreman of the jury.

Six: another woman—Mrs. Slight.

Seven: the chorister? I must also bear in mind that he was as tall as the captain. Could it have been he who danced with Polly Holford at Candlemas?

Eight: ?

I groped in my mind, feeling sure that I had discovered number eight. A person who stared . . . yes, it was the woman who had sat beside the cook at the coroner's court.

Eight: the lodgekeeper's wife—and now I remembered her name: Mrs. Davies.

Nine: Thompson the frightened coachman?

And four more—unknown.

I shivered, prayed, and found the congregation was streaming out into the brittle sunshine of a frosty noon.

"A capital run, yesterday," I heard Sir Abraham saying to another weather-beaten gentleman as he bent to set his gold half-hunter by the churchyard sundial. "Patchy scent—but a five-mile point at the last. Killed the other side of Horsefield in Old Buckley's country. Ay, he was there, shaking his fist at us. Buckler, is it? Dammee, but I've no head for names—and you none for faces, eh, Sir Jeremy?"

"I'll remember a pretty face with the best," leered the large country gentleman to whom he spoke. "I hear your niece is a toothsome morsel—that is the young lady who was in church with you, eh? The one who's something of an heiress, so they say."

A high-pitched laugh interrupted this interesting conversation and I turned my head to see the rabbit-faced young man, whose mother had given me the cut direct when I had met them in the drawing room at Pheasant's.

"By Jove, Sir Jeremy," cried Francis Sinclair-Stewart, "is it true that Miss Tremayne is an heiress? What a take-in for my mama, if so!"

"Eh, who's that? Oh, 'tis you, Sinclair-Stewart. Ay, well, no need for you to cherish hopes—Prendergast will have her in his eye for Mark, no doubt. But why ain't the young fellow with his regiment, eh, Prendergast? What is he doing at home, if he ain't wounded, eh?"

My aunt, who had been conversing with the lovely Mrs. Pole-Carter and her lively son, chose that moment to introduce me, thus saving me from the possible embarrassment of being discovered in the act of listening to what was very plainly not meant for my ears. Then, encouraged by Mrs. Pole-Carter's kindly reception of me, Aunt Margaret presented me to Lord and Lady Mortmain; and at last it was time to step up into the chaise and drive for home.

We were just leaving Lindenfold when we overtook the whole Latchington tribe on their way back to Abbotsford. Mrs. Latchington was leaning on the arm of a man whom I instantly recognized as the square-headed chorister whose odd behaviour had attracted my attention in church. I waved discreetly to the children, but my mind was occupied in trying to remember what Mrs. Latchington had told me of her husband's ways.

"We never know for certain where he is," she had said. "He's one who drinks deep and keeps his own council, is Latchington—not the sort you can dare question . . ."

I was subdued at dinner that afternoon; even the reflection that quite possibly the witches would be unmasked at their sabbat before many hours had passed could not prevent me from turning their possible identities over and over in my mind. The meal seemed endless; there were more dishes than usual, and Madame Beauregard helped herself lavishly from them, tasing each carefully before pronouncing judgment, and giving generously of her advice to my aunt as to how each might be improved. The squire drank heavily in an attempt, no doubt, to fortify himself against what promised to be an extremely cold and difficult evening, while my aunt bore all the signs of being about to succumb to a nervous headache.

"Well, monsieur," cried the squire suddenly. "What do you say to joining us this evening, eh? You've not had much exercise since you've been with us, would not hunt though I promised to mount you on a prime 'un; would not course hares with us, or go ratting. You can ride a horse, I assume— if you call that old rattlebones a horse?"

Rather angrily, Monsieur admitted he could ride.

"We need everyone—everyone who has no connection with the affair, that is," Sir Abraham added with a side glance at his son. "But I'd better lend you a horse. How would you like Thunder, eh?"

"Father!" shrieked Kitty, throwing down her spoon into the syllabub so that it splashed over the tablecloth. "If you do such a—a barbaric thing, I vow I shall never visit you again!"

"Now, now, my dear—'twas merely a jest. You know the horse belongs to Mark. Not but what I think that horse has been maligned," he added, draining his glass. "It pleases the stable boys to give him a reputation he does not quite deserve." He picked up the bottle with a somewhat unsteady hand. "Ay, Thunder can be very captious, 'tis true, but he is not quite unridable, as I have found."

"Father!" said the captain, in a warning tone. The squire

set down the bottle with a careless gesture that sent a ruby stream spreading across the cloth.

"You know I've ridden Thunder, my son. It is no secret, I suppose? Or would you rather have it said that only you have the art to ride him?"

"That was a long time ago," the captain observed evenly.

"D'ye mean he is growing more crabbed in old age? Besides, how do you know when I last rode him?"

Mark stretched out his hand across the table. "No wanton sacrifices, Father, if you please. And no more wine, if I may advise you, for you have work to do tonight."

"Tonight? Oh, ay, 'tis Sunday, to be sure—the sabbat. If I was not forgetting. . . ."

"Really, Father, how could you!" Madame Kitty protested.

He hunched his shoulder and raised the glass to his lips. I glanced at Aunt Margaret expecting to see her annoyed but instead surprised an expression of something like horror on her ravaged face. In a flash I realized that, far from supposing her husband to be attempting to sacrifice himself for his son, she really believed Sir Abraham had ridden Thunder to the church. Did she think he was a witch? Or did she merely suspect him of using the coven as a cloak for his own activities? And was it possible that she feared these activities to include murder?

I stared into my untouched glass of wine. Sir Abraham, I remembered, had no alibi for the time of the murder. Jem had encountered him on the road, quite close to All Saints. He had claimed that he had visited an inn or two after hunting—but hours must have passed since the horn sounded the homeward call. There had been time enough for him to have visited the White Lion, borrowed his son's horse to confuse the trail, and ridden to the church.

217

But it had been the captain upon whom I had fired, I reminded myself. Or was I absolutely sure of that? His father's build was very similar. I shivered and told myself not to be foolish.

"I will retire early, if you will excuse me, ma'am," I said to my aunt.

She started slightly. "Oh, by all means, Tansy, if you wish."

"And I will do the same," said Captain Prendergast, giving me a little conspiratorial smile for the pleasure of embarrassing me, I supposed. "You had better lock my door, Father," he added easily, "so you will know where at least one of your suspects is passing the evening."

"In that case, you had better lock Miss Tremayne's door also," said Madame Beauregard waspishly. "In fact, it will give me great pleasure to do it myself."

"Tansy is not suspected of—of anything," said my aunt quickly.

Her stepdaughter smiled, as one who knew better.

I felt my temper rising but fortunately the butler put a period to the conversation by announcing at that moment that a party of gentlemen had called to see Sir Abraham. These, of course, were the people who had agreed to ride with him to All Saints.

Once in my room, I poked up the fire and sat staring at the flames. In spite of my remarks to Aunt Margaret on the subject, I felt tempted to write to Miss Crofton's grandmother. It would not commit me, merely to make enquiries, I thought. It would take time, too, for my letter to travel to Yorkshire and be answered. It was not an irrevocable step. And yet how strange that I should be so reluctant to take it when one considered my adventures since I had driven into Sussex! One might suppose I positively enjoyed going in danger of my life, living beneath the same roof as a madman, in a locality where witches were a commonplace.

At that appropriate moment, I heard a key turn in the lock of my door.

"Madame!" I cried indignantly, running to beat against the panels. "How dare you! Unlock my door this instant!"

"She has gone, Cousin," cried the captain from the neighbouring room. "Don't distress yourself. I am in like case, but no doubt morning will soon come. Take my advice and compose yourself for sleep."

But I had, I realized, never felt less like sleep. I did not feel like writing my letter either. I paced about the room for a good while, and then took up my post by the window. The moon had just risen and was flooding the sky with light, pouring across the frozen meadows. It was beautiful, but there was no hope of concealment in it. How would the squire evade the sharp eyes of the witches? Where would he hide to ambush them? Who were they? And did the squire really expect or hope to succeed in his plan? These and other more personal thoughts occupied me while the moon rose with amazing speed, and a bank of clouds chased it from the horizon. They began to pass before it, and I gazed entranced at their beauty.

Suddenly a cautious sound attracted my attention. It came, I realized, from the room next door. Slowly, the casement beside mine opened to its fullest extent. I drew back a little behind my closed window. If the captain chose to breathe in the cold night air, it was no business of mine, I thought. But then there were further sounds of movement. What could he be doing? Escaping? But to what—and how? For I had assured myself when he had caught me in his room that it would be impossible to climb down to the ground.

Perhaps he had rope, or a ladder? I took advantage of a passing cloud to have a quick look sideways through my window, and saw the captain in the very act of climbing out —apparently without the help of either. If he dropped, he would surely break a leg if nothing worse, I thought, my hand to my throat. I remembered that he was very possibly a murderer and restrained myself from calling his name and pleading with him to return. A second glance showed me that he was climbing up, not down. The roof, not the ground, appeared to be his objective. A moment later there was a muffled thump above me, another sort of scuffling noise, and silence.

What now? Was he signalling, to warn the witches? Was he escaping in order to help his father? Or was he responding to the call of the moon and oblivious of all else, seeking to ride to join the coven?

Suddenly I knew that I must try to discover some at least of the answers to my questions. If he could climb to the roof and thence to the ground, I might not be able to follow, but at least I could attempt it. Besides, the thought of outwitting Madame Beauregard was too intoxicating to be ignored.

It took me but a moment to find my darkest cloak and to be sure the dagger was in my reticule. Then I opened my casement, gasped at the coldness of the air, and leaned out to look up. The parapet of the house was just above the top of the window, no very difficult feat to ascend to it, I thought, if only I could forget the drop that lay below me.

I shook the central pillar of the window and found it firm. I stood up cautiously upon the sill and a moment later had my other hand upon the parapet. Then I put my foot on the top of one of the casements, and pulled myself up.

I landed on my knees, huddled against the slope of the slate roof. I looked quickly about me, but luckily there was no sign of the captain, apart from the darker marks on the frosty whiteness of the slates where he had stepped. I followed his footprints cautiously, for the slates were slippery and the parapet low. I reached the corner, and looked down the slope of an outbuilding to the gutter, where I saw the dark bulk of the captain crouching. A moment later he jumped boldly down. There was a crash as a slate fell with him, dislodged by his boot, and I held my breath. On such a windless night, who would hear a slate fall from the roof without wondering as to the cause? But nothing happened. Perhaps, if anyone had heard it, they supposed it to be a cat.

The captain, reassured, no doubt, that the alarm had not been given, began to move across the yard below. I took a resolute breath and lowered my feet, in their inadequate slippers, to the steep slope of the little roof below. There came a moment when I was obliged to let go of the parapet, but I could not bring myself to do so. I might have been hanging there still if my fingers, gloved though they were, had not grown numb and betrayed me. Suddenly I was falling, sliding helplessly, then my feet caught in the gutter and I came abruptly to a halt, spread across the cold slope of the slates, which dampened me unpleasantly as the hoar frost melted beneath my body. I dared to twist my head in order to look again below me and saw with gratitude a rain barrel with a lid. The rest of the descent was easy, though I spared a brief thought to wonder how in the world I should return. Then I pushed aside that consideration and hastened to follow the dark trail the captain had left across the cobblestones. It led me round the corner of the stables and continued the length of the verge beside the kitchen garden wall, looking like tarnish on the silver grass, before leading on, into the wood.

Unfortunately the moon, which had been brightly lighting my way, now slid into a dark mass of cloud, leaving me palpitating on the edge of the trees. Should I go on? But I had not much alternative, I thought ruefully, moving forward again, for to stand still was surely to freeze. But where did this path lead, under the dark trees? It was in the opposite direction from All Saints. All the more reason then, I told myself, to follow it and discover if I could what motive prompted the captain to take it. This might be my only chance to discover whether he was good or bad, or somewhere between. That this was vastly important to me there could be no question. Besides, it was a matter of self-preservation—a matter, one might even say, of life and death.

I tripped over a root and returned rather painfully to reality. The moonlight had contrived to struggle through the cloud, but it was not strong and the trees cast a shadow. All at once I realized I was deep into the wood and there was no sign of the captain. The path I trod was mud, frozen like iron, and held no footprint. I could hear no sound beyond the usual ones of a wood at night that I remembered from my country childhood. I was suddenly very much afraid. Not only had I lost the captain, but I was lost myself.

I began to hurry on, hoping that each turn would show him some way ahead, but it did not, and again I had to suppress a strong desire to call him by his name. To feel his hand on mine, even though his words scathed me, would be comforting indeed. But there was no sign of the captain as I blundered on.

Suddenly my path was obstructed by a crumbling stone wall. I leaned against it, recovering my breath. Then, examining it as closely as I could, I discovered a pale scrape that looked newly made. Mark Prendergast had climbed it, I surmised; and I, therefore, would have to do the same.

It was not hard. Projecting stones made steps in the wall,

though I nearly turned my ankle on a fallen boulder when I jumped down the other side. Recovering myself, I made the unwelcome discovery that it was decidedly darker on this far side of the wall where the trees had a greater proportion of evergreens among them and grew far more thickly. I forced myself onward, reminding myself that there had not, so far as I knew, been any choice of path. Soon, surely, I must catch up with Captain Prendergast.

At just that moment I thought I heard the unmistakable chink of stone on stone as if someone had kicked a pebble out of his way. I hurried on, and stopped abruptly as I saw a figure ahead of me, walking slowly, with bent head.

Then as the moon slid out again from behind the cloud, my blood seemed to run cold. The man before me wore a long black garment that covered him completely, and his head was hooded by a slitted mask.

FOURTEEN

Instinctively, it seemed, I had stepped off the path and crouched with thundering heart in the frail protection of a thicket. Ahead of me the hooded figure moved slowly forward until it merged into the trees.

I stared after it, straining my eyes; and then the air became luminously bright and the moon slid out of the clouds, deepening the shadows but illuminating a glade a little way ahead and a huddled stone building that seemed familiar—the chapel, I suddenly realized, of Abbot's Grove.

A stick cracked sharply, and I sank into immobility, hardly daring even to breathe.

A high-pitched laugh sounded close behind me.

"Ha-ha! Oh, I say! But I'll wager to have her with us by then. Gives it a spice, don't it, to consider she's the sister—"

The voice hushed. I glanced up to see a flash of a gold ring in the moonlight only a yard from my startled eyes, as its owner's hand fell in remonstration upon the arm of—could it be Francis Sinclair-Stewart? Oh yes, that high-pitched giggling laugh—I would know it anywhere. And the ring, too, a curious ring of plaited gold on a swollen red hand—never would I forget that ring which once had even touched my skin as Mrs. George had dragged the kerchief from my neck in Hallchurch Gaol.

Number ten: I thought, seeing as if it lay before me in the moonlight the list which had been burnt—Number ten: Francis Sinclair-Stewart.

Number eleven: Mrs. George, whom her husband had re-admitted to the jail only a few minutes before my own arrival there, at Candlemas.

They passed on quietly down the path and disappeared under the pointed arch of the chapel door. Other hooded figures entered the glade from another track and joined them. This, then, was the new meeting place of the witches of All Saints—and Mark Prendergast was one of them.

I was cold, cold, and I did not know what to do.

Wait for the moment, yes—I had no choice in that. But once all were gathered in the chapel, what then? Tiptoe to the narrow window as I had begun to do that other time, at Candlemas, and peer within so that I might bear witness to what I saw? But this time the risk would be far greater, for there was no fog to cloak me if I were seen.

I ought really to fetch Lord Knevett, I reflected, but I found myself curiously reluctant to do so. It would be such an ordeal trying to explain matters to his apprehensive butler —a worse ordeal trying to evade him, tiptoeing through that mausoleum of a house, playing hide and seek with the mad Lady Knevett, and in the end being obliged to inform his lordship that what he feared and hated most was here on his own doorstep, in the chapel of which he was so proud.

No, I decided, I could not bring myself to attempt it. I must return to Pheasant's and send a servant from there to All

Saints to recall the squire and his men. But even that, I realized as I glanced over my shoulder, would be far from easy. The wood looked so dark behind me, even laced through with moonlight, how could I retrace my steps along the path alone, knowing that at any moment I might run into the unwelcoming arms of still another hooded figure? Yet I could not wait here forever. I must move, and soon.

There had been no new arrivals for a while. I stood up cautiously and looked all around. Everything was calm and still. Down to my right was a pale line that must be the carriageway to the house, I thought. It would not be so bad if I were to make my way to it, and return to Pheasant's by the road. The witches themselves, I reasoned, would hardly approach the chapel so openly; and I was beginning to step cautiously through the trees when a flying clatter of hooves sent me into hiding again. A man rode past me so close that a fleck of foam fell on my cheek, flung from his horse's bit. The man rode easily, his black cloak flying behind him, the hood fallen back on his shoulders so that I could see the glint of moonlight on his hair—red hair, I thought, again reviewing Kitty's list.

Number twelve: Mr. Brent—the groom at the White Lion.

I shivered violently, found I was again alone, and made my way towards the drive. I glanced to the right and saw it empty. To my left I could see one wing of the house, dark except for a single light moving from window to window. Could it be Lord Knevett, restless with the intuitive awareness of mischief on his doorstep? Or the chaplain, searching for some lost paper down the long corridors? Or Lady Knevett, seeking a snug roosting place for the night? Whoever it was, with a light in their hand they would not be able to see me out here in the moonlight; but I stepped a little faster over the smooth gravel of the drive. It seemed far longer now

I was on foot than it had done in the carriage, I reflected; but surely another turn would bring me to the gate.

At that moment I sensed rather than saw some movement before me. Again, without pausing to think, I found I had plunged into the nearest hiding-place, in this instance an exotic clump of rhododendrons beneath whose glossy leaves a small army might have hid. The person coming from the road became fully visible for just one moment before he too turned off into the bushes, on the other side of the drive. I pressed my hand against my heart. Was I mistaken, or had that hooded figure a hunched shoulder, a head held awry? But I knew Barney Clement was a witch, so why should the sight of him just then have shocked me? Perhaps, I answered myself, because it meant that not all were yet gathered at the chapel, and I might still run into the arms of one of them.

After Barney had passed, all was quiet, however. A few minutes later I forced myself to leave my hiding-place and moved on towards the gates. These, as I had expected, stood open. Indeed, they were so rusty I supposed they would fall if they were moved. I slipped between them and turned with a sense of vast relief on to the road. Only then did I remember that I had the ford to cross. Would it be ice-covered, or would the running stream have kept it open, obliging me to wade through icy water? At least it was moonlight, I comforted myself. I would not blunder into it unexpectedly.

I stopped suddenly, peering at a patch of darkness under the park wall a little way ahead. What could it be? It was too large for a sack, or a dead dog, though it lay still enough for either. It lay, inert, roughly bundled in a black cloth, for all the world, I thought, forcing myself onward, as if one of the witches of All Saints had come by his deserts. And then, as I drew closer, I realized that that was precisely what it was.

I stood still. What should I do now? If I had a rope I could bind the body and summon the authorities—but I had no rope. Should I try to ascertain whether the witch was dead or merely disabled? Should I risk leaving it there while I hurried home for help?

It was with relief that I became aware of the ringing of hooves on the frozen road, the rumble of approaching carriage wheels. Here, like the answer to a prayer, was the help I needed; and I turned with outstretched arms to stop the oncoming coach without a thought that I might be shot as a footpad.

"Lawks!" cried the postilion, reining in. "If it bain't the young m-miss!"

I gasped, recognizing Thompson, my uncle's nervous coachman, but before I could reply the window was abruptly dropped and my aunt pushed out her head.

"Tansy!" she cried. "My God, what are you doing there? And what is that, in Heaven's name?"

"Oh, ma'am—" I faltered, "please take me in, I will tell you all—"

"Is it—a body?"

"It is—I think it is—a witch!"

"Yes, I see the hood—but what devil's work is this? Thompson, get down directly and see if—that—is dead."

With extreme reluctance, he obeyed her, and thrust the reins into my resistant hands. He approached the body and bent over it, plainly prepared to spring away if it should turn out to be a trap set for an honest fellow. But the body did not stir, and he reached out to drag off the masking hood.

His shout made us all start, and for an instant I nearly lost control of the horses. Then my aunt was scrambling from the carriage. "The captain?" she cried out. "Good God, it *is* Mark, I do believe! Is—is he—dead?"

She bent over him while I found myself drawing in great

breaths of frosty air which perhaps were sobs, while I clung to the leather reins as if to a lifeline.

"He breathes—thank God!"

"Ay, my lady, but that's a terrible blow he has taken on the head, see there—that's more than a stick did that—more like an iron bar, I'm thinking."

"We must get him in the chaise, Thompson—get him home. Did he stir then?"

"Ay, he's beginning to rouse, my lady. B-best to move him soon, I'm thinking, before he comes to."

"But even between us—can we lift him?"

"Take the horses, Aunt, and let me help," I begged her. "I must be stronger than you."

A moment later the postilion was raising the captain by his shoulders while I bent to lift his booted legs. He groaned horribly, and I almost dropped him. Then his head fell back limply and we struggled with him to the carriage. Raising him into it was more difficult and Thompson had to loop the reins over his arm and enlist the help of Aunt Margaret before we were able to accomplish it, and then it was extremely difficult for us to fit ourselves into the chaise as well. I found myself crushed into a corner with Mark Prendergast swooning in my arms, his bleeding head against my shoulder; and could not forbear thinking it might have been more convenient had our positions been reversed.

"In God's name, Tansy," said my aunt in a trembling voice, "what were you doing here?"

I stared at the pale blur of her face in the carriage light. Did she think I was a witch? But perhaps it was not surprising in view of the circumstances in which I had first been discovered in this district. But, come to that, what was she doing, driving out at night, and on such a night as this?

"Answer me, girl," she said more sharply.

"My answer may not please you, ma'am. I began by following—the captain when I heard him escaping from his room."

"But Kitty locked you in—she boasted of it to me—"

"Mark Prendergast takes no account of locks, and I followed his lead—up to the roof and down by some outhouse. He went through the wood. Suddenly I found I had stumbled upon another witches' sabbat. They met tonight after all—not at All Saints, but at the chapel of Abbot's Grove."

"And Mark?" she breathed. "What did he there?"

"What can one suppose, but that he was one of them?" I murmured, looking down at the dark cloak on which his own bloodstains were now mingled, I supposed, with those of Polly Holford.

"You did not—hit him on the head?" she asked nervously.

"I, ma'am? No, indeed."

"But you were there together—when we found you. It seems rather strange—"

"Strange! It is like a nightmare. I followed him through the wood—God knows how I found the courage—or the foolishness, to do so—and then to see the others—"

"What others?" she cried sharply.

"Why, the witches, ma'am—I told you—"

"But did you recognize them?"

"No, how could I? They were hooded. . . ." I shivered, thinking of Barney, and the captain groaned in my arms as my convulsion shook him. I looked down on as much as I could see of him. "Do you think he was robbed?" I wondered aloud. "Do you have footpads in these parts?" I added, thinking that perhaps my years in London had made me too aware of thieves.

"What part does not?" she returned. "See if he still has his purse. He carries it in the left inner pocket, as I recall."

I slipped my hand into the warmth of his coat, and immediately felt the bulk of a purse through the satin lining. Before I could withdraw my hand, one of his had joined it.

"Robbing me, are you?" he demanded thickly, as if he were drunk. "Wait till I am myself, and you can have it all—adventuress. Oh God, my head."

I lifted my other hand to his forehead, which felt hot unless it was just that my gloves were thin and my hand cold.

"Ah, yes," he murmured. "Take off your glove . . ."

"Were you looking for me, ma'am?" I asked quickly to distract my aunt from the strangely caressing tone of the captain's voice.

"I, looking?" she repeated blankly. "Oh. Yes, of course, I was dreadfully anxious. Never do such a thing again!"

She had not been looking for me, I realized with a chill. What then had she been doing? Riding to join the witches' revel? She must trust her postilion rather more than was customary if that were so, but then, I remembered, he was probably a witch himself.

Aunt Margaret put out her hand towards me. Quite involuntarily, I shrank away from it. She caught her breath. "Tansy, you know—or have you guessed—?"

"No, no," I babbled, "I know nothing—have guessed nothing—how could I, indeed?"

"Calm yourself, love," commanded the captain in a firmer voice. "Stepmama, don't tease my bride."

"Mark," she said quickly, "are you awake? Can you tell us—did you follow Tansy, or—"

"I followed him," I said indignantly. "I told you so!"

"You followed me?" he repeated. "How flattering . . . how suitable. And where did I lead you, may I ask?"

"To the chapel at Abbot's Grove," I replied in a low voice.

"Did I so? I should not have led you there. And then, what happened?"

I shook my head, and then remembered that he could not see it. "I do not know. I thought I saw Barney Clement . . . at all events, someone or something, hit you on the head."

"Yes, and damnably hard, by the feel of it."

"It is—a horrid wound. You had better lie still. We will soon be home."

He gave a grunt that might have been a laugh. "How gentle you sound. I believe you have a soft heart after all. It seems a long time since anyone worried over me. Even my dear stepmother has other matters on her mind just now, I believe—"

I slipped my gloved hand over his mouth, hardly knowing why but feeling he should not be allowed to talk until his head was clear.

"He sounds quite tender," said my aunt sharply. "Might it come to a match between you, after all?"

I gasped. "We are hardly in a position to be thinking of the future, when the present is in such a tangle," I replied, recovering myself.

"But—you are not averse to him, I think?"

"To your stepson, ma'am? Why, if he were ordinarily pleasant to me I might contrive to be civil to him, but so long as he behaves as if he hates me—"

"But I don't want you to be civil to me," protested the captain freeing himself from my restraining grasp. "Civility is damnably dull."

"We are here," declared my aunt, looking through the window. "And—oh, God, Abraham is waiting for us! The hood— Oh, it is in my reticule. And the domino—get it under the cushions before he sees it."

She half-fell out of the chaise into her husband's arms. He tersely demanded an explanation of her.

232

"I found Tansy was out of her room, her bed not slept in—I had to look for her, you must own that, Abraham—"

"Yes, yes—but did you find her? Good God!" he added as I opened the door on my side, having blindly followed my aunt's instructions. "And who is that—Mark, as I live!"

"Yes, Father. I have been making love to Tansy as you see, but my stepmama was there to chaperon us—"

"What foolery is this? Mark, you are hurt!"

The story was soon pieced together, so far as it went, the captain maintaining he had been attacked while enjoying an evening stroll. My aunt cut short the interrogation and ordered the captain to be helped to his room and the doctor sent for. Meanwhile Sir Abraham explained that he had left a few men at All Saints, but was himself convinced the witches had met elsewhere and this was why he had ridden home in case further information had been sent for him.

I waited for Aunt Margaret to mention Abbot's Grove but instead she said, with a side glance at me, "I wonder where the witches met—or if indeed, they met at all?" and it immediately became impossible for me to divulge my evidence. She turned away, and a moment later the squire became aware of an obvious gap in the explanations he had heard.

"But you, miss," he demanded turning at the foot of the stairs to confront me. "What the Devil were you about, eh, to be wandering abroad at this time of night—and on such a night?"

I stared at him, my mind a blank. How could I say that I had been following his son? It was such a wild improbable tale, and for reasons of her own my aunt had indicated that she did not want the truth to come out.

"I—I—well, sir, the fact of the matter is—" I paused, waiting for inspiration. My aunt had gone upstairs after the captain. She could not assist me. I cleared my throat and looked helplessly around.

"Answer me, girl!" insisted the squire. His face was flushed with drink and rage; he looked quite capable of shaking some sort of reply out of me.

Deliverance came from an unsuspected quarter.

"Aha!" cried a triumphant voice from above. "So Miss has been making her rendezvous again, has she? Such a fine moonlight night—but you don't ask for Madame to accompany you again, I see."

"A rendezvous?" repeated Sir Abraham, stupefied. "I did not think this of you, Miss—Miss Tansy, dammee if I did! Sneaking out of the house like a—a scullery maid! Who were you meeting, then?"

I swallowed, and shook my head.

"Aha!" said Beauregard again, like a mischievous Puck. "Who else was out tonight, eh? Ask yourself that, monsieur!"

"Mark? Good God, girl, was it Mark you met in the wood?"

"Well, sir—it is true I—I did see him there, but—"

"You and Mark!" Slowly his anger subsided. "Well, well— but you need not go out of the house to speak to my son, you know. And he should not have encouraged you to do such a thing. H'm. I'll have a word with him in the morning, when he's better fit for it, the young jackanapes. As for you, Beauregard—well, I'm obliged to you for your suggestions, sir, but I'll thank you not to speak of what you have just heard."

The Frenchman assured him that he was the soul of tact and discretion, bowed to me and disappeared. The squire grunted a good night to us both and went upstairs. I unclasped my trembling hands and followed him, my mind still busy with Aunt Margaret's motives.

Was she protecting herself or Mark? I wondered, but when I reached my room I thought I had discovered the answer to my question, for the key was gone from the lock, and I could not open my door. Aunt Margaret had not discovered I was out of my oom before she set off for her drive, for she could not have entered it.

Wearily I turned to go to my old room where Kitty slept. Fortunately she was alone, snoring on her back; but she woke abruptly and sat up, the moonlight slanting through the curtains across her pale face.

"Lord, you frightened me, girl. What is it?" Her tone sharpened. "What are you doing out of your room? I locked you in."

"You have not unlocked the door since, or given another the key?"

"I have it here under my pillow," she said, pulling it out and looking at it briefly. "Why should I let you out? But how come you here? What witchcraft is this?" She was not afraid, but spoke sneeringly.

I sighed. "Please may I have the key? For I am now locked out."

"If you could escape, you may return by the same means," she informed me, smiling unkindly as she swung the key upon her finger.

"You are mistaken, ma'am," I told her, coming to the end of my patience and leaning forward to snatch the key away from her, "for I have broken my broomstick."

I left the room to her gasps of indignation, but she did not follow me and I was secure at least in the knowledge that Aunt Margaret would be on my side in the matter when it was referred to her in the morning.

As it happened, Kitty pretended at breakfast that she had slept through all the excitements of the night. She demanded explanations of her father, and professed herself unsatisfied with those she received. I was not altogether surprised to find that Aunt Margaret was confined to her room with another migraine, and was about to visit her when Barclay ushered in a visitor, causing me to pause on the stairs.

It was Lord Knevett.

"Ah, Miss Tremayne," he said, on seeing me. "The very person. What is this I hear of Mark's accident? Can you spare me a moment? I would rather not distress Sir Abraham by obliging him to go over it all again."

"No, very considerate of you, sir. I will come down."

He looked attentively at me as I stepped off the stairs and I felt myself blushing as I led him into the bookroom. It was not proper of me to receive him there alone, no doubt, but we seemed to have gone rather beyond such considerations since I came to Pheasant's, I reflected.

Lord Knevett closed the door behind us. There was a fire lit, I noticed gratefully. I crossed to it and warmed my hands at the blaze.

"Well, Miss Tremayne, is it true that Mark was hit over the head and left for dead not a stone's throw from my lodge last night?"

"I fear it is, sir."

"Who found him, do you know? I would like to question that person."

I turned, smiling a little. "You may do so conveniently, sir, for it was I."

"You!" He seemed thunderstruck. He strode forward and took my hands. "You found him? But how can this be?"

"It is hard to believe, no doubt—but the truth, nonetheless. The captain and I stayed in the house last night when Sir Abraham rode off to lie in wait for his coven—and when the captain left his room, I am sorry to say I was so officious as to follow him—secretly, of course."

"You—followed him?" repeated the baron in a stunned

voice. "My dear Miss Tremayne, you really should not take such risks."

"Oh, never mind that!" I cried, and wished I had not when I saw that I had shocked him by brushing aside so lightly his concern. "You are wanting to hear about last night—and I have a good deal to tell you, so let us get on before we are interrupted. Captain Prendergast left this house and took a path into the woods. I followed him at a distance—"

"Those woods to the west? Into my land?"

"Yes sir, we trespassed—but were not alone in so doing, I fear."

"What can you mean? Pray don't tease me, Miss Tremayne, but tell me what you saw. What occurred?"

"Well, sir—can you keep a secret?"

His dark eyes widened slightly. "Indeed I can," he said stiffly. "What secret is this?"

I put a hand on his arm. "It will come as a shock to you, I know, for I remember you have a peculiar horror of such things; but last night your chapel was used as a meeting place by the witches, while All Saints was guarded by the squire."

"The witches! By God, miss, you speak of this very coolly."

"I was not very cool at the time, I assure you."

"No, but—to follow a man in the dark—a man moreover who is under suspicion of murder! To find he is on his way to a meeting of witches! To—well, I don't know what you did then, but you did not do the one thing you should have done, namely to spread the alarm, let me know of it, give me a chance to rouse out my people—"

He sounded rather violent and I judged it time to interrupt him. "I would have done so but, bold as you think me—"

"Bold, ay—you are too bold. I fear I must have been mistaken in you—"

But I could not allow him to think that.

"I was frightened out of my wits," I assured him. "That is why I dared not go to your house. I could only think of getting home, to safety."

He stared at me. "Well, continue," he commanded, after a moment.

"Yes," I faltered, rather disconcerted by his tone. "Well, I got out on to the drive—"

"What did you see before that, by the chapel?"

I looked away. "Very little, I fear. Only hooded forms, black dominoes. I waited until it seemed there were no more coming, and then I crept out on to the drive and so to the road. There, a little way from the gate, I thought I saw Barney Clement coming from the road. I went out on to it and turned for home. Then I saw—a body."

"How far along?"

"Oh, I fear I am no judge of distance. About the length of this house from your gate, perhaps, or a little more—there I saw—someone lying by the wall. I did not know it was the captain, of course. Just another person in a hood and domino—"

He caught my wrists, his black eyes glittering. "A hood, you say? Do you know what this means?"

I shook my head. "Not really, sir. Was he one of the witches, or merely spying on them again? And then my aunt arrived on the scene a moment later in the chaise, with Thompson at the reins."

"Lady Prendergast was there?" His face drew into lines even more stern. "I did not know that. Ah, God, what a coil."

"She was looking for me," I said hastily.

"I see, but you—why did you risk yourself like that? It

238

might have been you lying there with a head wound. How could you follow your cousin as you did?"

I sighed. "I assure you, I wish I had not. Except that the postilion might not have noticed the captain, and I suppose then he might have lain out all night and died. But I felt I had to go. It is so desperately important to find out the truth and clear the innocent. As one who has been unjustly under suspicion, I know how important that is. The hangman waits . . . but he must not have the wrong person on his rope in the end."

Lord Knevett gripped me by the shoulders and stared into my eyes as if into a well of truth. "Whom do you suspect, Miss Tansy? By now you must have formed some opinion, however impartial you have striven to be? And it might be best if you shared your opinion with me."

"Oh, we have discussed it before—and it makes me feel so disloyal even to—"

"We have gone beyond such feelings, admirable as they may be."

"Perhaps you are right. The captain, then, must be suspect." I hesitated, but felt impelled to add, "But there is also my aunt. Oh, I know it seems impossible to doubt her, but I do not really think she was looking for me last night, as she pretended. And then Sir Abraham, if he was closer to Polly than he owns, might had had a motive. A case could even be made out against Holford, her father. Even you, sir, if the evidence of your friend cannot be called upon in court. Anyone who cannot account satisfactorily for that vital hour must be suspected."

"But I asked whom *you* suspected, ma'am. Does nothing seem to point, in your opinion, rather to one person than another?"

239

I turned away from him and went to the window. "I found a bloodstained dagger in this very room. I also found a bloodstained domino in the captain's bedchamber."

"Good God. That is serious, indeed. But how came you to venture there?"

Reluctantly, I told him what had occurred.

He did not this time reproach me for my boldness, though I thought it implied in the way he looked at me. He said merely, "Have you told the squire?"

"No, sir. What would be the object, indeed?"

"I think he should know of it." As if to himself, Lord Knevett added, "After this, he will have to stand down from the case. I wonder indeed, why he has not already done so."

"Because to stand down would have looked as though he was convinced that his son—" I broke off, the blood pounding in my cheeks as I stared at the baron.

The net was closing fast about Mark Prendergast as even his father would now have to own—and the final irony was that I could not bear to contemplate it.

With no word of apology to my visitor, I turned and stumbled from the room.

FIFTEEN

All that day it was extremely cold. I sat by the fire, stitching on my aunt's command at slippers for a man who would probably never wear them, while the doctor came to visit the captain, and shook his head and left again. Monsieur Beauregard tiptoed about and said that he had known sad cases of delayed concussion; at which point Captain Prendergast confounded him by appearing in the doorway, bandaged and pale but otherwise in apparent possession of all his faculties.

"So!" cried Monsieur. "You wish to speak with Miss—I understand! See—I go!"

He did, and the captain stared grimly at me, while I hid my sewing behind my back.

"You are the most foolish girl I have ever known," my cousin remarked bluntly. "I have got up to warn you—but I daresay you won't heed my warning—"

"No, sir—I fear I won't. And now you must excuse me. Through no fault of my own, your father was given the wrong impression last night, and I don't wish to encourage

241

everyone to suppose that—well, you heard Monsieur Beauregard just now—"

I faltered to a stop, and rose determinedly.

"Very wise," said the captain, tight-lipped. "I would be glad to think you would not let yourself be alone with anyone of the opposite sex at any time."

I stared at him. "Perhaps you are right. At all events, I am now going to my aunt."

I marched past him, and failing to discover Aunt Margaret at once, was obliged to spend the rest of the afternoon with Kitty, who was in a petulant mood, teasing her husband to distraction and vowing to go skating on the morrow if the frost continued.

Sure enough, there was a severe frost in the night and the following day dawned clear and bright. Work being impossible in the fields, everyone seemed to have gathered in the frozen meadows to make holiday and about the middle of the morning we went out in a party from Pheasant's to join them.

It was, as I was delighted to find, a sufficiently distracting scene. The clear air glittered with frost and fire, the ground was flint hard, the grass blades silver and crisp underfoot, trees blackly outlined against a sky of palest blue. To breathe was a cold pain that dissolved in the amusement of exhaling what appeared to be clouds. Cheerful voices rang almost echoing from the hard ground, the smooth black ice. The smell of roasting chestnuts, hoarded since autumn, drifted with the stinging smoke of the bright fires. The flooded meadows, armoured in ice, were alive with movement, as colourful and detailed as a painting of the Flemish school. It seemed as if all the villagers of Abbotsgate and the neighbouring hamlets were there, sliding and skating, warming their hands at great leaping fires, tumbling and falling, laughing and shouting, and behaving in general as if murder meant no more to them than a word read in a book long ago.

I hesitated on the brink, wobbling on thin varnished yellow blades which had been laced to my boots by Mitchell, who had discovered them in the attic together with the sable-lined cloak and muff which my aunt had kindly insisted on my wearing. I was wondering not only how one began to skate, but also where to go, so many people could I see whom I wished with cowardly fervour to avoid. There was the squire who, twenty-four hours after my conversation with Lord Knevett, had still not officially disassociated himself from the case. He stood, his face purple in the bitter wind, slapping his hands against his folded arms and stamping his feet as he talked to Carver the constable. There was Maggie Smith in the same black coat which I had worn to go to prison. There was the constable's brother, hunched over his flute; and though the airs he played were unexceptional, "Rule Brittania" and the like, the sound of that thin haunting music made me shiver. I could see young Jem skating clumsily but at great speed, causing more timorous folk to shriek and cling together as he hurtled past them; I could even see Mrs. George taking a holiday from jail-keeping, warming her red hands over an apronful of hot chestnuts.

My dilemma was resolved by Lord Knevett halting before me in a spray of ice cut from the surface by his skates.

"Come, let me instruct you," he commanded, his eyes shining with a glitter of excitement I had not previously observed in them.

"I have never skated before."

"That is evident. Put your hands in mine."

I did so, and he gripped them firmly. He began to skate backwards and I found myself gliding along as easily as if I had been in a dream. I could not take my eyes from his, fearing to fall if I were released from the spell. My cheeks glowed in the rush of cold air, my heart beat fast under the influence of this new excitement. Lord Knevett fascinated me; he was like some Russian prince in his fur hat, his fur-caped coat; and his dark eyes that admired without worshipping me were part of the magic which kept me ensnared for the very reason, I supposed, that the baron withheld so much of himself from me.

And then the spell was broken. Lord Knevett looked over my shoulder and his face grew, not hard, but remote. His grip slackened on my hands and I realized my feet and ankles were aching. The smooth movement, from being a delight, became an agony. I caught my breath and that hurt too as the icy air stabbed down into my lungs.

Lord Knevett glanced at me. "You are tired," he said curtly. "You had better rest here, by this tree. Just hold on to one of the branches."

He twisted his hands free from my clinging, helpless grip, and was gone, swooping expertly across the frozen meadow like a great dark bird, while I staggered and clutched at the frail willow boughs.

Other hands caught and steadied me, holding me firmly from behind. I turned my head to see that Captain Prendergast stood there, risen all too soon from his sick bed, and capped not in fur, but in bandages.

"Thank you, sir," I said, as coldly as I could. "But I am perfectly capable—"

His hands dropped abruptly, and I tottered. "Please!" I cried involuntarily, and with a triumphant laugh he drew me close and lowered me to a fallen log that lay half-submerged beneath the tree. I glared at him angrily; undeterred, he sat down beside me and lifting my foot began to rub it.

"I know how it feels," he said. "I used to do the same for Kitty and Elizabeth—and just look at Kitty now."

Diverted, I gazed across the meadows and saw his sister, forgetful of her condition, executing practiced figures. A man skating unsteadily by caught at her hands and they began to waltz together.

"Francis," murmured the captain. "I hope he does not mean to trip her. Perhaps I had better warn him . . . he is such a joker."

He stood up, and looked down at me again. "Are you quite comfortable, Cousin? If you will stay there a moment I will fetch you some chestnuts—or soup, if you prefer it."

I stared, suspicious of his uncharacteristic civility. "I want for nothing. But pray don't let me detain you, sir."

He smiled again, with infuriating warmth. If I had just met him, I reflected in annoyance, how charming I should have thought him!

"No, Cousin Tansy, I shan't let you do that," he said easily, putting me in my place. "I am sure Knevett will look after you—when he has concluded his conversation with my stepmother. Ah, no," he added quickly. "I see he is now with Miss Crofton—but I daresay he will not be long."

The captain bowed, and moved away with strong, firm glides, not gracefully like Lord Knevett, though it was equally impossible to imagine him falling. As for the baron, I saw that Captain Prendergast had been right. He was a little away from the main press of people, conversing with the nervous spinster. It was kind of him, I thought, for few would have taken the trouble to seek her out deliberately. A moment later he had turned away and I saw him speak to a pretty, fair girl, plainly dressed in a grey stuff gown half-covered by a black cloak. Then he turned quickly, caught me staring at him, waved a hand to acknowledge me, and approached rapidly to draw up in front of me before the blush had time to fade from my cheeks.

"How charming you look, sitting there—waiting so patiently for me," he said, smiling.

"Captain Prendergast suggested I should sit on this log," I explained. I was interested and gratified to observe a flash of anger distort his features.

"Indeed?" He loomed over me, and I felt a shiver of anticipation of—I knew not what. "Let me advise you, Miss Tremayne, to have nothing to do with that fellow."

"Why, sir, I should find your advice difficult to take, since Captain Prendergast and I reside beneath the same roof."

"A damnable situation." He frowned at me, and I was aware of that same delicious shiver. "I wonder now," he said slowly. "I wonder if it could not be arranged . . ."

He paused reflectively, and the silence lengthened. "What arrangement are you considering, sir?" I asked daringly, at last.

"You have a kind heart, Miss Tansy, I am sure. What would you think of coming to live at Abbot's Grove?"

My heart seemed to stop beating. What was he proposing? And should I like it if it were what I had hoped for? He fascinated me, I melted in his arms and longed for a closer acquaintance with him; but did I know him well enough for more, was I ready to advance our relationship, would that air of mystery which presently intrigued me survive our meeting at the breakfast table or even more intimate circumstances? Or would his tremendous presence, the state in which he lived, the grandeur of his house, to say nothing of the madness of his mother, unendurably overwhelm me?

I said faintly, "It is kind of you to suggest it . . ."

246

He caught his breath. "Ah! Then you will consider it?"

Inexplicably, I shrank away. "Aunt Margaret would not like—no, I fear I can't—" I broke off, finding I was not bold enough to ask him his intentions in so many words.

He knelt on the frosty grass and took my hand. I felt extremely confused; but after all the state of my heart was not then to be examined.

"I was going to ask if you would come to Abbot's Grove to be a companion to my mother—ostensibly, that is." He gazed deeply into my eyes. "You don't flinch from the notion," he observed in a low voice.

"No, indeed," I said quickly, longing to know quite what notion it was that he really had in mind, bending in embarrassment to unlace my skates.

He rose. "In that case I shall ask you again some other time, perhaps. And after all, Prendergast will soon be returning to the wars."

I said slowly, "But—how can he? Matters being as they are, I mean."

Lord Knevett shrugged. "It would be worth leaving the mystery unresolved, in order to be rid of him—or so I feel at this present time." He stared at me again, and I moved uneasily, searching about for a subject to distract him.

"Who was that young lady you were talking to just now?" I asked at random. "The pretty one, in the black cloak? She is skating now with Mr. Sinclair-Stewart."

"Ah! Were you jealous of her? There is no need to be. She is only Holford's daughter, sister of the one who was killed."

"Oh, poor girl."

The sister, I reflected. Francis had spoken of "the sister." Could it be this girl to whom he had referred? Then I recalled that it was Miss Holford who had confirmed Jem's evidence that her sister had met the captain, and I decided to make an opportunity to talk with her alone.

My chance came presently when Lord Knevett was claimed by Mr. Sinclair-Stewart to participate in an attempt to drive the latter's gig across the ice. I left the warmth of the bonfires by which I had been standing and approached the girl, who was now standing by herself staring rather wistfully at the reckless charioteers.

Peggy Holford was more sandy-haired than blond, I found, on closer inspection. Her pink skin was lightly freckled, and her face sharper than Polly's had been. She turned to me, her yellow-green eyes suspicious, as I spoke her name.

"Ay, that's me. And whom do I have the pleasure—?"

Her natural rustic charm had been ruthlessly veneered by the refined manners of the genteel school to which her parents had no doubt proudly sent her.

"My name is Tremayne—"

There was no need to introduce myself further. The colour came and went in Miss Holford's face. "Ay, I've heard of you. What do you want with me?" Plainly she distrusted me. At best, if she did not believe me responsible for murdering her sister, I reminded her of that wretched time. I looked at her more closely, wondering if she had been involved herself. Knowing little of witches, yet I did not think she could be one.

Her face was plainer than her sister's and her eyes were wary. She looked a little greedy, I decided, and somewhat unformed—innocent, no doubt, but perhaps she had not been seriously tempted yet. I thought of Francis Sinclair-Stewart and shivered for her.

I said quietly, "I am afraid you find it painful to meet me. I saw your sister, as you know, that night—and now I am living at Pheasant's Hall with my aunt. I make so bold as to speak to you because Captain Prendergast has lately come under suspicion, and I believe you yourself bore some evidence against him."

"I know he met Polly," she said sullenly. "Tain't no secret, as I knows of. Not now, that is."

I sighed. "It is a time of great trouble for your family, and now the Prendergasts also appear to be in trouble. I thought, as I am not related to the captain and only interested in discovering the truth so that the innocent may not suffer, that you might be so kind as to tell me what you know of his connection with your sister."

"That won't do no good. Polly is in her grave—and I've told Squire all I know."

"Please, Miss Holford. I assure you my aim is only to find out the truth, not to help—the guilty escape justice. You say you actually saw the captain meet your sister?"

She looked away. "I saw the note."

"The note?"

"Ay, the note that came from him, to arrange the meeting."

"You saw it?" I repeated carefully.

She looked at me again. "Ay, I read it."

There was a pause. "What did it say?"

She sighed. "That was pushed under the door at night. Polly read it, and showed it to me. She was laughing—happy. What did it say? Why, that she must meet him up by the elms at the top of the ten-acre—"

"Did it mention the captain by name?"

"No. But I knew it was him, later. Polly had a lover, see. I knew it was a gentleman, and that she got notes, but she didn't usually let me see them. This one was different. It made her laugh. She said it was all a joke—and that it would

249

be amusing to meet another gentleman. But it didn't look like any joke to me. She said it was in a different hand—besides, I saw the grey horse myself, up by the elms there—"

"The grey horse?"

"Ay, Thunder—the captain's horse. And that night, Polly told me it was him—and it was a joke, she said. 'But we got along well enough for all that,' Polly says, and tosses her head in that way she had. We was close, see, but she knew I didn't like her to be too free, and that it would kill Mother if she found out—and that Father would kill her, likely—" She seemed suddenly to understand what she had said and stopped abruptly. The colour drained from her face, leaving the freckles standing out like tea-leaves. "Father—oh, no—he fair worshipped Polly—he'd never have harmed her, even if he had found out."

"I am sure he would not," I said truthfully. The colour came back into her face, and she nodded slowly. "You are almost certain, then, that it was the captain your sister saw?" I persisted.

"Ay, no question. She said that night—'There's one thing I don't like about military gentlemen—they're not looking to be married.' I said, 'Have you a fancy then for a ring on your finger, Polly?' and she smiled, looking at her hand like this. 'Oh, there are means of bringing gentlemen up to scratch, even when they are reluctant,' she said. 'You'll see me going to the altar yet, young Peg, for all my wicked ways!' "

I shuddered. Polly had gone to the altar, indeed, and sooner than she reckoned. I felt cold and pressed my hands together within the muff. Across the ice I saw Kitty Beauregard swooping gracefully in my direction. She would, of course, be curious to know what it was I was discussing so earnestly with the sister of the murdered girl.

I said quickly, "That note—did your sister destroy it, or do you know where it is, by any chance?"

I was amazed when she nodded. "Ay, I have it—but I'd best not let it go."

"You have it with you—now?"

She put her hand to her waist and pulled out a folded paper from beneath her sash.

"You can look at it, if you've a mind to, but don't tear it up, mind."

"I swear I won't harm it. May I—" my voice faltered, "may I buy it from you?"

Her eyes gleamed with cupidity. Plainly it had not before occurred to her that the paper had a value. "Ay, perhaps. If so be the price is right."

What offer should I make her? Kitty was drawing closer. If my offer was too low, Peg might snatch the paper back and not even let me see it. Fool that I was not to have waited at least until I had read it! If my offer was too high, she might assume the note was even more important than she had supposed, and she might then refuse to part with it at all.

"Two guineas," I said boldly, for that was the amount I had with me, sewn into the lining of my reticule.

She gasped, and quickly smothered it. She pushed the note into my palm. Frantically with my other hand I began to tear at the firm stitches. I felt the worn satin rip beneath my fingers, and the heavy golden guineas slid into my grasp.

"Here," I breathed, wrapping them in my handkerchief and giving them to her. "Don't bite them now, look at them later. There will be nothing counterfeit about them, you will find, but if anything is amiss, you know where I live."

"Good afternoon, Miss Holford. Pray accept my sympathy on the loss of your sister," said Madame Beauregard, stumbling on to the rutted land. She bent to unstrap her skates. "Don't let me interrupt your conversation," she added, her face rather red from stooping.

"Not at all," I assured her. "We have just concluded it, have we not, Miss Holford?"

Peg looked uncertain. Then, her fingers tightly clenched about the handkerchief, she nodded and mumbled a farewell to both of us before turning away.

"Well!" Kitty exclaimed. "What in the world can you have been saying to each other?"

"The art of polite conversation is not so very hard to master," I informed her, and knew she would not soon forgive me.

"Indeed?" she said, standing upright and staring at me angrily. "Well, perhaps it may seem so from the level of a farmer's daughter and a—a—"

"Yes, ma'am? A what? I do hope you find the courage to be frank."

"A jailbird, then," she hissed. "Mark!" she cried to her brother, who was nearby. "It is time you went home, with that head. I will come with you. Beauregard! Oh, there you are. We are driving back immediately. I find I am fatigued."

Her husband immediately began to fuss about her, while even the captain remarked with unusual solicitude that he was not surprised, and hoped she had not exerted herself too much. He looked at me. "Will you accompany us, Miss Tansy? I believe my father has already gone home, but your aunt is going to walk back directly, if you prefer it."

"I do prefer it, thank you," I informed him, with perhaps more emphasis than was quite polite. "In fact, if you will excuse me, I will go to her now."

Aunt Margaret looked quite distraught when I joined her on the hard-rutted path which led across the fields to

Pheasant's. She pushed a wisp of hair out of her eyes as we set off, and began to subject me to a scold for having encouraged Lord Knevett by skating with him—a man of whom I knew she disapproved.

"But, Aunt," I protested, "he did not go beyond the bounds—there was really nothing to which you could object in his teaching me to skate."

She shook her head. "Mark was extremely put out," she declared, as if this should set the seal on my shame. I, on the other hand, was quite glad to think that I had angered my cousin, though sorry to have distressed Aunt Margaret.

"Furthermore," my aunt continued rather breathlessly as we walked briskly on, "it was scarcely tactful of you to single Peggy Holford out for your attention. I sent Kitty over to you to break it up. What in the world could you have found to say to her?"

I returned a soothing answer, but seeing that my aunt looked really upset I took her arm. "Forgive me, Aunt," I cried with more sincerity. "I have brought enough trouble upon you and have no desire to cause you further anxiety."

She bent her head and patted my hand. "No, no, my dear. It is not all your fault. I was a trifle harsh, perhaps. The truth is that I have had a narrow escape upon the ice, and it has unsettled me. It is still thin under the trees, you know, and I went too close."

I exclaimed, but she declared that it was nothing, it was all over, and she did not wish to dwell on it, nor hear it alluded to again. With an obvious air of searching to find another subject, she cried out, "Oh, and I had better warn you, Tansy, that Lady Sinclair-Stewart came over on purpose to talk to me about you. It is quite plain that she has heard you are something of an heiress and she is now quite eager for Francis to make your acquaintance. Only I hope you won't want to marry him," she added with an earnest look. "His father is a baronet, to be sure, but even so . . . his jokes alone would make him a very uncomfortable companion, I should suppose."

I assured her that I had no ambition to become a future Lady Sinclair-Stewart; but having been again reminded of Francis' reputation as a joker, it occurred to me to wonder if it might have amused him to bring Captain Prendergast and Polly Holford into each other's arms. I longed to open the note I had just bought from Peggy to see if the hand was at all like that of what I remembered of Mr. Sinclair-Stewart's—or if it had, after all, been written by the captain.

We reached the house and walked in through the side door. Barclay was in the hall, and Lady Prendergast enquired if the young people had returned. He shook his head.

"Sir Abraham has come in, but not the captain to my knowledge, m'lady, and I have been on the look out this last hour."

"Oh no, they would only have preceded us by a quarter of an hour or so. They must have gone on for a drive. Well, I think I will go up and change. The frost on my skirts will turn to water directly." She bustled off, the butler retired, and I hurried into the library.

The room was empty, a book lay on a chair, a fire crackled in the wide stone hearth. It was tempting to sit and read and warm myself—but I had work to do, and what might be an unrivalled opportunity to do it.

I took the folded note from my reticule. It was written in a firm black hand on heavy hot-pressed paper; a note, undoubtedly, from a man of means and education. It said merely, "Take pity on one who has long admired you, and meet him beneath the elms at the top of the ten-acre at the next fine sunset."

We had done Polly an injustice in assuming she might have written it herself, I thought, and I was also bound to own that the writing bore no resemblance to the spiky upright hand of Francis Sinclair-Stewart. With a sigh I began to search the captain's writing table.

In the first drawer of the desk was paper, very similar to that on which the note was written. I looked at it with foreboding and then, suddenly resolute, raised it to the light to compare the watermark.

The next instant came a heavy footfall, the rattle of the door handle. Before I had had time to think, I found myself hidden on the window seat, behind the curtain.

"So, Abraham," said my aunt's voice, shrill with suspicion, just an instant later. "What do you here?"

"Why, my dear, I came to get some ink—my well has run dry," replied the squire pleasantly enough.

"Are you sure it was ink? Not the paper knife? No, I see it has gone. Did you take it, Abraham?"

"No, why should I? Curse it, Mark's inkwell is nearly as dry as mine. Where does he keep the bottle?"

"Why should you take the knife, you ask?" cried my aunt, her voice trembling with passion. "Oh, don't try to hide it from me, Abraham. I know you better than you think—and found out more today. It was you, was it not? You spent enough time at Holford's place, in all conscience, you were forever saying how accomplished farmers' daughters are nowadays, and what a likely piece young Polly was. You got her into trouble, didn't you, Abraham? And, not content with that, you used your own son's dagger to get her out of it. Don't look so stunned, you dolt! Do you want it in plain words? Very well, then. I accuse you of murder, Abraham: the murder of Polly Holford."

SIXTEEN

In terror of discovery, I clasped my hands and trembled behind the curtain. Never had I so fervently wished myself elsewhere, not even when Mark Prendergast had found me prying in his room. It was far too late now to reveal myself, to make some light remark about having fallen asleep, and walk out past them. I knew too well how conscious I should look. There was nothing for it but to stay where I was, in silence and fear.

Meanwhile, the squire was blustering. "Ridiculous, woman! Why should I do such a thing? Because Polly was in trouble? But that was no doing of mine—I never touched the girl, do you hear me?"

"I hear you," she replied bitterly.

"The Devil!" he muttered. "Ay, there's only myself to blame for it, I know, if you choose to think I'm lying—but I'll swear there's never been another woman but you since Emily died."

"And you expect me to believe that, I suppose?"

"Oh, there's no object in this style of conversation, Margaret. Hasn't time taught you that? Only you should know me better than to suppose I would murder one of my tenants in such a damned melodramatic fashion—stabbed on the altar of a ruined church!"

It did, indeed, seem hard to imagine it of him. It was certainly easier, after the first shock, to recognize him as an adulterer. No wonder Aunt Margaret had changed, I thought. No wonder she had grown bitter and plain and unforgiving. No wonder that the squire drowned his guilt and despair in wine and punch. But an accusation of murder was a very different matter, and when it involved the squire's having worn a hooded mask and danced with witches—no, I could not believe it. Aunt Margaret, now, as she had just sounded, might more easily have been guilty of the crime. It was not too hard to imagine her becoming a witch on moonlight nights, learning their secrets for her own ends, masking herself in a cloak of convention at other times—and if she really thought her husband had put the girl in the family way, might not her obvious jealousy have driven her to the fatal act? And might she not be now accusing the squire in order to divert suspicion from herself?

But it was my mother's sister of whom I was thinking in such terms, I reminded myself, and shivered.

"You must have chosen to do it so because suspicion would then be thrown upon the witches, and not you," Aunt Margaret pointed out in a hard tone. "Or upon your son," she added coldly. "How you could involve Mark in this!"

"By God, Margaret, don't go on. Damn it, I did not kill the girl, and had no motive to do so."

"Oh yes, so you say—there has been no other woman since Emily, sure!"

"It is the truth," he muttered.

She said bitterly, "I suppose no one since has been good enough to take the place of Mrs. Horton, of sacred memory. Oh, God, it were better that she had lived. It is bad enough to be jealous of a living rival, but a dead one! She will never grow old, never become tedious through familiarity—"

"Her memory fades," he said morosely. "It was a passing madness. By God, Margaret, I believe I would never think of her now, if you were not so insistent on reminding me!"

"A passing madness! More like a recurring one, I think. You have forgotten, I collect, that your passion for this same woman killed your first wife, before it nearly caused the death of me."

"You are stronger than that, Margaret."

She said soberly, "I think you do not know what I am— nor of what I am capable. Oh, God, how could you fall twice into that woman's net? Do not you understand that any man would have done for her as well? And the Colonel, poor fool, still worships at her shrine and never suspects his idol had feet of clay. Oh, she was pretty enough, I'll grant you, and those soft blue eyes—"

She broke off abruptly. "Of course, you have seen the resemblance to Tansy," she suggested in a sulky tone.

"Do you mean that Tansy resembles Emily? I had not thought of it, but I suppose there is something a little similar—"

"Your Emily was taller and her eyes were blue—but their voices, their manner—even their smile is the same!"

"Well, if you say so, my dear."

"Abraham, you must have seen it. Tansy is more like her than Emily's daughter, Caroline—look me in the eye and deny it if you dare!"

"Well, well—perhaps. Ay, the thought did pass through my mind once or twice. Mark saw it too and mentioned it," he owned weakly.

"Of course! So that is why you encouraged that match from the first, regardless of their inclinations. You hoped to live again in them! And I was fool enough to think you were indulging me!"

"I was indulging you, my dear—and one cannot help being fond of the girl, for her own sake."

"I am sure you cannot!" she cried furiously. "And this explains why Mark hates her, of course."

Mark hated me! I had known it, to be sure, but to hear it expressed came as a shock. I bit my lip to prevent its trembling and reminded myself that I cared not a rap for him.

"Surely he does not hate her," the squire protested.

"Indeed he does. He did not admire your behaviour, you must know, in driving his mother into her grave and then taking up the affair again, after we were married. But at least he knew Mrs. Horton was not blameless in the affair. Unlike his father, he could recognize a wanton selfish adventuress masquerading as a sweet and loving wife, when he saw one! He could see that she was shallow, changeable as a cloud, at the mercy of her emotions, submissive one day, inconsiderate and demanding the next—all, no doubt, that made her so fascinating to you! At least Tansy has a warm consistent heart, I think; but Mark would think himself a fool to believe in it, particularly as Tansy is so much more beautiful than Emily ever was—and therefore, in Mark's eyes, even more dangerous."

"Hush, my dear—I think I hear them coming. There is someone in the hall—"

Seizing his opportunity, the squire opened the door, and Kitty's petulant voice could plainly be heard.

"I am frozen to the bone! I'll thank you not to drive off with me like a madman again, Brother, heedless of my pleas. What could have put you in such a rage, I'd like to know?

If it was that chit, your courtesy-cousin, flirting her eyelashes at Knevett, I'm sure you should wish them joy of each other. He'll never marry her, and by the time she discovers it she may have learned her lesson not to be so bold."

"Kitty, for Heaven's sake!"

"Why so squeamish, Mark? You told me yourself she would be the better of a beating."

"Oh, the Devil!" A door slammed. Kitty laughed, and I could hear her beginning to ascend the stairs. The squire's boots sounded on the polished floor, and the library door closed again. I peered cautiously through the curtain and saw my aunt, her face heavy with misery, approach the desk. She leaned on it a moment, looking down, and then with swift decision, pulled out each drawer in turn, looked through it and closed it again. Then, with a sigh, she left the room.

After a few minutes, I got down from my seat. I was stiff, cold, and shaken. It had been no pleasant experience, after all. But at least, I thought, I should be grateful to Lord Knevett for having given me a previous hint that it was my resemblance to another which was the primary cause of Captain Prendergast's antagonism.

I pushed that thought out of my mind and turned to the consideration of the squire's guilt. He had had the opportunity to murder Polly Holford; he had, if he were lying about his interest in her, the motive. He had access to the weapon—and he had been very drunk that night. But would he have allowed his son to be suspected? Would he have gone so far as deliberately to throw suspicion on his son? For only so could the presence of the bloodstained domino in the captain's room be explained, I reflected, if Mark Prendergast were innocent. The note, too; that could have been written deliberately to implicate him. No, I thought;

it was too horrible, too unlikely. As for my aunt, she must be innocent, for she had not been seen near All Saints that night, she had been shut in her room with a migraine. But then it occurred to me that might have been merely an alibi, after all. I remembered, too, that she had been out on Sunday, at the time of another witches' sabbat. I had seen for myself that she was fanatically jealous under her habitual air of calm and good breeding. Was she jealous of that paternal love as well?

A slight crackling sound reminded me that I still held the note—the note, I suddenly realized, that was far more valuable than the two guineas I had paid for it. It could very well be that whoever had penned this note was guilty of the murder. I had already ascertained that the paper on which it was written had come from Pheasant's, from, indeed, this very room. Now I must obtain samples of handwriting and minutely compare them.

A moment later I remembered that my aunt's hand was quite familiar to me. Round and flowing, spilling over the pages careless of the extra postage the recipient would have to pay for the pleasure of her letters, it could not have been more unlike the bold characters in which Polly Holford had been invited to an assignation under the elm trees at the top of the ten-acre. I sighed shakily. I should have to dare the squire's study, then; examine the inscriptions of books; hang about the post-bag in the hall; and then—but as a start there was the book that lay before me, cast down upon a chair.

I picked it up. It was *The History of Tom Jones,* by Henry Fielding. I opened it and there on the title page in faded but legible ink ran the inscription: To Mark Edward Abraham Prendergast, on the occasion of his sixteenth birthday, from his affec. Father, A.E. de C.P.

The script was squarish, the *e*'s Greek—that was the same, at least; but it was not this inscription which struck home to me but the letters that had been added by a different hand, in darker ink, on the top corner of the page—Mark Prendergast, His Book.

I did not need even to open the note I carried to be sure that the writing was the same.

So now I knew the truth, I thought, sitting down abruptly. Mark Prendergast had not been implicated in the murder by another's design. He had implicated himself. He was, after all, a simple soldier, too simple for the dangerous game he played—or perhaps too subtle for it. I must lose no time in showing the evidence I held to someone in authority—but not, I thought with a shiver, not the squire. And not my aunt, who had that ruthless streak in her and might, I feared, destroy the evidence—or even me, if it endangered one she loved more deeply. Could I trust even Lord Knevett to denounce his friend?

The dressing gong rang and I rose obediently, so strongly is habit engrained in one. With a feeling of guilt absurd in the circumstances I tore out the title page and put it in my reticule. Then I replaced the book as I had found it and left the room to climb the stairs slowly, my problem heavy within me. After all, Aunt Margaret was my mother's sister and had made herself responsible for me, I reflected. Was she not the proper person for me to approach with any problem, no matter how nearly it concerned her?

At the head of the stairs I hesitated and then with sudden resolution turned towards my aunt's bedchamber. I would tell her what I had learned, I decided, but I would not let her have the evidence. Her door was not quite fastened and as I paused before it with my hand raised to knock for admittance I heard her voice, soft like a girl's, soft as it used to be in my childhood memories of her.

"Do you truly mean," she was saying, "truly, Abraham—that there has been no other woman since—?"

I caught my breath. Was she giving her husband another chance? If only it were so, for surely they would need each other in the days to come as they had never done before.

Sir Abraham said earnestly, "I do, my love. If only you could forget the past I would do all I could to make amends."

I exhaled in relief.

"But, Abraham," said my aunt heavily, and my heart plunged again. "Abraham, I fear—I have a confession to make. I am a jealous woman. After I found out about—about Emily, I believe I ran mad awhile. I think—I think you do not know me; and it is my unhappy duty to tell you what manner of woman is this wife of yours—"

"No, my love," said the squire with a firmness unusual in him. "Do not tell me. Let us begin again. What's done is done."

"What, Abraham," she said, with a little laugh that sounded near to tears, "are you quoting to me? For that is from Macbeth, I think. 'Things without all remedy, should be without regard: what's done is done.'"

I whirled about at a sound behind me. Mitchell was walking down the corridor. I hurried towards her, thinking only that she must not be allowed to blunder in upon that scene.

"Oh, Mitchell," I said breathlessly, "I was just going to my aunt, but Sir Abraham is with her. I—I—" Inspiration came. "I have the headache," I finished in triumph swiftly suppressed, "and came to tell her I was retiring and would sup lightly in my room. But I don't want to disturb her."

263

"No, miss, and indeed you have a pale look and should be lying down, no question. Go to your room, miss, and I'll engage to explain matters to her ladyship. Shall I bring you some of my lady's leeches?"

"Oh no! I thank you but—it was only the excitement of skating. I shall be better directly, when I am lying down."

I quickly removed myself from the sphere of her solicitude and hurried to my room, congratulating myself on hitting on that particular solution. For it would, I realized, have been intolerable to have eaten at the same table as Captain Prendergast and his unsuspecting parents; intolerable to have endured Kitty's gibes and her husband's innuendos; and worse to have been forced to witness the happiness of the squire and my aunt, knowing myself obliged so soon to shatter it. I cast another log on the fire and drew the bed-curtains so that I should be able to retire behind them at a moment's notice. That done, I found myself wondering what it was that my aunt had been about to confess to her husband—something that lay in the past and concerned them alone, or could it be a graver and more recent matter?

A knock on the door announced the arrival of Susan, sent by Mitchell to disrobe me. I suffered her ministrations and accepted the tray she brought a little later with unfeigned indifference. I did not think I would be able to touch it, but contrived to drink the soup, at least.

When the tray had been removed, I lay back on the pillows, thinking. Something about one of my aunt's statements had chilled me, I realized. It was the manner in which she had said, "I think you do not know me," to her husband. If he did not, how much less did I. To whom, then, should I now turn for help? I reviewed the figures I had seen upon the ice-bound meadows, reviewed and rejected them, all but one. I had feared that Lord Knevett might be too partial towards his friend but now I recalled that he had told me to have nothing to do with the captain, and had described the fact that we lived beneath the same roof as a damnable situation. Belatedly it occurred to me that Lord Knevett, so far from being partial, must already have convinced himself of the captain's guilt, no doubt from the moment when I told him of the dagger and the domino. Once again, it was to Lord Knevett that I should look for help—and why not now, I thought recklessly, now before it grew quite dark, now while all the family sat at dinner?

It was some sort of a solution, and any action was better than none, I felt, springing from the bed and dressing again in haste. I put on my half boots and wrapped myself in the sable-lined cloak. Peering first through the crack and then through the partly opened door, I satisfied myself that the passage was empty, and slipped out into it. When I reached the stairs, a footman was crossing the hall. I waited until he had entered the dining room and then hurried down to the side door, which was still unfastened so early in the evening. A moment later I was outside, and turning up my collar against the chilly air.

It was beginning to be twilight as I stole out through the wood. There was no moon yet and certainly no witches would be abroad, I assured myself. It would be dark before I returned—but perhaps Lord Knevett would drive me home. Indeed, when he saw the evidence I had assembled, he would be obliged to present himself at Pheasant's Hall without loss of time to question and—there was no object in hiding the fact from myself—probably to arrest Mark Prendergast.

For a moment my steps faltered. I felt like a traitor, that I had not warned the captain of what I was about to do. But then, I told myself, if he were guilty of murder he deserved no consideration. Besides, it was even possible his anger this afternoon had been caused by seeing me with Peggy Holford and guessing the subject of our conversation; if he had witnessed the transaction between us he must have known it would be only a matter of time before I proved the handwriting to be his.

I hurried on, aware of the swiftly fading light—aware too that the weather was changing with the wind. A thaw was on the way and with it would come the fog. Already the distances were misty beneath the trees and I knew how easy it would be to get lost if I dallied too long.

The wall loomed before me, and I scrambled over it. By now, of course, I was fervently regretting my decision to come, but by forcing myself to think of nothing but putting one foot before the other, I contrived to drive myself onward through the wood.

At last I reached the glade wherein the crumbling chapel crouched like some great monster patiently awaiting the passing of its unsuspecting prey. I skirted it nervously, keeping under the trees, and came out near the maze, now barely visible save as another looming shape. I hurried over the lawn, whose frosted blades had already melted into soft damp grass, and realizing somewhat belatedly that Lord Knevett would probably prefer me to visit him by stealth rather than appear at his front door unchaperoned, I approached the outer courtyard of Abbot's Grove. I folded my cloak more tightly round me and stepped onto the mossy cobbles as silently as I could manage. An instant later I stopped short and sighed with relief. Silhouetted in an uncurtained window, Lord Knevett was standing in the drawing room, leafing through an enormous book. As I watched, he turned away and reached up to replace it on the shelf.

I quickly crossed the second courtyard and entered the passage to the hall. Fortunately no one was about and I flitted across the shadowy Great Hall to the drawing room door, which I flung open before I could lose my courage.

Lord Knevett, on the far side of the room, turned towards me with a blank look of surprise, which forced me into hurried speech.

"My lord—forgive my intrusion! Only the direst circumstances—" I stopped. Somehow my reception was not quite as I had visualized it.

Lord Knevett adjusted the spine of the book to the same level of the others in the shelf before he responded, and clarified his lack of welcome.

"Do come in, Miss Tremayne. Mama, we have a visitor."

With something like despair I saw his mother in her cage, swinging gently, her face soft and blank.

"I cannot stay—a word with you, sir, in private, if you please—"

He frowned at me and shook his head.

"No, you must join us for a while. Do sit down—not there, I am afraid the myna had an accident on that cushion. Here. Look, Mama, you remember Miss Tremayne?"

Lady Knevett cocked her head upon one side and a bright misleading intelligence returned to her dark eyes.

"Pretty girl, George."

"Pretty girl, pretty girl," reiterated the myna bird. There was a cackle of dissident laughter and I turned quickly to see a grey and red parrot chained by the leg to a high perch.

"Georgie Porgie, pudding and pie," announced this bird sagely when it had finished laughing. "Kissed the girls and made them cry—ha ha! Pretty Polly!"

Lord Knevett clapped his hands together and the parrot shook itself, rattling the chain and retiring into offended silence.

"Poor Polly," said Lady Knevett reprovingly. "You will

267

send her into a moult if you treat her so, George. She is a very sensitive and intelligent bird, you know. Do my feathers need preening?" she added, anxiously peering into a tiny mirror that swung from one of the bars of her cage.

I glanced at the windows. Whether or not because of the contrast of bright candlelight within, they were already dark. Lord Knevett caught my glance and went to draw the curtains.

"Don't do that yourself, George," cried his mother. "There are a dozen servants only waiting to perform such tasks. They will starve if we don't employ them, you know, and then they will cut off our heads, like their unfortunate majesties of France."

I touched Lord Knevett's arm as he passed close to me. "Please, sir, I beg of you—I think I have discovered who wrote the note to Polly—"

"Hush," he said swiftly, with a glance at his mother. "Of course I will hear you in a moment. It was only that it would have looked so singular to hurry you away before she had enjoyed a word with you. I will excuse us presently. But first—does anyone know that you are here?"

I shook my head, colouring a little at his expression of concern.

He touched my hand. "Impulsive creature! But we don't want your aunt worrying about you, do we? I think I shall send a note to someone at Pheasant's, only to be used if your absence is discovered, and destroyed when you return. Who shall it be? Mrs. Slight? I've scarcely spoken to the woman but she seems discreet. How will that do?"

"Quite well, I think." I was reluctant to hint of my suspicions concerning Mrs. Slight, though I supposed that presently I would not be able to be so nice.

"Then I will pen it in the library—and make sure there is no one about when we are ready to leave."

Leave for where? I wondered; but he had gone, closing the door behind him.

I waited, watching the birds and the cringing dogs, smiling at Lady Knevett when my glance crossed hers, starting nervously whenever the fire crackled too sharply.

"Young miss!" It was her ladyship, in a sharp whisper from the cage.

"Ma'am?"

"He does, you know. I've proof of it!"

"Have you, ma'am? I am sure you need not mind it."

"Not mind?" she screeched, sending the myna into a cackle of insane laughter. "Not mind it, when I find their little bodies still warm sometimes, their little wings still fluttering? He thinks I do not know—but I see more than he supposes."

"You are speaking of—a cat, ma'am?"

"A cat?" She shuddered. "I will have none of those. No, miss, I speak of George, my son. He kills us, you know—and so does your uncle—they said he was your uncle, did they not? Sir William? Or no, he's dead now, is he not? It's Abraham who has succeeded him, but he is as bad. He thinks I cannot see him, but I watch from the tower and weep for them—he has his dogs and guns, and they have nothing to protect them from him. Run and hide, miss, for you are one of us." She slid from her perch and began to approach me. "Shall I hide you? I know a place—a place where no one ever goes." She stooped, her soft face close to mine. The whites of her bright eyes were yellow and saliva ran from the corners of her mouth.

"It is the passage to the chapel. No one will ever find you there."

269

I sprang to my feet just as Lord Knevett returned and beckoned to me. I curtsied to his mother, bade her a relieved farewell, and hastened to the door. Lord Knevett snapped it shut.

"I am afraid Mother has upset you. I was sorry to leave you so long—first the note, you know, and then the place was full of people, as is always the way when one does not want them. Now, you have something you wish to say to me in private, I collect; but there is nowhere in this damnable rabbit warren where one may count on being alone for long. You would be seen, and we don't want that. At least, my butler did not announce you so I take it I am correct in assuming you did not enter by the front door?"

"No—I hope you will forgive me—I thought—"

He stopped and caught my hand. "Forgive you, child? But I am charmed that you chose to visit me clandestinely." He led me out into the courtyard.

"I was afraid you were angry. You must believe I would not have come—and so late in the day—but the fact is that I have just made a—a terrible and significant discovery—"

"Hush, my dear. No more until we are beyond the reach of curious ears. Can you walk any faster? We don't want you lingering on this wet grass."

Suddenly I realized where he must be taking me, and hung back. "We are not—going to the chapel, sir?"

"No, as it happens, but why should we not? We could have been sure of privacy there. Oh, you are thinking of—was it only on Sunday night? But I have been wondering if you were not mistaken about that episode. I examined the place very carefully next morning, and found no trace of that sort of invasion."

I stood still. "Are we not safe from eavesdroppers here?

I would rather tell you at once—it is about Captain Prendergast."

"Yes, I feared as much," he owned, halting reluctantly. "Have you discovered something more?"

"It is the note that Polly received. You remember that the captain said he had got one from her, arranging a meeting, only he threw it away; and she had one from him, but he said it was all a hoax and really neither had written to the other?"

"Yes, yes," he said impatiently, shivering. "You make a great muddle of it, but I know what you mean."

"Well, I have got the note that was sent to Polly."

"Good God, do you mean you have the original?"

"Polly's sister sold it to me, this afternoon, and I have compared it with the captain's handwriting."

"I take it you have the note with you?" He looked about him expectantly.

"Yes, of course, and a sample of the captain's hand."

"And you mean me to examine them, but I must have a light for that." He peered through the trees. "Ah, there is the carriage. Excellent, we can make use of the lamp."

"A carriage," I echoed, rather surprised. "Oh, you mean to send me back to Pheasant's, I collect?"

"I shall escort you. One moment, please." He moved towards the chaise, which had now drawn up near by, and spoke to the postilion, an indistinct figure, hunched against the cold.

Lord Knevett turned. "Well, Miss Tremayne, I had better just glance at these papers you mention."

I put them into his hand. He held them to the light while I peered over his shoulder at the two writings, to compare them in case I could remark any room for doubt.

271

They seemed horribly similar, however, written with the same broad nib in the same dark ink.

" 'My Dearest—' " and " 'Mark Prendergast—' "

Yes, the thick down strokes were the same, the Greek *e,* the neat *a,* the small arched *r*—and one must remember that the watermark was identical with that of the captain's own writing paper in his desk.

I sighed, and Lord Knevett smiled curiously.

"Yes," he said reflectively, "it is not a bad forgery, one must own."

I felt faint with relief. "A forgery? Thank God! I was sure they were the same, that Captain Prendergast had written them both."

Lord Knevett raised an eyebrow and looked at me in silence. "You may still be right," he owned. "In either event, the time has come for us to consult another authority. After you, ma'am."

He handed me up into the carriage and soon we were trotting down the drive.

Lord Knevett broke the silence after we had turned right, down the Horsefield Road.

"Have you your reticule with you, Miss Tremayne, and your faithful dagger?"

"Why—yes, sir, I believe I have."

"I am very glad to hear it," he said sincerely. "You quite frighten me, you are so impulsive; I have said so before."

"I assure you, sir, it was no subtle impulse that sent me to you. I considered for some while what I should do, before I acted."

"But to leave no note, no indication—however, you are not my daughter, I am glad to say."

"No indeed! That is—"

I was confused, but Lord Knevett only chuckled. Then I

reflected on what grim mission we were bound, and fell silent again.

After some while the ground became rough. "This is not the way to Pheasant's!" I exclaimed. "Where are you taking me?"

"To Colonel Horton's, my dear. This affair has gone too deep for us, and he is the only Justice here who is in no way involved. You do not object?"

I shook my head, conscious of relief that we were not to confront Sir Abraham just yet. Underhanded it might be, but the Colonel had looked both kindly and just, and was far better able than I to decide what should be done.

"Are we nearly there?" I asked, for the carriage had slowed.

"Nearly."

"We are stopping now."

And so it was. A moment later Lord Knevett had opened the door and himself let down the steps.

I descended and looked about, while he joined me and began to lead me forward.

"But—it is dark!" I protested, suddenly bewildered and even a little afraid.

"Fortunately it is the night of the full moon—only it is obscured by clouds at present. Get down, Brent," he called softly. "I may need your assistance here."

"Brent!" I exclaimed, stopping still. "I don't understand. Where are we?"

The postilion took my other arm. He had a foxy smell mingled with that of horses, sweat and spirits.

"Mind the gate there!" he said roughly. "Ay, that's right."

"The gate?"

Then I realized where they had brought me, and cried out as I was pulled under the dripping yew, and dark forms moved towards us out of the shadows and the mist.

"Don't be shy, Miss Tremayne," said Lord Knevett in a mocking tone. "It is so appropriate that tonight we meet in honour of Selene, for it means that we are all here to make you welcome at All Saints."

SEVENTEEN

They were all about me then, the hooded dark shapes, and
the tokens by which I was aware I knew the witches of All
Saints: Brent the groom, reeking of his foxy smell; the flash
of a gold ring on Mrs. George's swollen finger; Lord Knevett
looming tall against the light of the black candle the bowlegged tailor, Trimble, held aloft; Barney Clement, with head
awry; the fat cook quivering at the jest as I shrank back and
was impelled by ruthless hands through the creaking door to
a nervous giggle from Francis Sinclair-Stewart, and a steady
stare from Mrs. Davies, the lodgekeeper's wife. I could see
Latchington, the tall square-shouldered chorister, sitting sideways on the altar, his foot upon an open Bible, while Dick
Carver limped to the chancel steps, his flute to his lips as he
played a mocking phrase. Oh yes, I knew them now, though
they were cloaked and masked. Mrs. Slight stood silent in
the corner with folded hands—how many had I counted now,
and where was Mark Prendergast among them?

"It was you!" I cried, turning on Lord Knevett as he stood

in the ruined window, surveying me; he and I the only ones unmasked. "It was you whom I saw dancing with Polly—and whom I took for Mark!"

He shrugged. "When you came to my house tonight, I thought you must have guessed. I supposed you had come to Abbot's Grove to spy on me, as your cousin came on Sunday to the chapel. I assumed you had come to look in my desk in the hope of finding some more of the writing paper I took from Pheasant's—even, with luck, to find the samples I made as I strove to perfect my forgery, for it is certainly some time since I attempted Mark Prendergast's hand. But I am not to be trapped by a foolish impulsive girl, as you and . . . others have found."

I stared aghast. "No . . ." I breathed.

He looked haughtily down at me. "Now don't pretend you have never thought of suspecting me, after all. I am sure your aunt lost no time in warning you against me; and why else should you have shrunk from me, when you entered my chapel?"

"Are you saying that it was you who forged the notes; that you deliberately implicated Mark Prendergast?"

"Don't back away from me, Miss Tremayne. There is no object in it. We would catch you long before you reached the door—and even supposing anyone could hear your screams, they would be far too frightened to investigate their cause. We never have been interrupted until you came on us at Candlemas."

I grasped at the implication in his words. Lord Knevett was a witch, I told myself, forcing belief upon my unwilling mind. He had been here in the church, hooded and gowned, at Candlemas, and again in his chapel on Sunday while I watched the gathering from the wood. But his presence, I told myself, did not necessarily make him a murderer. Indeed, I remembered with relief, he could not have been here—he had an alibi, and a better one than Mark Prendergast had been able to provide.

"The friend you met at the White Lion," I cried. "The lady who could vouch for it that you did not leave the inn that afternoon?"

He smiled slightly. "Oh, you mean the obliging Miss Crofton?" He turned and beckoned to one of the hooded figures, tall and thin. "Lift your mask, Miss Crofton, and smile at this young lady. Yes, as you see, Miss Tremayne, she is one of us—a witch, that is to say, and a very promising one. She was glad to give herself an alibi with that letter, even if she did run some risk of her stern father discovering her supposed assignation with me."

After one glance I looked away from the spinster's light, mad eyes, her flickering pointed tongue. "You mean Miss—Miss Crofton was here at All Saints herself, at Candlemas?" I stammered.

"To be sure. It is an important date in our calendar."

I put a hand against my mouth. "Then it *was* you I saw—dancing with Polly?"

"Yes, Miss Tremayne, and I saw you. I was very angry with you, I must own, for making your inopportune appearance on the scene and threatening to spoil my careful plans. I had intended a special entertainment for my coven that night—and instead I had to drive the dagger home in haste after the others had rushed away when you shot at Prendergast." He raised an eyebrow. "Now you are flinching from me, I notice. I thought you were so bold and so adventuresome? Well, you may struggle as much as you please, for I never wanted a willing woman yet."

277

I forced myself to stand still.

"My aunt was right," I said slowly. "You are a dangerous man."

"Did she say that?" He glanced into the shadows. "It was rash of her—but Margaret does not matter any more. She would be dead now, if she had not been so suspicious of me. It is hard to kill when one's victim is on guard." He smiled, his dark eyes strangely blank. "I persuaded Margaret to skate with me today, but she was too wary to fall into the trap I had prepared for her, so I was obliged, for the time being, to be content with poisoning her mind against the squire instead."

"I thought—" I faltered, "I thought perhaps she loved you once." When would help come? I wondered desperately. If he talked for long enough, surely someone would look in my room and begin a search for me—but would they think of looking for me here?

"Oh, ay, to be sure, Margaret loved me," Lord Knevett went on. "When she was half-mad with her husband over his affair with the Horton woman, she took it into her mind to revenge herself on him with me—I daresay she had wanted me even before. I indulged her because the situation amused me—and she was an attractive woman then." He smiled again. "She has regretted it bitterly. I have enjoyed watching the change in her, as I am enjoying watching your shocked face just now. You will bore me soon, as they all do. Polly is a case in point—ah, you flinch again! Yes, Polly was a simple wench: at first, when she believed me to be the Devil, she resisted me finely and we had great sport. But she discovered my identity and when she became pregnant I was obliged to think of getting rid of her. Farmers' daughters are grown so fine these days," he added with distaste, "that I might have found Holford forcing me to the altar with a shotgun, and that, you must own, would hardly have done for a Knevett of Abbot's Grove! No, there was nothing for it but to force Polly to the altar instead—with a stiletto."

"Mark's paper knife," I whispered.

"Of course. If anyone were to hang for disposing of the girl, I did not intend that it should be me. Who better than Prendergast to take my place?"

"I thought you were his friend."

An evil look contorted the baron's face. "I have hated him for years—ever since I noticed that he was more popular, more fortunate, more wealthy—undeservedly more successful than I. Before Candlemas I set my trap, therefore, so that I could catch him in it if I chose. I sent that note to Polly, making sure they met where they could be seen; I borrowed Prendergast's stiletto, arranged a meeting at the White Lion with him, and tricked him into riding off to All Saints at the crucial hour complete with one of the two hooded dominoes I had taken care to bring with me. Does this interest you, my dear? I believe it does; and, besides, there are others here who would probably like to hear the full story of that night. Not all, perhaps," he added, looking round. "A few of them will be shocked—but they can never betray me."

Some of the black figures moved restlessly and then were still again, standing about us in a silent ring.

"When Mark left the inn," Lord Knevett went on, his eyes on mine, "I ordered wine so the waiter would witness I was alone, and to him I hinted of an assignation and commanded that no one was to be allowed to enter until I called. Then I left by the window, sped down the shortcut to the church, and did what I had to do, despite your attempts to ruin my sport. Afterwards I ran the whole way back and was just ahead of Prendergast and drinking at my ease when he returned to the White Lion. He made his report but did not seem to know he had witnessed a murder and I thought perhaps it would not have to be brought home to him after all. I even toyed with the idea of going back and disposing of the body—but then I reflected on the complacency of our community and decided there would be nothing to lose by a demonstration of the power of witchcraft. Later, when I changed my mind, Mrs. Slight was good enough to help me by returning the stiletto to Mark's desk, and by hiding my bloodstained domino in his room."

The baron's eyes seemed to flicker. He put out a hand and took one of my ringlets lightly in his grasp. "But you, my little dove—even when I was feeling lenient to Prendergast, I was determined not to let you off so lightly. Now, why do you shiver?" he asked in a caressing tone. "Is it passion? For you are in love with me, are you not?"

No! I cried within myself. I never loved you. I was bemused—enchanted—bewitched!

"It was quite a jest when I heard of your imprisonment," he went on. "A just punishment, it seemed, for your having stood in my way—but not enough, Miss Tremayne, I fear. No, not enough."

He pulled a hood from his pocket and put it on, instantly transforming himself into the sinister figure of my nightmares.

"What are you going to do with me?" I cried. "You may have succeeded in one murder, but a second would certainly be brought home to you."

He picked up the black candle from the altar and held it high, looking me over with an air of amused insolence.

"No one will know there has been another," he said slowly, "thanks to Miss Crofton."

"Miss Crofton?" I gasped, and there was a chuckle from behind me which I recognized as hers.

"None other, my dear. In payment for . . . favours received, Miss Crofton has prepared the ground for your disposal. Do you wish to know the details? What an inquisitive child it is! Very well, then. Miss Crofton has persuaded—never mind how—a young person to take your name and travel to Yorkshire to join Miss Crofton's grandmother's household, to prove herself unsatisfactory, to leave, and resume her own identity. Meanwhile, when I have done as I please with you and have caused you to be buried in one of the graves which so conveniently adjoin this place—how pale you are! Pray don't swoon, for I don't want you to miss a moment of this, the last evening of your life. Now, where was I? Yes, when you cannot be found, it will be assumed that you have run away, and in due course a letter will be received from Yorkshire, to say you have arrived and are settled in. If any come to ask questions there, they will be told that unfortunately you did not turn out well and have left, no one knows where. But I don't believe questions will be asked," he added complacently. "The household at Pheasant's will be fully occupied by then, with the trial and the hanging, for too much evidence has come out now for Mark Prendergast to avoid the rope, I am glad to say."

I look wildly round, but could see no chance to escape. Not only was I doomed but I was all that stood between Mark Prendergast and a shameful death, I realized. If I were to die tonight, if Lord Knevett were to dispose of me before I could speak of what I knew, Mark would surely hang—and Lady Knevett had warned me, I thought in despair, and I had thought it part of her madness.

The fog seemed to have thickened. I could almost believe I could hear the mournful voice of the postilion singing prophetically of the hangman, waiting by Tyburn Tree.

The screech of the church door opening made me spring

forward in a sudden hope that deliverance was at hand, but it was only Brent, the groom from the White Lion.

"All clear outside," he announced. "A fine still night, and a rising mist."

Dick Carver had begun to play again. The haunting music of the flute rose and fell, lilting through the shadowy ruins like a skein of silver in dark tapestry. A figure moved forward. I did not know who it was until a hand reached out to seize me by the shoulder, and I saw by the twisted ring it was Mrs. George, the jailer's wife. She bent her hooded face towards me and caught her breath on a little laugh. Then she gave me a push into the arms of Barney Clement. He lifted me high and swung me round. I thought he would dash me to the ground but he merely passed me on to Miss Crofton, whose thin fingers ran across my face like spiders.

"Pretty thing!" she exclaimed. "Pretty thing! Don't flinch, my dear, I won't spoil your beauty. You must be a fit toy for our leader." She brought her masked face close to mine. "Later, though, you won't look so pretty. Isn't it fortunate that we have an empty grave ready and waiting for you?"

I remembered the desecrated grave out there under the yew tree—but before I could sob or scream, she had thrust me from her and I fell against a softer form—a woman whose hands were twisting ceaselessly, and who had no chance to catch me.

Lord Knevett laughed explosively. "Embrace!" he cried. "Embrace! It is all in the family!"

He snatched the mask from the woman's head and her eyes met mine staring wildly from her blotched, contorted face.

It was Aunt Margaret.

She gave a moan, which drowned my cry of horror, and slid in a black heap to the floor.

"Drag her to one side," commanded the baron. "We have

finished with her ladyship, I think. Death by exposure will do for her—Francis, where are you? You have the replacement ready?"

"Oh, I say! Well, yes, I have, as it happens. I told her it would be for tonight—but I had to swear you would not harm her."

He pulled forward a slender shrinking form. Lord Knevett raised her hood.

"Peg Holford," he said in a thick, stirred voice. "Don't shrink from your master, child. Francis is right, I will not harm you but show you such delight you've never dreamed of. We'll have the initiation later. You've done well, Francis. You shall be rewarded in due course. Now, where's that meddling beauty? Ah, Miss Tremayne—" He slid the reticule from my wrist and dragged the dagger from its sheath. I gasped at my having forgotten it—my only weapon. Shock must have driven the memory of it from my head—shock upon shock; and now for that lapse I would surely die.

"The cup, Chivers," cried Lord Knevett. "The loving cup. Latchington—where the Devil is that chorister? Ah, there you are, man. I need you here, for you are the strongest of us. Latchington shall sing a canticle over your grave, Miss Tremayne. Barney—ay, come forward. Take her by the other arm."

They held me prisoner, forcing me back against the hard edge of the altar while Lord Knevett brandished the dagger, apparently watching the candle flames reflected in the yellow metal.

Then the baron loomed over me, his bright dark eyes piercing into mine through the slits in his black mask.

"Now, girl, your moment comes. Chivers! Ay, the cup." He forced a black and evil tasting liquid into my mouth, and raising his mask set his lips to the same place. He handed it on to the chorister and Latchington drank slowly before passing the cup to Barney, who stood giggling at my other side.

I struggled feebly. The chorister's fingers bit deep into my arm. Lord Knevett raised the dagger once again. Suddenly the chorister flung me violently against the idiot who still drank, smacking his lips. With a crack of bone on bone Latchington's fist pounded into the baron's face. Lord Knevett swayed and fell; while in the same movement the chorister swung round on Barney, and hammered a blow against the idiot's masked jaw. Half-fainting on the altar steps, I watched amazed in the dim flickering light as Barney shook his head and then with a sigh put out his arms as if to hug the chorister to death. But Latchington escaped him, evaded Brent and Trimble who had sprung forward to detain him, and leaped for the bell rope at the end of the aisle. He began to peal an urgent summons on the old cracked bell, while Francis pummelled him unavailingly.

I realized Lord Knevett was stirring and forced myself to move. I found the dagger half beneath him, and was standing with it ready when Francis dragged the mask from the face of the chorister who still rang the bell and gave a great shout that echoed round the mossy stone.

"Mark Prendergast! Out, coven, for your lives!"

The flute, which had been playing obliviously on, faltered and died. There was a rush like a flight of bats out of a cave, black skirts flying, feet pattering or pounding on the flags, confused squeals—and then nothing but the clanging bell, the heaped body of Lord Knevett, the dazed and stirring figures of my aunt and Barney Clement and—not Latchington, but Mark Prendergast and I staring speechlessly at each other.

An instant later the door screamed again as it was forced back so roughly that it sagged from one hinge. Wild-eyed, Sir Abraham stood swaying in the candlelight.

284

"Tansy, are you—my God! Margaret!"

In two bounds he had reached his wife and was raising her in his arms. "She tried to tell me," he said brokenly, "poor wretched woman, and I would not let her. This was her dreadful secret! Knevett forced her into this by blackmail!"

"Get her home," said the captain grimly. "Say she came to take Tansy back, and fainted from the strain. Her mask has gone, that cloak is suitable enough for a cold night. No one need ever know she was involved in this. God knows the others will not dare to say anything against her."

Aunt Margaret shuddered. "Abraham," she breathed, "can you ever find it in you to forgive me? I have been mad, I think. But I swear I did not know what Knevett intended with Tansy, until tonight. Oh God!" She struggled up on one elbow. "Were you in time to save her?"

"She is here, Margaret, and all is well. Your niece understands. It was only a nightmare, my love—a nightmare that can never come again."

"Abraham," she murmured. "You are strong—after all." She turned her face into his coat and fell limp again.

Sir Abraham rose with his wife held closely in his arms. "I'll send Carver and some others in for Knevett presently," he said gruffly, "when they have finished chasing away the rest. Tansy, there are questions you'll want to ask Mark, no doubt; then you can come out to the chaise when I've had time to settle your aunt comfortably."

I touched his sleeve. "She told me not to go to Yorkshire," I said softly. It was poor consolation, no doubt, but he looked grateful even for that.

"We'll wait here until the constable comes," the captain said. "If Knevett stirs, I'll put him out again—and that reminds me, Latchington should still be lying behind the font. I hit him pretty hard." He glanced at me. "I was fortunate to have the chance to disable him while you were all dancing, for he was the only one of the coven I dared impersonate."

Sir Abraham began to walk towards the broken font, his wife in his arms. "Wake up, Latchington," he called in a harsh voice. "You have two minutes in which to leave this place and forget all your past."

He kicked at the recumbent form and slowly, cursing, the chorister rose, rubbing his jaw and shaking his square head as he followed the squire from the church.

Alone with the captain, I found it strangely hard to meet his eyes. "Captain Prendergast," I said eventually, "how did you know I was here?"

He started slightly, as if his thoughts had been far away, though I had been aware of his scrutiny. "Why, you owe that to Kitty, in the first place—she was very quick to report your vandalism of the book she had been reading. Almost at once I realized what your business with Peggy Holford must have been and therefore why you had torn out that page. I hurried to your room to demand to see the note—and found you were not there."

I felt my face grow scarlet. "I thought it was you," I confessed. "The writing was the same. I thought I ought to tell—"

"I guessed as much. I knew you would have gone to Knevett—and at the same time I recalled that he used to amuse himself with forgery at school. I saddled Thunder and galloped to Abbot's Grove—only to find you had already left. But old Lady Knevett waylaid me while I was arguing with the butler—she told me you had been taken here, to All Saints, where the coven was to meet to celebrate full moon. George meant to kill you, she said. She knew his habits, and his look. But she assured me there would be plenty of time, as George liked to draw out his pleasures, like his father before him. Nevertheless, I galloped home, roused out my father, put on that bloodstained domino and hood, and rode here like the Devil. I have never been so relieved as when I saw you still alive. I waited my moment to pull Latchington behind the pillar, and then—what a pleasure it was to knock him down! I am sorry you had to wait a little longer to be rescued but my father had gone to get Carver from the village, and I was alone."

"I am extremely grateful to you," I said in a stiff little voice. "Are the witches to be imprisoned?"

"No. They will be obliged to behave differently in future, now they are known. It is enough that Knevett will hang. Remember that the act of murder was his alone, however much the witches may have helped him later, and even if some of them would have connived at another death tonight."

I shivered. "I hate the thought of facing Mrs. Slight."

"I think you will find that she has gone by the time we return to Pheasant's."

"I hope you are right. And what of the rest? Your father's coachman?"

"You were mistaken in him—he only feared and obeyed the witches. The coven was Knevett; my stepmother; Miss Crofton; the idiot, Barney Clement; Latchington; Trimble the tailor; little Dick Carver; Mrs. Slight; Chivers the cook and her friend, Mrs. Davies from Lindenfold; Francis Sinclair-Stewart; Brent the groom; and Mrs. George, the jailer's wife."

"So those are the thirteen. Miss Holford was to replace my aunt, of course." I shivered again. "How she could—!"

"She fell in love with Francis, poor misguided girl. Ah, Barney's up."

The idiot stood swaying, grinning, shaking his great head in bewilderment.

"Out," ordered the captain, pointing to the door. "Go home, Barney, and stay there."

To my relief Barney shambled obediently to the door, turned to favour us with a last grin, and tottered out into the night.

I heard the squire call my name an instant later, and drew my cloak more closely about me.

"Did you know Lord Knevett was the murderer?" I asked, feeling strangely reluctant to leave.

"It gradually occurred to me."

"And I was certain it was you," I burst out. "At the meet at the White Lion you were speaking to all the people I suspected. I thought you must be warning them not to go to All Saints on Sunday night."

"I was hoping to provoke them into some action by subtly reminding them that I had seen them here. I might not have been so foolhardy if I had known then what it felt like to be hit on the head and left for dead."

I felt worse than ever at this instance of the captain's courage. I wished that I could tell him how much I despised myself for ever having thought Lord Knevett was the better man. But the words would not come, and I found myself relieved to see the swinging shaft of lantern light which heralded the approach of Sid Carver, the constable.

I forced myself to look up into the captain's cool grey eyes.

"We meet—tomorrow, then?" I murmured.

"Tomorrow, Miss Tremayne," the captain agreed. He smiled with unexpected warmth and added, "Remember that I too harboured the deepest suspicions against you—and I also have been obliged to revise my opinion."

It was the memory of that smile which enabled me to walk boldly away from the ruined church for the last time, and cross without faltering the troubled moonlit graveyard of All Saints.